I0633780

PROLOGUE

Ever ask yourself, "How in the world did I end up here?" Yeah, that's me right now. I remember how I got here, it's just that the how part is kind of, well, unbelievable. I'm a vampire slayer—a job that's synonymous with kickass and dangerous. Instead, I find myself playing the part of a smitten werewolf whose soulmate happens to be the Vampire King.

Sounds like something straight out of a soap opera, doesn't it? I mean, don't get me wrong, I can binge-watch a good drama like the best of them, but this is my life we're talking about, not some TV show.

Let me rewind a bit for you. It all started with a couple of drinks—as most memorable nights do. Except, instead of ending up in some dreamy guy's bed, I found myself face-to-face with a bunch of bloodthirsty vampires, all ready to rip me apart.

Why, you ask? Well, I was doing my job—slaying a vampire who'd killed an innocent. But his other half didn't take too kindly to that and decided to come after me. My only saving grace? My mate—a vampire whom I'd never met before—came to my rescue.

I won't lie, it was a pretty romantic moment. We even shared a kiss. A hot, unforgettable, steamy kiss. Even now, thinking about it sends chills down my spine.

Then I found out that someone put a hit on Gabriel, my knight in shining armor. Now, I don't believe for a second that Gabriel broke any laws. He's a king, for heaven's sake. It's not like he's sneaking out at night to gorge himself on human blood. Granted, I don't really know him. What I *do* know is that his lips are magical. Soft. And...perfect.

But I'm getting ahead of myself.

To make matters worse, the slayer tasked with

Gabriel's case is Chris—one of my best friends, and the top slayer in the Academy.

Cue my inner panic.

My loyalty has always been to the Vampire Slayer Academy and to my friends. They're my family. But Gabriel is my mate. The man I'm supposed to spend the rest of my life with. See the pickle I'm in? I can't let Chris kill Gabriel. Or let Gabriel kill Chris.

So, here I am, caught in a predicament of epic proportions. Which is how I found myself here. Trapped again. Only this time, I'm with my mate—who I may have knocked unconscious and kidnapped—in a tiny, one-bedroom cabin I *borrowed* from Jaden. Yep, you heard that right. I clubbed him and dragged him here. Quite a revelation about myself, isn't it?

This probably ranks pretty high in my list of worst ideas ever. One cabin means one bed, and as much as I want to re-live that epic kiss, I'm not ready for a one-bed situation.

On the bright side, he's safe here. Only those I trust with my life know we're here.

Sadly, I have no idea how long this'll take. While we're hiding out, Anna and Vlad are searching for the person who put the hit on Gabriel. Because that's what this an—an assassination attempt, plain and simple.

I refuse to stand by and let someone murder my mate. Even if he does look like an angel and possesses a power unlike any other vampire I've met. However, power doesn't make him invincible. If anything, it attracts trouble.

Which is why I'm here.

I may not be ready for a mate, but I sure as hell can protect him. Then, once we have our answers, we can all move on. I mean, I'm a werewolf, he's a vampire. We aren't exactly a match made in heaven.

In the meantime, it's the loveseat for me. Gabriel barely fits on the bed, let alone a two-seater couch. It makes my back ache just looking at it.

Ugh. Remind me again, how did I land myself in this mess?

1

THREE DAYS AGO

Come on, Maddie, get your shit together," I hissed at myself as I put on another burst of speed. My legs ached and my lungs burned from the chase this demonic little vamp was leading me on, but I couldn't give up. In all my years as a slayer, I hadn't missed a single target, and I wasn't about to start tonight.

Fuck, I hated running. I knew people who loved it and even saw it as a recreational sport, but I wasn't one of them. I didn't even enjoy it in wolf form—which, according to my sister and her husband, made me one odd duck. But I hated everything about it. The sweat, the panting, the muscle cramps, the post-run agony, *all* of it.

Unfortunately for me, running was a huge part of my job.

As much as I would appreciate it if they did, vampires didn't stand around waiting for slayers to stake them for their crimes. And apparently, *this* one had been training for a marathon, cuz sweet Jiminy Cricket, he was fast. I mean, all vampires were fast. But this little turd was faster than Usain Bolt.

We tore through LaFleur's Bluff State Park at speeds humans wouldn't be able to track. Luckily for me, it was nighttime and the middle of February. Mississippi winters were mild, but people still tended to avoid the chillier temperatures. Meaning, the park was quiet, and no one was here to witness me running at top werewolf speed. That would change, though, when we crossed the highway and entered the 'burbs.

My target threw a quick glance back my way, surprise widening his eyes.

Guess he thought he'd lost me back in the brush.

Guess again, fang-daddy.

I would have loved nothing more than to shift right now, but I couldn't waste the precious time. It wouldn't take long—I'd mastered the art and reduced my shifting time to thirty seconds—but those thirty seconds were pivotal right now. I couldn't lose track of this vamp. Not after what I'd seen tonight.

The vamp stole another glance back at me, cursed, then banked a hard left turn, toward the Museum of Natural Science.

Damn it!

The museum sat right next to I-55, and on the other side of that was housing. Which meant people. And that put me at a disadvantage. The public knew about vampires and had been quite accommodating to them, but they didn't know jack-shit about werewolves. And no one from my community seemed willing to reveal that little secret. I certainly wouldn't be the one to expose us. If he crossed over into a populated area, I'd have to slow down and risk losing him.

No way in hell would I let that happen.

This dude murdered three women. And when I found him tonight, he'd been chomping down on number four. Thanks to me, she would survive. But I refused to let him escape.

The sound of traffic rose to my ears, and I swore.

I wouldn't catch him now.

Luckily, I had one last ace up my sleeve.

"Hey Siri," I called quietly to my cell phone, hoping I was loud enough for it to pick up my voice, but not too loud that the vamp overheard me. "Call Jaden."

"Calling Jaden, mobile," chimed Siri's voice through my Bluetooth earpiece.

Thank the stars for virtual assistance because I knew from experience I couldn't keep sprinting and dial Jaden manually. Last time I'd tried, I'd dropped my phone on the pavement and shattered the screen. Hence my shiny new device, complete with Siri.

The call connected, and Jaden's whispered voice carried through the speaker. "Maddie?"

"Where are you?" I demanded through a wheezing breath, praying that she was where I hoped.

"I'm about to leave class," she said. "What do you need?"

Relief nearly had me tripping over a stupid tree root. About a year ago, Jaden had started taking night classes at Belhaven University, which was a little more than a mile from here. It chapped my ass that I'd have to slow to human speeds, but I had no other options. I wouldn't catch him before he crossed into the nearby residential area.

"I'm in pursuit," I told her. "We're passing the Museum of Natural Science and heading in your direction. This bastard's fast. I think I can herd him down Riverside if you can cut him off?"

I listened as she gathered her books. "I'm on my way now. Josh is here too, so we can both help."

"He is?" Then I shook my head. Not important. I could ask about his presence later. "Meet me at Linden and Riverside in a few minutes. Can you make it there in time?"

"It'll be tight." But she was already on the move. I heard her repeat my directions to Josh right before the call disconnected.

The vampire shot across the interstate without any difficulty. My gaze immediately darted to the oncoming vehicles. Shit, this was going to be close. Gritting my teeth, I dove across the highway. Brakes screeched behind me, and I waited for the sound of metal crunching, which, thankfully, never came. Traffic resumed after a few honks.

I blew out a relieved breath and continued my pursuit, sadly at slower speeds now that I had to weave through a throng of pedestrians.

God, I hated this.

I'd petitioned the alphas more than once to reveal our kind to the public, but they refused. Keeping this secret made my job difficult, but they didn't care. My job's challenges didn't trump the safety of every other werewolf in the world. Hell, my friends didn't even know I wasn't human. And believe me, that was a hard secret to keep.

When the vampire started heading north, I cursed and altered my course, pushing him back toward Riverside. Who knew I'd make a good vamp herder? At least I had him headed toward the college now, because my reduced speed meant the gap between us kept widening. It wouldn't be long before I lost track of him.

The vamp and I crossed St. Ann Street when he made a sudden break for a huddle of college kids. Screams echoed a second before they scattered. Soon after came the unmistakable glows of smartphones. Because of course they'd decided to record us instead of, oh, I don't know, *helping* me. Lucky for the fanger, cameras and his kind didn't mix, so he didn't have to worry about going viral. I, however, wasn't so lucky.

My phone rang, and Siri announced Jaden as the caller.

"Answer," I said, connecting the call.

"Josh and I are in position," Jaden immediately said.

"We're almost there. You won't miss us."

"I'll leave the line open in case he changes direction," she said.

I nodded, even though she couldn't see that, and pressed onward. The leech was a full block ahead of me, but I grabbed Sir-Stab-A-Lot from my tactical belt and gripped him hard, preparing myself for the kill.

"I have visual," Jaden quietly murmured.

"Good. Take him down," I ordered.

"Go!" Jaden hissed.

Rustling carried over the phone line, and I watched as Josh and Jaden appeared out of nowhere and tackled my target. The three tumbled to the ground in a mess of limbs.

Screams erupted from the crowd surrounding us, but Jaden and Josh ignored them, and focused on the target.

I forced my legs a little faster, hoping no one questioned my speed, then came to a stop next to the heap.

Josh and Jaden were both human. But like me, the Vampire Slayer Academy had trained them. They knew how to take down a vamp. Which is why, without any direction from me, Josh wrenched back the vamp's arms, giving me a clear target. I gripped Sir-Stab-A-Lot and slammed him down, right into the vamp's black heart. His eyes widened, then with a slow breath, he went slack on the pavement, his eyes glazing over.

"It's okay!" Jaden shouted, waving her badge—the one we carried in case the real police ever questioned us. We weren't true law enforcement, but they respected us. "We're with the VSA."

The screams faded, but college students gathered around us, gasping in horror and fright at the sight sprawled before them.

Staking a vampire wasn't clean. Nor was it anything like what they showed on television shows. When we staked them, they died the same as everyone else—in a heap of blood and gore. I'd never once seen a vampire turn to dust. Unfortunately.

Breathless from my impromptu marathon, I yanked Sir-Stab-A-Lot free and slowly rose to my shaky feet.

"How long were you chasing him?" Josh asked.

I bent at the waist and flattened my palms against my thighs. "About thirty minutes or so."

"At top speeds?" Jaden asked, her voice filled with awe.

I merely nodded. It wasn't like I could tell them the distance. Ten miles in thirty minutes wasn't possible by human standards.

"Good for you!" Jaden said, clapping me on the back. "It's too bad you won't wear a smartwatch. I would have loved to look at those stats and compare them to mine and Josh's."

Which was exactly why I didn't wear one. They didn't know I wasn't human—and I needed to keep it that way.

Straightening, I grabbed my phone, then sent a quick message to the Body Retrieval Team. An automatic response pinged back, giving me an ETA of ten minutes.

Oh, thank goodness. Usually, BRT took longer than that.

Relief had me plopping down on the ground next to the dead vampire. I grinned at the sight of his lifeless eyes. Maybe I shouldn't take such pleasure in a kill, but this bastard had murdered his fair share of humans. It felt justified to celebrate.

"You shouldn't sit," Josh advised. "Come on, get up. Keep moving around. Trust me, you don't want lactic acid building up. Stretch your muscles out. Otherwise you won't be moving too well tomorrow or the day after that."

Yeah, yeah, I knew all that. But couldn't I have a few moments to collect my breath first?

Jaden hauled me to my feet and pushed me forward. "Get moving, girl."

Guess not.

Ugh. I truly hated them right now. I was a werewolf. I wasn't even sure we produced lactic acid. But I had a guise to maintain, and that meant stretching out my quads after a particularly harrowing run.

Jaden turned to the gawkers and waved her hand. "Okay, people. Come on. There's nothing left to see here."

And this was why we tried not to slay vampires in public. It attracted far too much attention. People pretended to be horrified, but inside, they were fascinated.

"Let's go!" Josh shouted. "I'm sure you all have better places to be."

About half dispersed, but the other half wouldn't budge until BRT loaded the body into the van and drove off. Humans were an odd lot—and I should know. I used to be one. Always so captivated by the macabre.

Once I completed the required stretches, I turned back to my friends. "How much of a cut do you want?"

Jaden waved a dismissive hand without even looking at me. "Don't worry about me."

"I'm good too," Josh said.

"No, seriously. I wouldn't have caught this dickhead without your help."

Jaden chuckled, then tucked her curls behind her ears. "I think you deserve it all. We can hardly get you to run a mile with us, but this guy led you on a merry chase. It's all yours."

"So funny," I muttered.

My hunts didn't normally pan out like this. They always ended in a chase, sure. But since I could easily keep up with vampires, I usually caught them within a few minutes. This guy, though, had the legs of an antelope on him.

The real problem had been me. I *may* have been a wee bit inattentive at the start of the hunt. So much so that he'd spotted me first, giving him the upper hand. Usually, I was more careful than this, but I'd been a bit distracted recently, unable to think of anything other than what'd happened two nights ago.

The night I'd met my mate.

I shook my head. I couldn't keep going down this road. Couldn't keep thinking about *him*.

17

Yes, I'd met Gabriel. And yes, he'd kissed the ever-loving-bejesus out of me. But I refused to turn into some sloppy, lovesick woman who couldn't think of anything else.

So, I slapped on my game face and turned toward Jaden.

The concerned furrow of her brows startled me.

"You okay?" she asked.

"Me? Sure. Why?"

Her pale blue eyes narrowed on me. "Josh and I were talking to you, and you completely spaced out. Did you even hear what we said?"

I blinked, a flush warming my cheeks. I hadn't heard a damn thing. Because once again, I'd been thinking of Gabriel. Jaden and Josh knew absolutely nothing about him. Which distressed me all the more, considering they'd actually met him. They simply didn't remember, thanks to Gabriel compelling them to forget.

"Earth to Maddie." Jaden snapped her fingers in front of my face.

I forced myself to focus on her. "What?"

"There you go again," she said, shaking her head. "You've been acting really oddly lately. Ever since your last hunt. Are you sure you're okay?"

"I'm fine. Just tired," I said, lying through my teeth. I *so* wasn't fine.

And why?

Because not only had I met my mate, and we'd shared this amazing kiss that haunted my dreams, but he was also a vampire. I didn't hate vampires as a general rule, but I didn't love them either. No one in this business did. How could I be a vampire slayer, and fall in love with one?

Whoa. Pump the brakes. No one had said anything about falling in love with Gabriel. Just because he was my mate didn't mean we had to be together, right?

I really needed to call my sister about this. Lucy would know. She had her own mate. She knew how this blasted connection worked.

Maybe with time, the longing would dissipate?

"Maddie!" Jaden shouted.

I shook my thoughts clear and focused on her and Josh again. Now both stared at me, concern etched on their faces.

"I'm sorry," I told them both. "That run really exhausted me."

"What are you thinking about?" Jaden asked.

"My bed," I said, laughing. "Ooo, or maybe a bath first. Soak these muscles. Or maybe we should eat. We could get some waffles! Isn't there a Waffle House nearby?"

Jaden chuckled. "I always forget how hungry you get after running. Maybe you need some electrolytes or something."

"Yes, those!" I glommed onto that like a duck on a June bug. Anything to keep her from asking what I was thinking about again. "Anyone carrying?"

Jaden chuckled and shook her head, her beautiful, dark, curly locks bouncing against her shoulder. "We weren't out for a run, so no, sorry."

No, they'd been at school together. Except Josh wasn't a student. I eyed the two of them and noticed the faint color to their cheeks. Josh rubbed the back of his neck, as though afraid I'd question his presence here.

Innnteresting.

"Oh, uh, there's a shop nearby," Josh said, his words rushing together. "I'll run and get you a Gatorade."

"Aw, thank you."

With a smile, he started down the street at a slow jog.

Before I could question Jaden, she hopped back into the conversation with, "You sure you're okay?"

This time, I chuckled. Distraction and avoidance, much? "Yes, Mom."

"Don't give me any attitude, Missy," she teased, imitating what I assumed was a mother's voice. Seeing as how I'd never had one, I had no idea. But I'd seen movies.

She cleared her throat and wrung her hands together. Something I'd never seen her do before.

"So, I guess you're wondering why Josh is here, and well, I've been meaning to talk to you about this."

Well, that sounded serious.

"He and I have been spending a lot of time together. You know, without you and Chris." She scratched her cheek, her umber color deepening. "We get along really well, and I think there may be something more to it. I've been wanting to ask him out for a while now, but I'm... Anyway, I wanted to get your opinion on that." She shot me a shy glance. "On whether or not I should...you know, do that."

Surprise lifted my brows.

Jaden liked Josh? In our five-year relationship, she'd *never* expressed liking anyone. Sure, men flocked in her direction—she was downright gorgeous, with her dark skin and striking blue eyes. But six years ago, a vampire had murdered her fiancé, and that had broken her. Afterward, she'd taken herself entirely off the market.

Until now, apparently.

My gaze flicked over her shoulder to the man jogging down the street to fetch me a Gatorade. Josh was a sweetheart, and my initial reaction was to squeal at the thought of them together. But then reality reared its ugly head.

We were all friends.

Me, Jaden, Josh, and Chris. A foursome that had been together since we all started at the Academy. What would happen if they didn't work out? Would we all split up? Or would it force the two of them to see each other daily? Flashes of Ross and Rachel from the show *Friends* rose to mind.

"I know," she said. "It could get messy."

It could get hella messy. But who was I to talk? My mate was a vampire, for cripes' sake. Hell, I didn't even know where he was currently. His deeply British accent suggested he wasn't from around here. Which had me wondering if he'd returned home. That thought unsettled me, which upset me even more. I shouldn't care so much! Not after *one* kiss.

The memory of that kiss resurfaced. His arms around me, his lips firm against mine, the feelings he'd awakened within me. My body yearned for him, if only to explore the heat between us.

"Maddie?" Jaden asked.

I cursed inwardly and forced all thoughts of Gabriel aside. My friend needed me right now. I had to stop thinking about *him*.

"Well, there's a risk," I said. "But if you like him and don't act on it, wouldn't you regret it?" I almost laughed at my advice.

"Yeah," Jaden said. "And I've felt like this for a while. I *think* he's into me too, but I'm afraid to find out."

"You won't until you ask. We're all adults here."

She chuckled. "Adults do stupid shit."

That we did.

I took her hands and gave them a reassuring squeeze. "The only thing you can do is ask. If it works out, at least you'll be with someone who understands your lifestyle. Someone you mesh with. Could you imagine explaining all this to a normal person?"

That made her laugh harder. "Too true."

Movement caught my eye, and I glanced up in time to spot Josh closing the distance between us, a Gatorade bottle sloshing in his hand.

I gave Jaden a smile, then released her hands. "Incoming."

Jaden's smile vanished, replaced by something that resembled fear.

"Hey. You got this."

Because honestly, what man would be crazy enough to turn her down? Jaden was an amazing person through and through.

"Thanks," she said.

I nodded, eager to see where this led.

Now, if only I was this excited about my own love connection.

2

I COULDN'T FOCUS ON THE MAN POISED ABOVE me, only the sensations he awoke within me.

Silk sheets enveloped me as firm hands ran down my body. Soft lips brushed my skin, tasting every inch of me. His leg slid between mine, his coarse hair rubbing my sensitive flesh, and his thigh pressing against my center.

I gripped his shoulders, my fingers digging deep, pulling him closer. I hauled his mouth to mine and moaned when his tongue slipped past my lips.

Sweet manly vamp, I wanted him.

Gabriel.

My mate.

Not an ounce of doubt fluttered in me. And when his thick, hard cock nudged my entrance, I was all rainbows and unicorns. Bliss, they called it.

This. This was where I belonged. With him.

He pressed his mouth against the hollow of my throat, his fangs positioned in the perfect spot. I arched into him, feeling the rounded head of his cock edge inside me.

"Bite me," I whispered, delirious with need.

"Maddie...." The sound of his deep voice rumbling my name had me shivering in his arms.

"Bite. Me," I whispered again, a fervent whisper in the dark.

It was my heart's deepest, darkest yearning. To feel him buried inside me, to consume me, to know I was the only one who sustained him.

"Maddie!" he shouted, his voice rising in pitch. A voice that didn't belong to him.

I blinked up at Gabriel, then gasped when his image began to waver, and the room began to dissolve. I choked back a cry when he vanished, taking with him all the fuzzy feelings he'd evoked within me.

"Maddie, wake up!" Another shout, and the one that finally jolted me awake.

My eyes shot open, and I scrambled up in my bed, my hand already cupping my throat. My fingers probed the exact spot where Gabriel had rested his fangs, but I found nothing except smooth skin. Relief had me slumping back against my headboard and closing my eyes.

What in the name of garlic bread had just happened?

Had that seriously been a dream? I'd never felt anything like that before. Hell, it'd felt like he was physically here with me. Even now, I could feel the pressure of his hands on my body and the lingering heat from his kisses. My core ached from the emptiness I felt inside.

This was insane.

Vampires weren't able to invade your dreams, were they?

To the best of my knowledge, they weren't in the dream invasion business. But then again, I hadn't known compulsion existed, and that was something I'd recently witnessed firsthand. Gabriel had wiped my friends' minds clean of our strange meet-cute. They hadn't even noticed the gaping black hole in their memories.

What if he'd somehow fiddled with my dreams? To make me crave him like I craved chocolate?

"Maddie?" came the high-pitched voice again.

I peeled open my eyes to find Jaden standing at the foot of my bed, clad in her winter coat and gloves. Guess the weather was still rocking the chilly temps.

"Jaden," I croaked. "How'd you get in here?"

She laughed. "C'mon Maddie. At least rotate where you hide your spare key. Even a half-brained burglar would think to look under the welcome mat."

I shrugged. Honestly, I wasn't too fussed about home invaders. I could handle myself. Besides, the last thing I wanted to do when stumbling through the door at ungodly o'clock was dig my key out of the bottomless pit that was my bag.

"Alright. What's up? What do you need?"

"Didn't you hear your phone ringing? We've been calling," she said.

They had? I shot a glance at my nightstand and spotted my phone. I picked it up, and the screen flickered awake, revealing missed calls from Jaden and Josh as well as a slew of unread text messages.

"Huh. I guess I didn't hear it." 'Course, that could be because it was on silent.

Jaden chuckled. "Some dream you were having. Who was the lucky guy?"

"Guy? What guy? Who said anything about a guy?"

She lifted a brow. "You're telling me I didn't just stumble into your room while you were having a sex dream? Girl, you're sweaty, your sheets look like they survived a tornado, and the sounds—"

"Okay!" I interrupted, really not keen to hear my BFF's play-by-play commentary.

"Mr. Dream must've been giving you the ride of your life. So"—she plonked down on the bed, a mischievous grin spreading across her face—"who was he?"

Oh god. Nope. That was one conversation we weren't having. "Uh. I don't know. I never actually saw his face." A white lie mixed with some truth. I knew who he was. But had I actually seen Gabriel's face in the dream? Not really. Too engrossed, you know. It did make me wonder, though. Would he look and feel as good in real life? Or had I... exaggerated things?

"Damn." Jaden smirked. "Still, I wouldn't mind a little of that action myself."

I tossed her a wan smile, then swung my legs

over the side of the bed and stood. Thank heavens I believed in pajamas.

"Okay, so why the call fest?" I asked, heading to the bathroom for a much-needed cleanup. I definitely needed a shower. I smelled of sex sans the actual act. Luckily for me, human noses weren't as sensitive as a bloodhound's. Unluckily for me, mine was, and I didn't particularly fancy a constant reminder of the dream.

"Chris asked us all to meet him for coffee. Apparently, he's got something up his sleeve and needs our help."

I cranked on the shower, then stepped under the icy spray with a suppressed yelp. I could have waited for the water to warm, but I wanted to wash away this scent now. Somehow, I smelled of *him* even though he hadn't actually been here. Maybe it was all in my head, but either way, it needed to go.

"What's he need our help with?" I called out to Jaden.

Her reply echoed in the bathroom. Nothing weird about it—we'd been bathroom buddies before. Girls had that advantage.

"He finally got a whiff of his 'big fish'."

Oh, right. Jaden had mentioned this big fish during our chat the night I'd met Gabriel. Needless to say, my mind had been a little preoccupied, and I'd forgotten to follow up with Chris.

I quickly scrubbed down, then killed the shower and stepped out. Jaden leaned against the counter, staring at her phone with a dreamy smile.

I swaddled myself in a towel, then stole a peek at her screen. Upon seeing Josh's name, I laughed.

"So, finally popped the question, did'ya?"

Jade's dark skin color deepened. "I did."

"And judging by that goofy grin, he said yes."

"He did." She chuckled. "Gosh, why do I feel like I'm back in high school, giggling over boys?"

"Because we're standing in a bathroom, literally giggling about a boy," I teased. "Was he surprised when you asked?"

"Um. Not...exactly," Jaden admitted.

"No?"

"He planted one on me."

I froze. "He what now?"

"I asked him out, and instead of a simple 'yes' or 'no'—like a normal guy—he opted to kiss me."

I held my tongue even though *so* many questions rose to mind. After a pause, I flung my arms up in dramatic fashion. "Well? Did he pass the kissing test? Please say yes. It'd be a crying shame if after all this, Josh kisses like a guppy."

"Oh, it was good," she said, her voice dropping a pitch and her eyes glazing over in a dreamy haze.

I recognized that gaze. I'd worn it once or twice myself. She was reliving their kiss. Well, at least someone could bask in all their smooching glory.

And that totally killed my buzz.

Suddenly, I didn't want to talk about boys anymore. Especially when I couldn't even dish about my own twisted love life to my bestie.

Clearing my throat, I retreated into my bedroom and dressed at warp speed. "Where are we meeting the guys?"

"Urban Fox," she said, still rooted to my bathroom. Guess the kiss had been *that* good.

"Alright." I snagged Sir-Stab-A-Lot, my faithful stake, and strapped him on—a girl never knew when a stake could save the day. "Then let's get a move on."

JOSH AND CHRIS HAD ALREADY SNAGGED US A table and pre-ordered our preferred drinks. Jaden and I strolled toward them, but as we neared, she veered toward Josh, and planted a whopper of a smooch on him. Publicly.

I merely rolled my eyes, but poor Chris almost died choking on his coffee, spraying the brew across the table. Evidently, Josh had failed to brief him.

"What the hell!" Chris sputtered.

I nabbed the nearest napkin and dabbed at his chest.

Chris swatted my hands away, then stared at the two lovebirds. "When the hell did this happen?"

"Last night," I replied. "Roll with it."

"Roll with it?" His accusatory glare ping-ponged between the three of us. "A heads up would have been nice." He eyed his cup with a sigh. "That was a six-dollar coffee."

I snorted. "Aw, a little hard up for cash, buddy?"

None of us were hard up for cash. Slaying vampires paid the bills and then some. I never had to work another day in my life if I didn't want to.

Chris shot me a glare. "You should have warned me."

"Nah, I figured it would be funnier this way."

"Oh, very funny," he groused. He rounded on Josh. "We've been sitting here for, what, twenty minutes? And you didn't think to share this?"

"I thought this would be funnier?" Josh winked at me.

Chris folded his arms over his chest, and

slumped in his chair, sulking. "You guys suck. All of you."

I laughed, then pulled up a seat. "Okay, so Jaden and Josh are an item." I glanced their way to ensure they were okay with that label. Both beamed at me. Yeah, they were over the moon. "Let's accept it and move on. We've got bigger fish to fry, right?"

Chris didn't seem thrilled by my suggestion. Instead, he glowered at Josh. "You screw this up, and I'll knock your lights out."

Jaden and I laughed, but it was an uncomfortable one. The sort people made when they wanted something very much not funny to be funny. Chris had sounded almost possessive. Like he cared about Jaden more than he was letting on.

And it seemed Josh thought the same. His eyes widened and his focus darted from Chris to Jaden. "What? Did you two ever...?"

"No, never!" Jaden blurted out.

Yep, we were *definitely* back in high school.

I rested my chin on my palm, relishing the drama. Real life soap opera. Fantastic.

"We're family," Chris said. "The four of us are all we've got."

I winced. His words dampened my spirits. Chris, Jaden, and Josh weren't *all* I had. I had Lucy and

Sam and their kids. But Chris wasn't entirely wrong, either. These three had all lost their families—and tragically so. As for me? I'd never had any family to lose. My father—the man Lucy called our sperm donor—had left me on a church doorstep when I was a baby. And my mother, sadly, had died soon after my birth. I didn't know anything else about her. As for my sperm donor, I didn't care to learn anything else about him. I had all the information I needed. So, I'd grown up in foster care—never adopted.

My friends, however, had idyllic lives once. Until vampires wrecked everything. One had slaughtered Chris's entire family right before his eyes. Another had murdered Jaden's fiancé. As for Josh, one had turned his mother into a vampire against her will, and Josh had put her down himself. We didn't know much else about that situation, as we tried not to discuss them much. Some things were better left unspoken.

So when Chris said we were family, he was right.

I adored Lucy and her family. She was my sister. But I'd lay down my life for these three.

"All I'm saying is don't mess this up," Chris continued. "None of us want to lose what we have."

That was heavy-duty pressure on them. But thankfully, they seemed unfazed. With a bit of luck, they'd be *it* for each other. Best friends to lovers to spouses. So romantic.

"Okay," I said, steering the conversation back on track. "Jaden mentioned you have some intel to share?"

Chris nodded, then pulled out his phone. He tapped the screen and pulled up an email. "I recently received an email from Vera"—the woman responsible for assigning us our targets—"which details my latest mark."

He snuck a glance around the café.

The three of us did the same, though I wasn't sure why. We weren't breaking any laws. Our kills were one hundred percent sanctioned.

"Everything I say here needs to stay between us," Chris whispered. "If word gets out, I won't get within a mile of this bloodsucker."

I frowned. Who on earth was he talking about?

"This contract is going to be the toughest I've ever had. That's why I called you guys. I think we'll need to team up on this one."

That raised my brows. "Really? We don't usually work like that." Last night had been an exception. Generally speaking, slayers operated solo. The Academy seemed to prefer it that way, though I wasn't sure why. Teamwork would certainly simplify things. But I'd never questioned it, considering I had my own little secret to keep.

"The payout is more than enough to cover all four of us," Chris said. "If we nail this guy, we're looking at a cool half-mil *each*."

"What?" Jaden gasped, leaning in. "You're telling me your target has a two-million-dollar bounty?"

Even *my* eyes bulged. I'd never heard of a bounty that high. The vampire had to be some big wig then. Like the pope. Except, as far as I knew, the pope wasn't a fanger. Big fish, indeed. I was dying to know who it was.

"Here's the thing. It isn't going to be easy getting to this guy. From what I can tell, he has round-the-clock security. The other challenge is our window. He's not American, and if he leaves the country, we're done."

I nodded. We weren't authorized to slay outside our borders. Each country had its own jurisdiction rules.

"So, this will require a lot of work," Chris continued. "And a lot of research."

"Who is it?" Jaden asked.

Chris took another quick glance around, then

produced a charcoal-sketched image from his jacket and showed it to us.

My heart screeched to a dead halt at the sight of the familiar face. I gripped the edge of my seat and fought to control my quickening breath.

No, this couldn't be. It just *couldn't*.

"Who is that?" Jaden asked, oblivious to my impending panic attack.

"Gabriel Roche," Chris said, his voice tinged with awe. "The Vampire King."

And my mate.

3

Could anyone hear that noise? Or was it just me?

It sounded like static in my head. Like someone was crinkling tinfoil right next to my ear. And who on earth had turned down the thermostat? A second ago, it'd felt like a cozy eighty degrees, and now, the temperature had dropped to a level of frigid no amount of thermal undies could combat.

My mate...was the Vampire King?

I honestly had no idea what to make of that.

Shouldn't I have recognized him the night we'd met? The night we'd *kissed*?

The king of vampires.

Damn.

The voice in my head told me to worry about his royal status later. It didn't matter as much as the bounty. I had to focus on *that* first and let the rest fall into place later. It explained so much, though. The power he'd demonstrated, the way the other vampires had fled after he'd killed their leader—it all lined up. But I'd been too blindsided to piece it all together. Some detective I'd make.

I reached out a trembling hand and touched the picture Chris had laid on the table. Whoever had drawn this must be a talented artist, because it nailed Gabriel to a tee. Sure, I'd only met him once, but in that small amount of time, my brain had committed his face to memory. Hard not to when the man was so beautiful, it almost hurt to look at him. And this image was most definitely him—right down to his stormy gray eyes, aquiline nose, and plump lips.

Tearing my attention away from his face, I focused instead on the top of the page, where it read in bolded capital letters: **WANTED FOR MURDER**.

My heart dropped.

Murder?

What? When? And who had he supposedly killed?

I scanned the page for a victim's name, but there was nothing. Huh. How odd. The Academy always gave us a name and the circumstances surrounding their death.

I couldn't see Gabriel being a killer.

Okay, scratch that. That was one of the dumbest things I'd ever thought. Of *course* he was a killer. He was a vampire. He'd literally killed someone right in front of me. I needed to get my head on straight. I couldn't romanticize him.

The real question was, was he a murderer? Because a killer and a murderer were two different things. Gabriel had killed to protect me. That was different than murdering an innocent person. He'd saved not only my life, but the lives of my friends too. And when I'd asked why he'd helped me in the first place, he'd said, *"Because I could."* In my experience, murderers weren't that altruistic.

"Who'd he kill?" Jaden asked, shattering my train of thought.

"That information wasn't provided," Chris

admitted. "Vera said that was on a need-to-know basis, and I didn't need to know."

I dragged my gaze from Gabriel's picture and stared at Chris. Didn't need to know? That made no sense. The Academy always listed the victims' names when issuing us our bounties. An extra little motivation to slay our target.

"Odd," Jaden murmured. "Maybe they're trying to keep this as quiet as possible? He is royalty, after all."

I frowned. What did his political stature have to do with concealing his supposed victim's name? The two weren't mutually exclusive.

"Not only royalty," Josh interjected, holding his mug in front of his mouth. "He's also the leader of every vampire worldwide. This is quite the task. And it's gonna be dangerous. Think you can handle it?"

"That's why I called you here," Chris replied. "As Maddie pointed out, it isn't normal for us to hunt together, but I'm going to need help with this one. Because he's royalty, his people will protect him. And last I heard, his guards are a mixture of human and vampire. That's going to make it even more difficult."

Employing both made sense. Vampires "died" at

sunrise. Of course he'd also hire humans. Who else would protect him during the day?

"It'll make escaping after more difficult too," Jaden commented. "Not to mention, every last vampire will want your head once word gets out."

She leaned back in her chair, staring at Gabriel's portrait. For one insane moment, I wanted to rip it away from her and hide it somewhere safe.

Yeah, I definitely needed to get my shit together.

I reached for my mug and noted my weak grip. I had to brace the bottom of my cup with my other hand and force them to work together to lift it to my mouth. Thankfully, no one seemed to notice.

"Maddie?" Chris asked, his gaze swinging in my direction. "You've been really quiet. What are you thinking?"

I could only imagine the looks on my friends' faces if I told them the truth. I needed to inject some reality into the conversation. I carefully lowered my mug, then leaned forward. "I think this is above our pay grade."

All three stared at me as though I'd grown a second head.

I bit back a wince and tried to infuse my voice with as much confidence and steel as possible. I *had* to talk them out of this. And not only for Gabriel's sake, but for theirs too. Gabriel's guards would slaughter us. This was like a real-life *West Side Story*, but without all the singing and dancing.

"Guys, Gabriel is the king," I said, stating the obvious. "Do you honestly think he ever strolls around unprotected?"

Except, apparently, he did. He'd been alone the night we'd met. He'd appeared from thin air, staked the vampire trying to kill me, then chased off the others. And he'd done it all alone. Not a guard in sight. But maybe rescuing werewolves in distress qualified as his 'me time'.

I massaged my temples, trying to dull a sudden headache. "His guards, whether they're human or immortal, have all likely undergone top-notch training. Otherwise, why would he employ them? Trust me, they won't stand by idly while you kill their employer-slash-sovereign."

Chris's lips curved into a triumphant smile. "I know. I've been giving that a great deal of thought. I wanted to have a plan before I brought this to you guys."

He reached across the table and reclaimed the picture. It took all my inner strength not to snatch it out of his hand.

"I only see one solution," Chris continued,

completely oblivious to my internal struggles. "This needs to be a covert operation as opposed to our usual chase and stake."

My blood ran cold.

"Are you serious?" I demanded. My fingers clutched my mug so tightly, I heard the ceramic crack. Cursing, I put it down on a napkin and watched as coffee started trickling out. Shit. I needed to get control of myself. Humans didn't walk around shattering mugs with one hand.

"What's wrong with you?" Chris asked. "I thought you'd be on board with this. Maddie, we can't pass up this opportunity. This is their *king*. Their head honcho. If we take him out, we'd..."

We'd *what*? Cause destabilization? Start an interspecies war?

"Chris, if you kill Gabriel, you'll become a walking target for anything with fangs. No vampire would forgive you for killing their leader. Hell, for all we knew, they'd wage open war on us out of spite." Okay, maybe I was only seeing the worst-case scenarios here. But I certainly didn't see any good ones.

Chris stared at me, bewildered. "Maddie, what's going on with you? Why are you so freaked out by this?"

Why? *Why?*

Because one of my best friends was plotting to assassinate my mate. And if that wasn't good enough of a reason, he was going to get himself killed while doing it.

No, I had to put a stop to this. I had to make Chris see reason. Somehow. I couldn't lose him. Or Gabriel.

A quiet voice intruded on my thoughts.

What if Gabriel is guilty?

Good question. I needed to learn the truth. That was the most important thing here. If he was innocent, I'd do everything in my power to protect him. But if he was guilty...I'd run a stake so deep in his chest, his people wouldn't be able to pull it out.

I could do that, right?

The mere thought was a punch to the gut. The thought of killing Gabriel seemed unfathomable. But I couldn't sit back and let him murder people. That went against every oath I'd pledged to the Academy, not to mention broke my own moral code. Yes, we were mates, but that didn't mean I could turn a blind eye. On the other hand, I also wasn't about to let anyone else harm him.

If Gabriel was guilty, *I* would be the one to end him. Not Chris.

"This bloodsucker's a murderer," Chris continued when I didn't respond to his question. "And we dust murderous vamps. That's the job. Nothing else matters. The Academy protects us. So his people can hate me all they want."

"How do we even know he actually killed someone?" I blurted out. Heads swiveled our way, their eyes shockingly wide. I gritted my teeth and leaned in, lowering my voice. "For the record, we don't even know who the so-called victim is. Don't you guys think that's weird?"

Silence befell our little group. Jaden, Josh, and Chris all stared at me like I'd sprouted a second head. I grimaced and leaned back in my chair. None of us had ever questioned the Academy before, so I understood their shock.

"Maddie, are you okay?" Jaden touched my forearm. "This isn't like you."

No, I imagine it wasn't. I didn't feel like myself at all. It was like every bone in my body wanted me to run to Gabriel and warn him. But doing so betrayed my friends and the Academy—the life I'd dedicated myself to.

"You look a little flushed," Jaden continued. She pressed the back of her hand to my forehead. "And you're really warm. Sweetie, you look sick."

Werewolf metabolisms ran a little faster, which made us run a little warmer than humans. But she didn't know that. To her, it probably seemed like I was running a low-grade fever.

"Do you feel sick?" she asked.

Not physically. But emotionally, I was a wreck.

I merely nodded.

"You do look a little out of it," Josh pitched in. "Your eyes are weird. They seem a bit...yellow."

Oh. *Shit*. I slammed my eyes closed. If my friends were seeing yellow instead of green, then my wolf was far closer to the surface than I'd realized.

I slowly counted to ten in my head, all the while begging my wolf to back off. I reassured her that no one would get their hands on Gabriel without going through us first. That seemed to appease her.

Geez, I hadn't even felt her try to take control. I needed to pay better attention.

"Maybe you should go home," Jaden suggested. "We can fill you in on the plan later, when you're feeling better."

No, going home wasn't an option. I couldn't afford to miss out on anything. Especially not when Gabriel's life was at *stake*. I needed to stay, include myself in the plans and help strategize so that I could...

Could what?

Save him?

The thought struck me, but the answer came to mind in a resounding *yes*. My wolf wouldn't accept any other outcome.

And neither would I.

I could argue with myself until the cows came home, but I knew I couldn't turn my back on this. I had to save Gabriel. If it turned out that he had murdered someone, then I'd do the deed myself, no matter how much it hurt me to do it. But if he hadn't harmed anyone, then I'd protect him.

Even from my own friends.

Fuck. What a mess.

I was desperate to put a stop to all this. To convince Chris to drop this bounty. But he would *never* give it up. He abhorred vampires. Jaden and Josh loathed vampires too, but their hatred wasn't as intense as Chris's. Of the four of us, I was the only one who hadn't suffered a loss at their hands, so I wasn't as bloodthirsty as my friends. I only hunted guilty vampires. Chris, however, was on a self-declared crusade to eradicate every last "bloodsucking leech" from the planet. Slaying the king of said leeches would up his rep and mark a personal win for him. He wanted this. There'd be no reasoning with him.

Which left me with one option.

Warning Gabriel.

I could tell him about the bounty and ask him to leave. Surely he'd understand, right?

"Maddie?" Jaden called, waving a hand in front of my face.

I blinked, pulling myself out of my thoughts. "What?"

"I asked if you wanted a ride home."

She had? My mind was so chaotic, I couldn't recall her asking me anything.

"Oh," I mumbled. "Um, no. I'd like to stay, if that's alright. I want to help." The lie tasted bitter on my tongue. They were my friends, my family. But I couldn't let Chris kill Gabriel. Nor could I let Gabriel kill Chris.

"You sure?" Chris asked. "You do look like you're about to hurl."

I *felt* like it too. "Since when has that ever stopped me?"

Chris grinned, as though my response reassured him. "That's our girl." He shifted in his chair, then cleared his throat, bringing our conversation back on track. "Here's everything I know. The king is definitely in town. He arrived about two weeks ago."

"How did you find that out?" Josh asked.

"Through the wonderful world of social media," Chris said, shaking his head. "I guess even the undead can't escape it. Nothing's a secret anymore. He's famous, so people have been posting sightings. From what I've read, he's brought a full guard with him, and a few vampires have come from out of town to visit with him. Namely, the infamous Dracula and his wife. They're all holed up in the Westin."

I sucked in a sharp breath. Not only Gabriel, but Anna and Vlad were here too? Christ, that complicated things. They were personal friends of my sister. If they found out about my involvement in this, they'd hate me.

"Posh place," Jaden commented.

"Well, when you're a king," Josh added casually.

"Word is, Count Dracula, his lady, and our Gabriel are going to a charity thing tonight. *Pints for Pints* or some such," Chris continued. "He'll likely be flush with guards. I propose we scope out the hotel tonight *before* they head to the event. That'll give us a clear idea of his numbers and how his squad operates. Then, when they're out of the picture, we'll have full access to the hotel. I've got a buddy who manages the hotel and he owes me a solid. He slipped me a few staff badges, for maintenance and cleaning staff."

Holy. Shit.

With those badges, Chris could waltz right into Gabriel's suite.

This was escalating way too fast.

"We'll go in unnoticed, find Gabriel's room, study the floor plan, the whole shebang," Chris rattled off. "All this will give us a leg-up when the time comes to take the bastard out. This is the mother of all gigs, folks. No room for mistakes. We need to soak up every bit of info we can before we drive the stake in."

Every inch of me squirmed with anxiety. I gripped the table to keep myself still. My wolf wanted to bust free and kill all three of them. My friends. Simply because they were a threat to Gabriel. I couldn't let that happen. Couldn't lose control of myself.

"What if someone catches us?" I asked.

Chris shrugged. "So what if they do? We're executing a bounty. There's no law against any of this."

I bit my lip to keep from arguing. It was one thing to ask legitimate questions, but I couldn't question him too much. It'd raise suspicion. I had to play this cool. "This all sounds good. But attacking him at night seems dicey. We need to catch him during the day when he's at his most vulnerable. Recon only tonight. No staking. Agreed?"

Just saying the words sickened me.

Chris nodded. "Good idea."

Relief had me slumping forward in my chair. Now I had some time to come up with my own plan.

"If all goes well, we'll go in tomorrow afternoon for the finale," Chris finished.

Tomorrow? That soon? My heart skipped a beat. Good thing my friends weren't werewolves. If they heard my heart going haywire like that, they'd know something was off.

"We also need a headcount of his human guards," Chris continued, "and we need a clean way to do this without hurting them. Once we have all this figured out, we can slip into his room during the day and make the kill."

My mind whirled. Chris's plan had promise. Unless we wore t-shirts saying, "Vampire Slayers Unite!" Gabriel's crew wouldn't know who we were, or what we were planning. Posing as hotel staff, we'd blend right in. No one would question us.

All this meant Gabriel was on borrowed time.

Fear had my foot tapping an erratic beat under the table. I struggled to hold back the urge to run to him.

I needed to continue playing this cool.

And if *I* succeeded, Gabriel wouldn't be there when Chris went in for the kill.

I just needed to get to Gabriel first.

I LEANED AGAINST THE SIDE OF A RED-BRICKED
building across from the Westin and watched the
hotel entrance. The sun had just clocked out for the
day, and a surge of raw energy pulsated beneath my
feet. Jackson wasn't quite as flamboyant as New
Orleans. It didn't boast vampire dens on every
corner, or sell bottled blood on the street. But those
of us in the know *felt* it when the city came alive at
night, beckoning all the monsters to come out and
play.

Monsters like me and Gabriel.

I stared at the hotel, watching as people came and went. No vampires, though. Not yet anyway. The lingering daylight needed to burn off a little more before they'd venture outside. But I was ready.

After my coffee-infused rendezvous with my friends this afternoon, I'd gone home and come up with a plan. One that had soothed my anxieties enough for me to function. I'd written it all down, because it made me feel better to check things off, then tucked it into my pocket.

Step One: Stakeout the hotel. Easy.

Step Two: Extract Gabriel. Doable.

Step Three: Verify if my 'soulmate' is a murderer. Awkward.

Step Four: Depending on the results of step three, either slay Gabriel or get him the hell out of Jackson. Oh boy.

The first step had been a piece of cake once I'd separated myself from the group. I'd fed Chris some line about wanting to study the perimeter and establish an escape route. He'd agreed, telling me we'd meet after they'd investigated the interior and swap notes. I'd texted back a thumbs up emoji. With any luck, by the time we regrouped, Gabriel would be high-tailing it out of town.

I couldn't even think about the *other* scenario.

My functionality relied on my to-do list. Step two was manageable, in theory. But steps three and four were giving me hives. The thought of slaying Gabriel....

Get your head on straight, girl. You have a job to do. Now isn't the time to let some guy fuck with your head.

Easier said than done.

My wolf scratched at the surface, unhappy with the emotional roller coaster we were stuck on. One moment, I was as cool as a cucumber, the next I was sweating like a woman caught in the throes of menopause.

I had to focus instead of fretting over all the possibilities. Grabbing an elastic band out of my pocket, I raked my hair into a low pony, and straightened. Time to smarten up.

With luck, it wouldn't be much longer, considering Gabriel's plans this evening.

That afternoon, while coming up with my to-do list, I'd taken the time to do my own research. Chris had been right about the vampire fundraiser tonight. According to the website, *Pints For Pints* brought in humans from all over. In exchange for donating their blood, they'd receive free pints of root beer. This was an annual event, and one of the largest organized blood drives. Half the supply would go to local hospitals, while the other half would go to the vampiric community. A little morbid if you asked me. But hey, the donors were willing, and that was all that mattered.

With the Vampire King set to grace the event this year, participation had sky rocketed. I wasn't privy to his schedule, but from what I'd been able to suss out about him, he didn't seem to enjoy being in the limelight. It seemed safe to assume he'd show up, shake a few hands, give a speech, then bail.

Unfortunately for me, the event complicated things.

First, I lacked an entry pass, which they would be checking for at the doors. Sure, I could sneak in, but that wouldn't be easy. The next challenge was separating Gabriel from his security squad. They'd be stuck to his side like glue. On the bright side, Gabriel and my friends wouldn't be in the same building tonight. That gave me a small sense of relief. Chris had promised to keep all stakes holstered tonight, but I didn't trust him to keep his word. The guy had a vampire-slaying itch, one he loved to scratch.

All this had left me with a decision to make. Either we spoke before the event, or after. I preferred before. The sooner I spilled the beans, the sooner he'd get the hell out of Dodge. Theoretically.

Movement caught my attention.

I wedged myself deeper into the growing shadows, concealing myself from sight. The Westin's doors swung open, and a quartet stepped out onto the pavement. Unfortunately, I stood downwind, so I couldn't catch their scents. But the preternatural glint in their eyes told me they were vampires. And the action-movie-worthy arsenals strapped to their sides told me they were Gabriel's bodyguards.

Geez, these guys were giants, each one sculpted like a Greek god clad in a sleek black uniform. They moved with a lethal ease and a predator's grace. These men were warriors. There was no way I could win a fight against this Fab Four, not even in wolf form. If one got their arms around me, it'd be lights out. Gabriel had a keen eye for hiring.

One of them paused and raised his head, his nostrils flaring. His eyes narrowed, and he bared his pointed teeth, catching a whiff of something he didn't like.

"What's up?" one asked.

"Wolf," was his succinct reply.

I tucked my nose into my armpit and inhaled. My scent differed from other werewolves, since I hadn't been born one. Perhaps Gabriel's guards knew the scent of both types? Gabriel had seen me shift the night we'd met. Could be he'd passed that knowledge onto his men. Or, and this seemed more likely, maybe there was another werewolf nearby. Jackson's pack wasn't small by any means.

"This whole city reeks of wolf," another guard remarked in a British accent. He sniffed, then shrugged. "Smells like the same ol' shite to me."

The first guard's gaze swept across my hiding spot. I quietly swore, then edged deeper into the shadows. For a second, I swear he'd spotted me, but eventually his gaze moved on. A few moments later, he gestured, and the Westin's doors parted once again.

My heartbeat stuttered to a stop the second Gabriel appeared. He cut a striking figure in a charcoal suit that mirrored his eyes. Its tailoring accentuated his physique, highlighting the muscular lines of his body. Even his hair was perfectly styled, falling in dark waves to his cheekbones.

Sweet Jiminy Cricket, I'd almost forgotten how beautiful he was.

It'd only been three days since we first met—three days since we'd shared that world-changing, life-altering kiss. Yet, I still had to fight the urge to go to him. I yearned to touch him, as if he was some irresistible force I couldn't ignore. It unnerved me to hell. I barely knew this man. But my body didn't care. It *wanted* him.

Before I could do something stupid like throw myself at him, a black Lincoln Navigator rolled up to the entrance. Gabriel, flanked by his guards, moved toward the vehicle. I cursed, my eyes flicking to the lot behind me where I'd parked my car. I'd hoped I'd have a chance to speak with Gabriel before they left for the venue.

I bit my bottom lip and considered my choices. My friends were already inside, so I couldn't risk speaking with Gabriel here. If they spotted us, it would ruin everything. I also didn't want his guards to overhear this conversation. If it turned out he'd murdered someone, I'd handle it, fast and painless— or so I kept telling myself. His guards wouldn't allow that to happen.

I needed to get him alone.

But how on earth was I supposed to separate him from his entourage?

I only had one option here. A really, *really* stupid option.

I pulled my hood up over my head, sucked in a deep, steadying breath, then stepped out of the shadows. Nonchalantly, I walked past the red-bricked building across from the Westin, hands casually tucked into my pockets. *Just strolling by. No biggie. Nothing to see here.* I passed by the group of vampires, but kept Gabriel in my periphery, *hoping* he caught whiff of my scent.

Thankfully, Mother Nature did me a solid and shifted the wind, wafting my scent in his direction.

Gabriel halted, his hand resting on the door handle. He lifted his head and turned slightly in my direction, sniffing the air. A slow smile curved his lips, one that set my insides on fire.

Oh yeah.

He knew I was here.

But from the expressions on his guards' faces, they did too.

I barely had a chance to curse before one of them snarled quietly, "Werewolf!" and went all medieval on me, drawing his sword.

The other three reacted instantly. Two moved to flank Gabriel and shove him into the SUV, while the other two charged toward me, their fangs glinting in the streetlight.

Shocked, I went for my stake. My wolf rushed forward, eager to take over, but I couldn't shift here. We were in public. Too exposed.

Easy girl.

She reluctantly obeyed.

I gripped my stake, ready to strike, when Gabriel sprang into action. I barely saw him move, but he suddenly stood in front of me, shielding me from his guards with his own body. And from his steel grip dangled one of his men whose feet hovered in midair. I inched around Gabriel and stole a glimpse at his face. A shiver rolled down my spine at the sight of his murderous expression. His face had thinned back until nothing remained but the vampire within. His eyes blazed like hot coals, his fangs on full display. He looked...monstrous.

And lord help me. It turned me on.

Clearly I had issues.

"If *anyone* lays a finger on her, I will eviscerate you *and* all your loved ones," Gabriel announced in a voice colder than ice. "Do you understand?"

The guard Gabriel held nodded, while the other three sheathed their swords and stepped back.

Fuck. That was hot.

Was I twisted for thinking that?

Absolutely.

Did I care?

Not in the least.

After sizing them up, Gabriel slowly lowered the

guard. The instant his boots hit the pavement, he sheathed his sword and stepped back with the others.

"Leave," Gabriel ordered.

His security team shared a concerned glance. "Sire, it's our job to take you to the fundraiser."

A blistering growl tore from Gabriel's throat. "I said *leave*. Do *not* make me tell you again." He stared them down until one by one, his guards dropped their gazes. "I will meet you there. Do not disobey me."

His tone very much suggested they wouldn't live to see sunrise if they did.

His guards bowed. The leader's glare found me, and it was a look I knew well. He didn't like me one bit and probably planned to kill me the next time we crossed paths. I'd like to see him try.

All four guards snapped straight, then quickly piled into the SUV and drove off, leaving me and Gabriel alone on the street. I should have felt relieved. Except Gabriel was now without protection, and I didn't like that one bit.

He was vulnerable. Exposed. Easy prey. And my friends were here.

As though to remind me of that very fact, my phone chimed. Twenty bucks said it was from one of them, telling me where to meet them. Little did they know, I had no intentions of meeting them anywhere.

Gabriel turned, his eyes meeting mine. For a moment, the city's noise dimmed, and everything else fell away. This moment was all that mattered.

"You," Gabriel whispered, almost reverently.

He reached for me, his hands gently framing my face. His touch sent me into a dizzying spin and muddled my brain. This wasn't me. I wasn't the sort of girl who let a boy screw with her head. But Gabriel was no boy. And he utterly overwhelmed me.

He held my gaze as he eased my hood back, exposing me to the streetlight. His palms cradled my cheeks, and I leaned into him, my eyes fluttering shut.

He felt like...*home*. Or rather, what I assumed home felt like.

I'd never experienced this sort of connection before. No matter how many homes I'd bounced between, no matter how many foster parents had taken me in, I'd *never* felt welcomed or loved. Not until the Academy. My friends loved me and would die for me. But this felt *different* somehow. More soul consuming. And I wanted more.

Gabriel rested his forehead against mine. I

sighed and listened as all my many broken pieces fell into place.

We hardly knew each other. But something unexplained drew us together. His touch felt as vital as my next breath. I craved his touch. Craved *him*. It was all so surreal.

But then reality invaded, reminding me of my purpose here tonight.

I blinked open my eyes to find Gabriel's steel-gray ones boring into mine.

"We can't stay here," I whispered. "It's dangerous."

He straightened, severing the connection between us. "I have a room—"

"No!" I shouted.

Gabriel arched a brow, clearly confused by my outburst.

I shook my head. "We need to talk. But it has to be somewhere we can be alone."

He studied me, as though trying to solve a riddle.

I shot the Westin a panicked glance. Chris, Jaden, and Josh were somewhere inside. And here we were, standing beneath the streetlight, exposed.

"Please, Gabriel," I said.

That damn grin of his spread across his face.

"What?"

"I like hearing you say my name." He leaned closer, amusement twinkling in his eyes.

I scoffed. "Let's go."

He immediately fell into step beside me. "And pray tell, my lovely mate. Where are we going?"

I stole one final glance at the Westin. I'd made my choice. "Anywhere but here."

5

Without a word, I took Gabriel's hand, my warm werewolf flesh contrasting starkly with the icy smoothness of his vampire skin. I found it particularly interesting that our differing temperatures didn't bother me. His cool temperature complemented my warmth as though we were two halves of one whole. I squashed that sentimental thought. Now wasn't the time for poetic analogies. I had other lethal matters to deal with first.

Afraid of crossing paths with Chris, Jaden, and Josh, I dragged Gabriel to my car and stuffed him into the passenger seat. Then I jumped behind the wheel and sped away from the Westin, driving us into the heart of urban Jackson. My destination? Good question. I hadn't given this part much thought. In all my planning, *this* was the part I'd blanked on.

"Where are we going?" Gabriel asked.

I glanced over to find him leaning against the passenger door, his attention trained wholly on me. He looked...amused. Whereas I was as anxious as a cat on hot bricks. I had no idea where we were going, but I needed to decide, pronto. It needed to be somewhere secluded. Private. Somewhere no one could expose our location.

The first place that immediately sprang to mind was the same one I'd chased the vampire through last night. It was also the same place I'd used as a hideout during my foster care days. A place where I'd gone to get away from everything.

My body reacted instinctively. I swerved onto the I-55, muscle memory guiding me to Lakeland Terrace, then to the parking lot. I opened my door and stepped out, the sound of rushing river waters filling my senses.

"Nice place," Gabriel observed.

"Yeah," I replied. "It is." Last night, I hadn't had

a chance to reminisce, but now the memories came flooding back.

My wistful tone caught Gabriel's attention. He cocked his head as he regarded me, as though trying to puzzle me out.

I reached toward him, smiling when he took my hand without question. Together, we moved deeper into the park until the sound of the city faded, replaced by the soft rustling of bare trees in the winter breeze. This haven was so different from the concrete jungle we'd left behind.

Crossing a rickety bridge, we neared a long-abandoned wooden cabin tucked away amidst the overgrown brush. This hideaway had served as my sanctuary countless times over the years. It had weathered numerous Mississippi storms and probably even more teen angst. As far as I knew, no one had ever claimed it, so I'd adopted it as mine. But it'd been nearly a decade since I'd last visited.

Pausing in front of the weather-worn door, I turned to Gabriel. His figure struck a dark silhouette against the moonlit landscape. Pushing the door open with a gentle prod, I winced when it fell to the ground with a heavy thump. Guess the cabin hadn't weathered the years well.

"Okay, in you go," I commanded Gabriel.

His brows rose, and he snuck a quick peek inside the cramped space. Barely enough room for the two of us, but we'd manage. This was a conversation that required privacy.

He ducked into the cabin, his large form occupying most of the space. When he stood, his head brushed the weathered roof, his hair catching on the broken slats.

I followed quickly after and gently shut the door. The cabin was far from soundproof, but it offered a hint of privacy. And with luck, we'd hear anyone's approach before they heard us.

"This is...romantic?" Gabriel teased.

He faced me, humor twinkling in those damn eyes of his. He stood before a small, crooked window, his hulking body engulfing the width of the frame and blocking the moonlight. We stood in complete darkness, yet we could see each other perfectly. My gaze traced the hard line of his jaw and the sensual curve of his lips.

God, those lips...

No. Concentrate.

Gabriel stepped away from the window and moonlight spilled into the cabin, illuminating the rough floor. His hand rose, and I knew he had every intention of touching me. But I couldn't allow that.

Not yet. If I let him touch me now, I'd never learn the answers to my questions.

"Did you murder someone?" I blurted out.

His hand froze midair. "I beg your pardon?"

"It's a simple question," I mumbled, my voice cracking. "Yes or no. Did you murder someone?"

He blinked slowly. "Might need some specifics on the timeline there, luv. Are we talking recently? Ever? What's the scope we're referring to here?"

I bristled, but understood his question. "Recently. It would have been since you arrived here."

He cocked his head, his smile slipping. "You're serious?"

"Dead serious."

His brow furrowed, and I could have sworn his gray eyes turned black, as though angered by my question. His jaw tightened, and a muscle throbbed near his temple. "The only person I've killed since stepping foot on American soil was that vampire at the bar. You might remember her? Long red hair? Lethal fangs? Tried to murder you? In case you've forgotten, I staked her to save you."

Heat flushed my cheeks. I remembered. And he knew I did. Immediately afterward, we'd shared our first—and *only*—kiss.

"It wouldn't have been a vampire," I told him, fidgeting with the hem of my sweater. The weight of his gaze had me squirming, and I hated it. "It would have been a human."

He jolted, as though taken aback by such a suggestion. After a moment's silence, he shook his head and chuckled bitterly. "Shouldn't really bother me that you'd think I'm capable of that. But it does."

"I need an answer on this, Gabriel," I told him.

He sighed and stared at me, his eyes narrowing. "No. Okay? I haven't killed a human in ages."

I sagged in relief. I hadn't realized how much this had been weighing on me.

"Was this some sort of test?" he demanded. "Some slayer nonsense? To see if I'm worthy of you?"

My head snapped up. "What?" I waved a hand. "No, Gabriel. Listen." I took a deep breath and dropped the bombshell. "The Academy's put a bounty on your head."

He slate-gray eyes widened slightly.

"They're hunting you, Gabriel. Slayers. You're in danger."

A smug smile crossed his features. "I'm always in danger, Maddie. It's part of being king."

His arrogance irked me, but I knew he had a point. He was a king. Danger was never too far away.

"This isn't about your ego, Gabriel. You're not invincible. And the slayer who's after you is one of the best. He'll—"

"Who is it?" Gabriel interrupted, moving closer.

His sudden approach startled me, and I took a step back, pressing myself against the decaying wall.

"Who's after me, Maddie?" he asked, his gaze practically pinning me to the spot. Sweet lord, the way he said my name made me weak in the knees. I wanted to melt into him and tell him everything. But I couldn't. I *wouldn't*. I'd never betray Chris like that.

I cleared my throat. "You need to leave the country."

His grin vanished, replaced by an aggravatingly annoying look of defiance. "And what? Run? Hide? No."

"Not hide," I bit out, exasperation simmering beneath the surface. "Just don't be *here*. Once you leave the Academy's jurisdiction, the contract defaults. You'll never be able to return to the States, but that's a small price to pay—"

"The hell it is," he snarled.

I froze, startled by his vehement response. "Why do you care so much? You don't even live here, right?"

"But *you* do," he said.

Shit, I almost swooned right there.

He lifted his hand once more and tucked a stray strand of hair behind me ear. His touch sent a thrill down my spine. "You're here. So I'm not going anywhere."

That sparked my temper. "You're not safe here."

"I'm not safe anywhere," he shot back. "That's why I have guards."

"And where are they now, huh?" I retorted, matching his tone. "You sent them away. And what about a few nights ago at the bar? You were alone then too. You aren't as safe as you think, especially if you keep taking risks like that."

"I didn't know there was a bounty on my head," he murmured. "And going back to that—who am I accused of murdering?"

"I don't know," I confessed, defeat rounding my shoulders. "We weren't given the victim's name."

"We?" he asked. "Who else knows about this?"

I snorted. Solid attempt, Gabriel. But I wasn't falling for that.

"And the Academy has deemed me guilty?" he continued.

I nodded.

He placed a forearm against the wall and leaned

forward, his presence enveloping me. He brushed his nose against my cheek. "Who's the lucky slayer, Maddie?"

Fury rushed through me. I lifted my hands and shoved him. Much to my surprise, Gabriel didn't so much as budge. My eyes shot wide, and I stared up at him. I was a *werewolf*, for frick's sake. I wasn't weak by any means, and he hadn't so much as twitched.

His mouth curved into an arrogant half-smile.

A grin I wanted to punch right off his face.

"Keeping it a secret, huh? Fine." He pushed off the wall and strutted across the room. "Let's think this through. The Academy thinks I'm a murderer, but someone must have pointed their finger at me first, right? That means someone is pulling the Academy's strings."

I scoffed. "You've got it all wrong. The Academy doesn't play favorites. They investigate, find proof, then render their verdict. No strings attached."

Gabriel shot me a glance over his shoulder and tsked under his breath. "Everyone has a price, luv."

Anger pulsed through my body. "You have no idea what you're talking about. Look, all that matters is your safety. If you leave—"

"I already told you, I'm not going anywhere."

I threw my hands in the air and started pacing.

Stubborn, stubborn vampire. Were they all like this? I'd killed my fair share of them, but I'd only ever formally met Vlad and Anna. And they'd seemed normal—for vampires.

"Is this why you dragged me here?" Gabriel asked. "To tell me to leave town?"

"Well"—I turned and dropped my arms to my sides—"that seemed the better alternative."

"Than what?"

"Than seeing you dead," I bit out, my lips curling into a snarl.

That damn grin returned to his lips.

"Oh, for crying out loud. Now what? What's so funny?"

"Not funny, per se," he said. "But it's nice to know you're concerned about me." He stopped and clasped his hands behind his back. "You like me."

I sputtered. Like him? What? No. I—I... "I just don't want to see you dead."

"I'm already dead," he oh-so-helpfully pointed out.

I rolled my eyes. "I don't want to see you double dead."

"Double dead?" he teased, revealing a set of sharp fangs when he smiled.

My attention was involuntarily drawn to his

teeth. I had fangs too, only mine were bigger, and they vanished when in human form. His were always there.

"Look, you may think you're this awesome god-like vampire who can't be killed—"

"God-like?" he repeated. "I like the sound of that."

"I said you may *think* you're god-like," I corrected. "But you're not. We're slayers for a reason. We're trained to take you guys down. No matter what you think of yourself, *we're* better. Because we have to be."

A glint twinkled in Gabriel's eyes. "You think you can take me?"

I knew I could. "Are you going to leave town or not?"

His smile wavered. "Not."

I cursed and tipped my head back, praying to whatever gods were out there for patience. Had fate really determined *this* man to be my mate? He made my damn blood boil.

What the hell was I supposed to do now?

My phone chimed.

Muttering a quiet curse, I flicked a glance at my watch and noted the time. Seven forty-five. I dug my phone out of my back pocket and illuminated the screen. It lit up the dark cabin, blinding me for a moment. When I could finally see, I read the messages scrolling through our group text.

Chris: King G a no-show at the fundraiser event. Guards in hotel. King G missing.

Josh: What are you thinking?

Chris: Heard talk from the guards that he's out on his own.

Jaden: Wanna track him down?

Chris: Anyone heard from Maddie?

Josh: Negative.

Jaden: Ditto. She's probably busy scoping out the escape route.

Chris: Okay. If King G is somewhere in the city, unprotected, we should track him down and get a feel for the situation.

Josh: And if we find him?

Chris: We take the shot. Meet in the lobby in five minutes.

Shit. Shit. *Shit!*

I gripped my cell and slid it back into my pocket.

"Bad news I assume?" Gabriel asked.

"Word has spread that you're out here unprotected. Who would do that? The message said the intel came from one of your guards? Would one of them betray you like that?"

Gabriel's eyes narrowed. "My guards would *never* betray me."

Well, someone had.

My friends weren't werewolves, so I didn't have to worry about them following our scent trail, but they *would* track us down. Chris was the best damn slayer in the Academy, with me coming in second. I wasn't a bodyguard, though. This was so out of my wheelhouse.

I pinched the bridge of my nose and contemplated my options.

I *needed* to get Gabriel the hell out of here. LeFleur's was a fairly big area, large enough that a person could hide here for a few days, but I didn't have the luxury of time. Sunlight was a vampire's worst nightmare, and our makeshift cabin wouldn't protect Gabriel from the lethal rays. He would burn, and I'd have to stand here and watch. I also couldn't send him back to his hotel, not with my friends waiting in the wings.

I unleashed a string of curses and resumed pacing.

"You seem a bit wound up," Gabriel said. "I could help with that, ya'know."

I shot him a droll look.

"What?" He cocked a brow. "I'm a talented man."

"Great, you're a comedian."

He shrugged. "It's only funny if you don't take me seriously."

Ignoring him, I smoothed my hands down my face and resumed strategizing. If Gabriel wouldn't willingly leave Jackson, then I'd force him to. It was as simple as that. I needed him somewhere safe while I figured out how to fix this mess. And if that meant risking his anger, so be it.

"Do you need a massage?" Gabriel questioned, his tone still teasing. "Or a hug?"

A hug? I didn't hug people. Probably because no one had ever wanted to hug me growing up. But it did give me an idea, one that would likely end with me dealing with a pissed off vampire.

I spun to face him. He stood near the door, hidden in shadows, watching me.

"A hug?" I repeated, braving a step toward him.

Gabriel eyed my movements, a smirk lighting his handsome face. "Sure. A hug could help. Works wonders for the nerves."

My heart pounded as I stood there, torn between *actually* wanting the comfort of his arms and fulfilling my plan. A part of me doubted myself, doubted that I could do this. He was my mate, after all. But if he refused to believe he was in danger, then that left me to take charge of the situation.

I took a slow step toward him, my lips curling into a shy smile. The dizzying scent of him filled my senses as I closed my eyes and nestled into his chest. He hesitated for a moment, but then his muscles flexed beneath his shirt as his arms closed around me. He was a pillar of strength, one I felt I could forever lean on. And I was about to destroy that. After this, I doubted he'd ever trust me again.

A pang of regret hit my chest, but I pushed it down.

This was for his own good.

I slipped one arm around his waist while the other rose slowly, purposefully. I leaned back and gazed up at him, then cupped his cheek. It took every ounce of skill I possessed to keep my expression from giving me away.

With a whispered apology, I grabbed his head and smashed it, *hard*, against the doorframe. The cabin shuddered from the strength of the blow, and for a moment, I thought the whole thing would come tumbling down around us.

Gabriel released me and stumbled backward, clutching his poor head. But he didn't go down.

Strong bastard.

But then, I already knew that. I'd seen him in action.

He growled under his breath and shook his head, as though trying to clear his thoughts. My wolf gave a small whimper, one that almost slipped past my lips. I hated hurting him. But what choice had he left me?

Committed to my plan, I dropped into a fighting position and bided my time. The instant he lowered his hands, I struck. I whipped in a tight circle and snapped my leg out. My heel connected with his jaw with enough force to kill a human. For Gabriel, though, it merely sent him spinning into the nearest wall. He staggered. Teetered. Then, with a shocked expression, went down like a ton of bricks, dust pluming around his body when he landed.

Remorse cut through me. I hated that it'd come to this. Hated that he'd left me no other option. He'd thought himself invincible, and I'd proved otherwise. Of course, I was probably the last person in the world he'd expected would hurt him, so I wasn't sure this qualified as fair game. But I still hated that it'd come to this. Better me than my friends, though. They wouldn't have stopped until he was dead.

I crouched next to him and brushed his hair back from his face.

Blood flowed from an inch long gash next to his temple.

Ouch. I'd gotten him good. He was going to be royally pissed when he woke up. His Majesty wouldn't appreciate that I'd rung his bell so spectacularly. And yes, I did feel bad about it. But he hadn't left me much of an option.

Now came the truly challenging part.

Getting him the heck out of here. Thank goodness my car was nearby. Vampires were notoriously tough bastards, so I couldn't imagine he'd stay unconscious for long. And I needed to get him somewhere safe before he woke up. Then I just needed to figure out who accused him of murder and call off the bounty, all before my friends found him.

Good thing I liked a challenge.

6

I PULLED OFF THE HIGHWAY AND ONTO A GRAVEL road, one that led me toward a rustic cabin surrounded by a wall of pine trees. In the dark of night, the cabin didn't quite look familiar, but that didn't surprise me. It'd been years since Jaden had last brought me here, and we'd only come the once. From the looks of it, no one had been caring for the property in her absence. The weeds and tall grass now overran the grounds. It felt like the right place, though. I only hoped I didn't bust inside and scare the bejeebers out of some innocent resident.

After a quick glance back at the still unconscious Gabriel, I climbed out of my car and approached the cabin. There weren't any lights on inside, but that didn't mean much. It was well after midnight, and any sensible person would have tucked themselves into bed by now.

Guess I wasn't a sensible person.

Approaching the door, I lifted my fist and gave a solid knock, one loud enough to wake the dead.

Nothing.

No sound of movement, no lights flicking on, no whispered questions. Nothing but dead silence.

I tried the doorknob, unsurprised to find it locked.

I peered through the main window, relieved to find Jaden hadn't closed the curtains the last time we were here. I could see right into the living room, and thankfully, it all looked familiar.

Phew. I was in the right place. Jaden had brought me here about a year after her fiancé's death to help clean out his stuff. But after that, she'd refused to ever step foot inside again. They'd bought this place as a sort of sanctuary—a home away from home. Instead, it'd become a haunting memory, but one she refused to sell.

The last time I was here, Jaden had shown me

where she kept the spare key. And seeing as how she hadn't been here since, it seemed a safe bet to assume the key was still there. I crouched in the overgrown garden bed, grasped the one big rock, and turned it over. *Aha*! There it was. And to think she'd razzed me about not rotating where I kept my spare key. Tsk, tsk.

I plucked the key from under the rock, then approached the door, and slipped it into the doorknob. With a quick turn, the lock disengaged, and I opened the door. The smell of musty air and stale linens wrinkled my nose, but I stepped inside, relieved it was the right place.

Pocketing the key, I returned to the car and stared inside. I had a feeling this wouldn't be easy. Popping open the door, I hooked my arms beneath Gabriel's armpits and hauled his ass out of the vehicle. My god, the man weighed a ton! Thank the moon for my wolfy strength. Without it, there was no way I could drag him inside.

I grunted as I pulled his taller, heavier, and inconveniently limp body across the terrain. I was far stronger than a human, but nothing could have prepared me for the comatose Vampire King.

"Okay, Gabriel, let's do this," I wheezed as I hoisted him up the porch stairs. But as soon as we reached the front door, his body came to an abrupt halt as though meeting a brick wall.

I grunted, pulling harder. Was he caught on something? Or just too damn big to fit through the narrow doorway? Cursing, I gave another hard pull, but something invisible slammed against Gabriel's prone form. I stumbled, his slack body dropping me onto the porch with a thud that rattled my bones.

What on earth...?

I peeked over my shoulder at the door and saw literally *nothing*. Vexed, I shoved my hand inside, meeting no barrier. But when I did the same with Gabriel's hand, it thunked off *something* and ricocheted back at me. Only my werewolf reflexes saved me from a hard punch to the face. A story no one would ever let me live down.

I scowled at the vampire. "Even in your sleep, you're a royal pain in my ass."

Something was preventing him from entering—something magical. No doubt about that. I could pass. But he couldn't. Why?

Had Jaden warded the cabin? Vampires had killed her fiancé, after all. Maybe this was her way of keeping them out. But that didn't make sense. First, she never used this place anymore. She wanted nothing to do with it. In fact, she'd once told me to make use of it as I see fit. *Mi casa, su casa*, and all that. And second, she would have told me if she knew of such a ward. Hell, the Academy would have loved to get their hands on that kind of knowledge.

"Shall we give this another try?" I asked the unresponsive vampire sprawled at my feet.

I stood and jumped over the threshold without any issue. I hopped back and forth between the porch and interior, as though to show myself all was well on my end. The problem definitely wasn't me.

Then I hooked my arms under Gabriel's and hauled him backward. Once again, he slammed into the invisible barrier and slid down.

Brushing dirt off my clothes, I glared at the vampire's serene, moonlit face. My foot tapped as I considered my options. I certainly couldn't leave him here until he woke up. Who knew how long that would be? And the sun would be rising in a few hours. At least I didn't have to worry about any nosey neighbors.

No, there had to be a solution to this. One I wasn't seeing.

Okay.

Straightening, I blew out a breath and propped my hands on my hips. Something was barricading him from the house. Something that didn't affect me.

I was a werewolf, he was a vampire. Did that play a factor in all this?

A second later, understanding dawned, and I smacked myself in the forehead.

"Idiot!" I scolded myself.

Vampire one-oh-one. They couldn't enter residences without permission.

Wow. I couldn't believe I'd forgotten that. Guess the cabin in Fleur's park didn't qualify since no one actually owned it.

But that presented an even bigger problem. I didn't own this cabin. Jaden did. Could I even invite Gabriel inside? And would it count if he wasn't conscious? If not, I'd have to come up with a different solution, and quickly.

Only one way to find out. I only hoped her *mi casa, su casa* comment allowed us to enter.

"Gabriel, please come in."

Absolutely nothing happened to tell me whether it'd worked.

I stepped out onto the porch, took his hand, and waved it over the barrier. *Presto.* His hand passed through without any obstruction.

I dropped his arm and straightened, practically cackling at myself. Some vampire hunter I was. I'd forgotten one of the main rules. In all fairness, it wasn't as though I'd dealt with this before. It wasn't like I invited them inside for tea and crackers. Gabriel was the first.

Well, that was one obstacle down. Only about a million more to go.

Gathering him up as best I could, I dragged his handsome butt into the cabin, kicked the door shut, then deposited him onto the loveseat. His long legs hung over the loveseat's armrest on one side, and his head propped against the other. If he were human, I'd worry about the inevitable neck crick, but lucky for him, those sorts of maladies didn't affect the undead.

At least he was inside now, though. And away from Jackson. No one would even think to look for us here. Jaden barely thought of this place, and Gabriel's people didn't know it existed. So long as no one had followed us, we'd be fine.

I rested my hands on my hips and stared down at the vampire clocked out on the loveseat. It'd been about an hour since I'd knocked him out. There really wasn't any reason for me to worry. Sure, I'd clocked that poor noodle of his and he probably had a brain injury his body was fighting to heal. But since there were only a few ways to kill a vampire— beheading, fire, sunlight, and staking—I knew he would be fine. I'd just expected him to wake up by now.

I crouched by his side and stroked his cheek, hoping for some movement. An eye flutter, a lip twitch, *something*. But he remained as still as the dead.

Pursing my lips, I stood and considered my predicament. Sunrise was still a few hours from now. Hopefully he woke before then. I'd never seen a vampire during the day before, and to be honest, the idea of seeing him "dead" made me nervous. My sister had once told me that it was the most unnerving thing she'd ever seen—watching Anna and Vlad "die" at sunrise.

Sunrise.

Shit.

I spun around and inspected the living room, wincing at the sight of the massive window across from the loveseat. I flicked the nearest light switch and prayed the lights turned on. When they did, I sighed in relief. This place brought Jaden immeasurable pain, but it seemed she cared enough to keep the electricity up and running. That would certainly make life easier.

I hurried through the rest of the cabin, taking stock of our situation. It didn't take long considering the cabin only consisted of a kitchen, living room, bathroom, and—*gulp*—a single bedroom. Oh man. How could I have forgotten that little tidbit? *One* bedroom? And not only one bedroom, but one bed too. That was going to be a problem. A *huge* problem. But not the most pressing one at the moment. I'd worry about that after I made this place hospitable for a vampire. If such a thing was possible.

I ferreted out the linen closet and ravaged it for any kind of covering sturdier than the thin curtains Jaden had hung in the windows. Lo and behold, I had a few choices, most of which were adorned with baby animals. A tad creepy for a grown woman, but hey, beggars can't be choosers. Up next, I needed hardware. The kind I'd need to fasten these blankets over the windows.

I strode into the kitchen and rummaged through the drawers. I'd never known relief quite like what ripped through me when I found a single hammer and a box of nails tucked in the back of what looked like a junk drawer.

The next item on my mental checklist required me to sprint back to my car and pop the trunk. As a rule, I kept an emergency roadside kit and a spare vampire-extermination kit in there. Between the two, I was the proud owner of a tarp—for disposing bodies if needed—a fireproof blanket, extra stakes, and, um, shackles. I hadn't needed to use any of this stuff yet, but it seemed their day had finally come.

As I charged back inside with my backup slayer kit in hand, I had to admit, I was totally winging this. I had no idea what consisted of a safe-haven for a vampire. All I knew was I had to make the place as dark as possible. Worst-case scenario, maybe I could bury him in the backyard until the sun set.

I shuddered, imagining that conversation.

"Where's your mate, Maddie?"

"Buried in the backyard until the sun goes down."

"Oh, how...nice?"

Shaking off that disturbing mental image, I got to work. First, I shackled Gabriel's legs to the loveseat. The restraints wouldn't hold him for long, but perhaps it would slow him down and give me enough time to reason with him. Then I hung the tarp over the living room window, ensuring it was nice and taut before hanging a blanket over it. Next, I tackled the bedroom. I didn't have a second tarp, so I hung two blankets instead, covering every bit of the window before stepping back and studying my handiwork. I turned off the bedroom light and was promptly enveloped in darkness. However, given that it was nighttime, it didn't offer me much insight as to whether my work would hold up during the day.

Now I *really* wished Gabriel would wake up already, if only to assure me he would survive the day.

I snatched the fire-retardant blanket and stretched it across the bed. If any light trickled into the room, I could swaddle Gabriel like a vampire burrito—or a *vampurrito*. Ha. I cracked myself up.

But the list of remaining issues was longer than a Monday morning. My spur-of-the-moment kidnapping meant I'd broken the first rule of the Boy Scouts. I wasn't prepared. We had no spare clothes, no food for me, and no blood the esteemed Majesty out there. That wasn't exactly something I stocked in my vampire kit. Yes, my veins were pumping with the stuff, but that hardly meant I was willing to turn myself into a buffet for him. I wasn't a walking Happy Meal.

A quick search on my phone told me there was a small town about ten minutes away by car. But that meant leaving Gabriel behind, unguarded. And that didn't sit well with me.

Huffing under my breath, I stood in the living room and glared at the sleeping vampire. He'd simply have to make do without. Pure and simple. At least until I could think of a better solution. We were in the woods, so maybe he could feed on the animals or something. There were plenty nearby. I could hear the deer rustling around in the bush.

Then came the mother of all problems. The one I'd been resolutely ignoring while fortifying the cabin.

My gaze flitted uneasily between Gabriel and the bedroom. Somehow, the bed that had seemed big enough to fit a small family the last time I was here now suddenly seemed half the size. And it didn't help that the man was enormous. At least six-foot-three.

But what other options did we have?

The living room offered a loveseat, an overused chair, and a table. That was it.

The loveseat could hold me, but it would make for quite the uncomfortable sleep. I had a few blankets left. Perhaps I could make a bed on the floor? Or sleep in the car? No, that wouldn't work. I needed to be close in case things went sideways.

Ugh. This was one can of worms I hadn't expected while kidnapping my soulmate. Safety had been my only concern. But cohabiting in a small cabin in the heartland of Mississippi took things to a whole new level of intimacy I *knew* I wasn't prepared for.

I sank into the well-loved chair and stared at Gabriel's features. He seemed almost peaceful, whereas I was fighting to keep from chewing off my fingernails. I tried to mentally prepare myself for the moment he woke. How did I explain that I'd knocked him out, kidnapped him, and taken him to a cabin hidden deep in the woods for his own good? I'd stolen him from his people and security detail, kept him from appearing at the fundraiser tonight, and injured him.

A great start to our nonexistent relationship.

"Okay, Maddie," I whispered to myself as I let down my hair. "You're not a deranged abductor. You're protecting him from your friends." Well, I kind of *was* a deranged kidnapper. I'd acted purely on instinct. And now here we were, in a cabin with no supplies and only one bed.

I leaned forward and brushed the hair back from his forehead, gently tracing the sharp arch of his eyebrows. It was strange how fate played out, how it'd rearranged our lives so completely to bring us to this moment.

The universe sure had a sick sense of humor. But then, I'd always thought so.

My phone rang, shattering the silence. I jumped at the sound, then laughed at my foolishness and dug my phone out of my pocket. At the sight of Jaden's name, my stomach twisted with anxiety.

Great. Just great.

I wasn't ready for the third degree yet. She'd called me earlier, when I'd no-showed at the post-hotel rendezvous. I'd been on the road then and hadn't answered. If I didn't pick up this time, they'd assume the worst and kick off a city-wide manhunt. They'd report me missing to the Academy, who would then mobilize all the other slayers. They took the safety of our people quite seriously.

There was only one option here—one I wasn't thrilled about.

I accepted the call and held the phone to my ear. "Hey, Jaden."

"Oh, thank god! She answered." I heard movement on the other end. Footsteps. "Maddie, where the hell are you? And why haven't you been answering my calls or texts? We were all supposed to meet over an hour ago!"

"I know," I whispered. "I'm so sorry."

Ugh, what in the world could I tell her? The truth, "*Hey, my bad, but your vampire target is actually my soul mate, so I ran away with him,*" would likely blow up in my face. They'd think I'd lost my mind. Hell, maybe I had.

"What's wrong? Are you okay?"

"Yeah. I, uh..." I took a deep breath, then went for a lie that was the staple of TV dramas, but new to my repertoire. "I've got a family situation." It wasn't *entirely* a lie. Gabriel was my mate, and we definitely had a situation developing.

"What do you mean? What happened? Are Lucy and the kids okay?"

Jaden's worry only made me feel so much worse. She'd met them a few times now, thanks to my dream of having a big family. Having been a foster kid, I'd never had one before. So when I met Sam and Lucy, I'd immediately introduced them to my friends. Lucy and Jaden had gotten on well enough, but it was Josh and Sam's bromance that was straight out of a rom-com.

I made a mental note to call Lucy after all this. She'd have my back. She always did.

"I'm not sure of all the details," I lied again. "Lucy called and said she needs me, so I'm on my way to her place now."

Silence stretched over the line. I heard movement, then the sound of muffled voices. Jaden must have cupped the mic to talk to Josh and Chris. Even with my werewolf hearing, I couldn't pick up on what they said.

When Jaden returned, I heard Chris's voice clear as day, insisting Jaden find out what'd happened. The fact they cared about me so much was touching and lying to them made me feel like shit. I mean, right in front of me was the very vampire they were hunting.

I needed to end this call. Now. "Jaden, I have to go—"

"What? No, Maddie. Tell us what's going on."

"I love you, and I'll call you soon, okay? Tell Chris I'm sorry. I don't think I'll be able to help him much with his contract."

Understatement of the year.

"Maddie—"

"I really do have to go. I'm driving, and I don't have you connected to the speaker. Bye, Jaden."

I ended the call, then slumped back in the chair and sighed.

No sooner had I hung up than a barrage of text messages assaulted my poor phone. Concern dripped from every message. The guilt knotted my stomach, so I flipped my phone into silent mode and put it away. I couldn't deal with them right now. Or the guilt. I needed a clear head for the impending shitstorm when Gabriel woke.

I WAS ABOUT TO DIAL LUCY'S NUMBER WHEN Gabriel came awake, sitting bolt upright on the cramped sofa. I choked back a gasp and pressed a hand to my chest. He'd scared the ever-loving crap out of me. Who woke up like that? Just shooting upward like some possessed mummy?

Vampires, I guess. Especially a vampire I'd recently injured and was now likely on full alert.

Gabriel scanned the cabin with a dark scowl, his gaze landing on me with a look of complete and utter betrayal.

"Have you gone mad?" were the first words he uttered, his sharp canines glittering with a dangerous sheen. His gray eyes held a preternatural edge, one that might have sent me running for the hills had he been any other vampire. As it stood, I knew he wouldn't hurt me—well, I knew he wouldn't *kill* me. I hoped he wouldn't anyway. Really, I knew nothing about him, other than he was a king, and my mate.

As though to prove my own inner strength, I crossed my arms over my chest and lifted my chin, adopting my own haughty expression. Sure, guilt still gnawed at me, but I'd been right to bring him here. I knew that without a doubt. I did wish, however, that I could have done it without hurting him.

My attention flicked to his forehead. The gash had sealed a while ago, about five minutes after I'd hauled his ass into my car. But that didn't mean he'd healed completely. I'd practically bashed his skull in, after all. At least he looked well enough. I wasn't sure I could have recovered from a head wound quite so quickly.

"How are you feeling?" I asked.

His mouth twisted, and his eyes narrowed. "Absolutely spiffing."

I...had no idea what *spiffing* meant, and I didn't feel like asking. "Any lingering headache?"

Gabriel growled a nonsensical response, then shoved to his feet. But the moment he tried to take a step, he froze. His eyes widened before his gaze dropped to take in the shackles wrapped around his ankles. Okay, maybe I felt a little bad about *that*. But what else was I supposed to do? I knew he'd tried to leave the moment he woke. I'd needed something that would give me a fighting chance until I could get him to listen.

But the sight of the chains seemed to awaken the beast in him. He lifted his head and unleashed upon me what I assumed was his alpha stare. Fury blazed in his eyes, and his lips curled back to reveal those damn fangs again.

He looked downright terrifying, and I had to fight the urge to scramble into another room.

"Maddie," he snarled, his voice alarmingly deep.

Yikes.

"Unchain. Me. *Now*."

I had to summon every bit of inner strength I possessed not to follow his orders.

Screw that noise though.

Sure, he was a vampire. And yes, he was a king. But he wasn't *my* king. And I was a vampire slayer. I didn't cower before his kind. They cowered before mine.

Thankfully, I had my inner beast to rely on. The instant I called to my wolf, she came roaring to the front of my mind, backing me up. I stood and matched Gabriel's inhuman stare, even though it was like trying to out-stare a statue. After a tense pause, one of his eyebrows slowly crept up, like he was amazed I hadn't crumbled under his glare.

Scared many people, did he?

"I'll take the chains off if you promise to sit down, put your vampire face away, and listen to me."

He blinked. "My what now?"

"Your vampire face," I clarified, motioning at him. "Flashing fangs, creepy eyes, the snarly thing you do with your lips, all that stuff."

A cocky grin curved his lips. "You'll know when I'm showing you my *vampire* face, luv. In fact, unchain me and you'll never have to see it again."

I tried not to show how much that hurt to hear. Instead, I lifted my chin. "Why? So you can leave?"

"Contemplating it," he mused, his sharp gaze watching me for my reaction.

I tsked under my breath. "And stumble right into the slayers who are hunting you. Genius plan, Einstein."

Gabriel sighed and raked a hand down his face.

"You realize how ridiculous this is, right? I'm a bloody king. I can look after myself."

I let out a rather unladylike snort. "Really? Because your current circumstances suggest otherwise. Need I remind you that you're in chains?"

I rested a hand on his shoulder and pushed him down onto the couch. He dropped with a huff, one that made me laugh. He'd allowed me to push him down. The man was a foot taller than me and weighed likely a good seventy-five pounds more. The only reason I'd been able to take him out earlier was because I'd surprised him. Twenty bucks said he'd never underestimate me again.

"Going to behave now?" I asked.

"Doubt it," he drawled with a low chuckle.

At least he was honest.

"How about you stop playing games?" I asked. "We both know you could easily break those chains. Which means there's nothing stopping you from waltzing out that door."

Another cocky smirk. "And?"

I rolled my eyes. "And, obviously, you want to stay and talk to me. Promise you'll stay, and I'll take them off."

"Fine, fine." He waved a comically regal hand. One that had me nearly cracking up.

I grabbed the key from the nearby shelf and unlocked the chains. They fell from his ankles with a quiet clatter. Then I returned to my chair and sat.

"So, let me get this straight. You show up at my hotel. Separate me from my guards. Take me to that peculiarly romantic shack by the river. Knock me unconscious. Then drag me to this"—he cast a speculative glance around the cabin—"place. And now you fancy a chat?"

"Yes," I confirmed, dropping my hands to my lap. "First, I need to apologize for hurting you. You weren't listening, and I needed to get you the hell out of Jackson."

"We aren't in Jackson anymore?" He drew in a deep breath, his nostrils flaring as he scented the air. "Ah. We aren't."

My eyes widened briefly. "You can tell?"

"The air smells earthier here. Less urban. I can smell trees and plenty of wildlife. Jackson smells of werewolves, body odor, and cement."

Well, didn't that sound lovely? I scented the air, but only smelled Gabriel—and boy, did he smell delicious.

Gabriel leaned back against the loveseat and placed one ankle over his knee. "Fine. You have my attention. Let's talk."

Success. Maybe now I could convince him to take this seriously. I only wish it hadn't required a brain injury to get him to cooperate. Maybe I'd lobotomized him, and this was the friendlier Gabriel?

"Okay, so like I said back in Jackson, you have a bounty on your head."

He nodded, but said nothing.

"The Academy thinks you're guilty of murder."

Another nod, slower this time.

His expression never so much as changed. He seemed almost bored.

"And you're in danger." I added for good measure, hoping for *some* sort of reaction. When he said nothing, I threw my hands into the air. "Well?"

"Well, what?"

Wow. I stared at him, anger churning in my blood. Why was I the only person worried about this? Chris only cared about the kill, and Gabriel seemed entirely unconcerned. Like this sort of thing happened to him regularly.

Sighing, I pinched the bridge of my nose. "*Well*, what are you going to do about it?"

"What can I do about it?" he asked, shrugging. "Do you know who accused me of murder?"

"No," I said, my shoulders deflating. "That's not information we're normally given. Usually, we're only given the target's—I mean, vampire's—name, along with the names of their victim or victims."

Gabriel fell silent, but he held my gaze without blinking. After a few moments, I started to squirm in my seat. I might be a bad ass vampire slayer, but I'd never loved intense, prolonged eye contact. Probably something to do with my childhood and the countless times someone had hit me for daring to openly challenge them. I thought I'd overcome that little tic of mine, but apparently not.

"Do you know of anyone who would falsely accuse you of murder?" I asked.

Gabriel repositioned himself on the couch, stretching out on his back and dangling his feet over the edge. He clasped his hands and rested them on his chest, but he kept his focus on me. Guess he knew how to make himself at home. He seemed almost at ease now.

"It could be any number of people," he replied. "I'm a king, Maddie. There are plenty who would love to dance on my grave, metaphorically speaking. And more I probably don't even know about. I'm sure my enemy list is longer than most."

My brows knitted. If that were the case, then there was no chance of us finding a simple solution like I'd hoped. "Let's start with the most obvious," I suggested. "Who would be the person at the top of your list?"

Gabriel sighed. "You realize I have people who handle this sort of thing for me, right? People who are experts in these situations and are literally paid to protect me?"

"Yes, and look where that got you," I snarked. "You aren't untouchable."

"You sucker punched me," he countered.

"Kicked you, actually," I emphasized. "And smashed your head into a wall."

He blinked, then shook his head and stared at the ceiling. "There must be something wrong with me that I'm actually proud of you."

Proud of me? What the what? I'd knocked him bloody senseless, and he was *proud*? Vampires were a strange breed. But then again, I was also an odd one, since I *liked* that he was proud of me.

"But here's the thing"—he turned his head and stared at me—"I'm no safer here with you than I was with my own people. One might argue I'm less safe here, since we're only two people. I have an entire team back at my hotel. And they would have done the job perfectly fine had I not sent them away—a mistake I won't make again. Not to mention, and truly, I can't stress this enough, I can protect myself.

I've been doing it for more years than you've been alive. The only reason we're even in this situation is because I never imagined you'd harm me. A second mistake I won't make again."

His words struck deep, but I forced the ache aside. "That's exactly it, Gabriel. The people hunting you won't come after you directly, either." I leaned forward in the chair and decided to hit him with a little honesty. "Do you know what they were doing while I was luring you away from your guards?"

Gabriel's face tightened.

"No, you don't. And that's the point. We're trained to slay vampires, Gabriel. We're stealthy, crafty, and intelligent. We have to be in order to survive. Your security team might be able to handle an outright attack, but what about a subtle one?"

His expression darkened.

"You had no idea that a team of slayers had infiltrated your hotel tonight. Does your security detail check every single hotel employee—maintenance, room service, desk attendants? Hell, what about the restaurant staff? Do you think your security team knew someone was canvassing you? My people were watching your every move. They were taking count of how many you have working for you, memorizing shift changes and patrols, and scouting your room. The second that sun comes up, you're vulnerable."

"I employ human guards," Gabriel snarled. "They would have—"

"What?" I cut in. "Stopped us? Do you honestly think a handful of human guards would present a challenge for us? Do you know how easy it is to pay off guards? Blackmail them? Me and my people do this professionally, you know. You have complete faith in your people. It's a weakness. Believe me, we would have found a way around all of them. And then there would have been nothing stopping us from accessing you."

His lip curled.

"And because daylight renders you completely defenseless, you wouldn't have been able to defend yourself. By the time anyone caught wind of the trouble, you'd be dead, and we'd be long gone. Because that's what we're trained to do."

Gabriel sat up and leaned forward, hitting me with a piercing stare. "Trusting people is a weakness, eh? So what about you? Are you trying to trick me into trusting you so *you* can kill me?"

I sucked in a sharp breath. "What? No. Of course not."

"How can I believe you?" he demanded. "You admitted that slayers are masters of deception. And did you forget that you knocked me out and abducted me? How do I know this isn't some trick?"

His words pierced me, and this time, it was *my* lip that curled. I felt my fangs pressing against my gums, demanding I free them. I wanted to snarl at him, but I knew that wouldn't accomplish anything. He'd likely snarl back. "If I wanted you dead, you'd *be* dead," I snapped. "I certainly wouldn't have risked *everything* to get you out of Jackson and bring you here, you inconsiderate *asshole*."

He startled, clearly rattled by my outburst.

"And for the record, I never said I was a liar."

Gabriel whipped a hand through his hair, mussing up his waves. Guess my words had unnerved him.

"Look, I don't know who's accused you of murder. Nor do I know why the Academy would think you're guilty. All I know is that you aren't safe in Jackson. Not until we get this mess figured out."

"And you want me to hole up here with you?" he asked, his voice soft now. "So you can play bodyguard?"

"Yes," I murmured.

"And if I don't want a werewolf nanny?"

"Good, because you're not a child," I snapped. "If you choose to stay, then we're working this problem out together. I would expect you to help me figure all this out, especially considering it's your life in danger here. Not mine."

"You realize my guards are going to lose their minds when they discover me missing?" he asked.

I nodded. "They've probably already figured it out." I glanced at my watch. "It's five a.m. You've been MIA for most of the night."

Gabriel cursed and dragged his hands down his face. "They'll tear up Jackson looking for me."

"I hope they do."

He dropped his hands, his gray eyes trained on me. "How is that good?"

"Their reaction will convince the slayers that you're actually missing. Otherwise, they might think this is some sort of ploy. It'll take the heat off you for a bit while everyone tries to figure out what's going on. My people will wait for you to resurface before making their move. It'll give us time to figure out who's behind all this."

"You don't think the slayers will come looking for me here?"

I stole another glance around the cabin. "If all goes according to plan, this place won't even register on their radar." There'd be no reason for Jaden to assume I'd come here.

"Is this place yours?" he asked.

"No," was all I said.

He frowned. "Then how did you get me in here?"

"Don't worry about that," I said, waving a hand. "We've got bigger fish to fry."

"Oh?"

I stood and strode toward the far end of the living room, peering into the attached bedroom. "Have a look."

His footsteps echoed behind me, but it was the weight of his presence pressed against my back that made me shiver. "What's the problem, luv?"

What's wrong? "One bedroom, one bed," I choked out. "That's what's wrong. There's no spare bed anywhere. And the couch is too small for you."

"Hmm." Gabriel chuckled then. "I fail to see the issue here."

I almost cracked a smile. Of course he didn't. Guess all men were the same no matter the species. "I'm not sharing a bed with you."

"Then you can take the couch," he said.

"Excuse me?"

He gave me a devilish grin, stirring up a storm

inside me. His eyes sparkled with mischief as he leaned down. "You brought me here. That makes me the guest and you the host. Therefore, I get the bed. You can take the couch. You're petite, after all. If you're not keen on that arrangement, then we can share the bed. I assure you, I won't object."

"You...you..." I sputtered, at a loss for words.

"Oh, come on now. I can make it worth your while. Trust me."

I jerked back, then scoffed when I caught sight of his grin. He was playing me. Teasing me. I wanted to smack him, but I'd already made a silent promise never to hurt him again. I couldn't break that promise the first night we were together, no matter how badly I wanted to.

"I'm kidding, Maddie," he said. "Besides, the bed isn't going to be a problem. I'm a vampire remember? I sleep during the day. And I assume you'll be keeping guard or whatever you plan to do during those hours. We can switch off as needed."

Oh. I...hadn't thought of that. I really wasn't on top of my game here, was I?

Gabriel glanced at my face, then laughed. "You were really worried about that?"

I gave a slow nod. What was happening to my brain? Ever since I met Gabriel, it hadn't been firing on all cylinders. I needed to get my head back on straight.

Gabriel snickered, then stepped into the room. He studied the blanket I'd hammered over the window. When he shot me a glance, I merely shrugged.

"Had to improvise," I said. "I'm not even sure if it'll work."

He strode toward the window and fiddled with the blanket. "We could add a few more nails as an extra precaution, but this should do. For now. I wouldn't want to live like this permanently."

No surprise there. He probably had a castle and throne and all that *royal* stuff back home in England. This place likely looked like a shanty to him.

"So, you're staying then?" I asked. "You trust me to protect you?"

He glanced at me over his shoulder. "Would you let me leave if I said no?"

It went against every instinct I had, but I forced a nod. "I've explained the situation and the dangers to you. If you still wanted to leave, I'd…I'd step aside."

His mouth pursed, and once again, the desire to know what he was thinking hit me. He crossed the room and came to a stop in front of me. "Really? You'd let me walk out that door?"

I swear, the entire universe seemed to hold its breath in anticipation of my answer. It grew so quiet, I could hear a pin drop. Finally, I jerked a nod. "I wouldn't like it. But I would respect your decision."

Gabriel smirked, as though I'd passed some test. "Well, I guess it's a good thing I'm staying then. I wouldn't want to do anything you wouldn't like. Besides...." He took another glance around the small cabin. "I'm due for a vacation. Being a king gets old. It could be fun to hang out here. For a little while, anyway. Plus, it gives us some time to get to know each other."

Relief had me leaning back against the wall and sighing.

"That concerned for me?" he asked, winking.

I sputtered for words. "No, I—I... It isn't safe out there!"

He chuckled, then turned back to the window. "Don't worry about it, Maddie. Your secret's safe with me."

"What secret?"

He inclined against the wall, delight shining in his eyes. "You like me."

All the heat drained from my body. "I like you?"

"Mhmm. But it's okay." He held my stare, and

heat ignited in his eyes. "Because I like you too. Even when you're giving me a swift kick in the head."

Oh god. I wasn't prepared for *this*. I'd brought him here to protect him, not flirt with him! And I wasn't about to start now.

"I need to go to the store," I blurted out, grasping at straws. "Get supplies. And uh, stuff."

"Yes, *stuff* is very rather crucial," Gabriel retorted in a droll voice.

"Right. Stuff." I hurried into the living room, then stopped and turned back to face Gabriel. "Um. You stay here."

"Oh? All by myself? I thought it was super dangerous for me out there, though? And you're here to protect me, remember? Hard to do that if you aren't here, wouldn't you agree?"

I cursed under my breath. "Well, I can't take you into town with me. Everywhere you go, you're recognized. And we can't let that happen. I'm a nobody, so I can get in, get us some supplies, and get out."

Gabriel laughed again. "Do I really fluster you that badly?"

"Huh?" My head shot up and I stared at him. "What do you mean?"

"Maddie, it's five in the morning, remember? There's nothing open for a few more hours yet."

Well, fuck me. He was right. About the time, *and* that he flustered me.

"Guess I'll have to go while you're…asleep?" I ventured, not sure if that was the right word. Vampires didn't sleep when the sun came up. They died. But there was something far too macabre about that for me to say the word.

Gabriel lifted a brow at my choice of phrasing. "You look and sound exhausted. How about you get some sleep, then?"

I blanched at the suggestion. "You want *me* to sleep?" Why, so he could leave when I wasn't paying attention?

"Surely you don't expect to stay awake the entire time we're stuck here?" he asked, chuckling. "That'd be quite the feat. You'll need to rest if you plan to be of any use."

He wasn't wrong. But I still didn't love the idea of sleeping. I'd only been awake for twenty-one hours or so. I could hold out longer if needed.

"Maddie," Gabriel said. "You can trust me. Get some rest. I'll keep watch until sunrise. Granted, that isn't a lot of rest, but it's better than nothing."

My eyes shot to the bed. The bed that Gabriel would die on soon.

When I didn't respond, he waved a hand in front of my face. "Maddie?"

I blinked and tore my focus away from the bed. The couch was safer. "What?"

He frowned. "Did you hear me?"

"Yeah, Okay, fine. I'll take a quick nap on the couch, if that's alright."

He shrugged. "Your choice."

I moved toward the loveseat, then froze after kicking off my shoes. I turned and faced Gabriel, only to find him leaning against the bedroom doorframe, watching me. "You'll be here to wake me, right? You won't leave?" Ugh, I hated how weak that sounded.

He gave me a questioning look, one I refused to acknowledge. Yes, I had some major abandonment issues, but he didn't need to know that.

"I'll wake you around six-twenty," he assured me.

I curled onto the couch and tucked my hands under my head. My eyes drooped, and I felt myself drifting off when words I'd never meant to speak aloud left my mouth, "Don't leave me."

A light touch brushed my cheek. "I'm not going anywhere, Maddie."

I WOKE WITH A START. DISORIENTATION GRIPPED me as I took in the faded, lumpy couch beneath me. An unfamiliar pillow supported my head, and a flannel blanket draped over my lower half.

What on earth? Where was I?

Light from a single lamp glowed across the room, but it was the sight of the log walls that sparked my memory of last night. I jolted into a sitting position and jerked my head toward the bedroom where a dark figure lay sprawled on the bed.

I leapt to my feet and approached the bedroom,

my eyes immediately drawn to the accompanying window. Not a sliver of sunlight infiltrated the room —thank goodness. And for good measure, Gabriel had covered himself in the flame-retardant blanket.

Relief had me slumping against the door frame, and I gave myself a moment to breathe and reorganize my thoughts.

He was alive—well, not exactly. Not right this second, anyway. But he wasn't crispy from the sunrise, which in my books counted as a win.

Why hadn't he woke me up though, like he'd promised?

I turned back to the couch and eyed the mysterious blanket and pillow. Those hadn't been there when I'd fallen asleep. He must have fetched them from the linen closet and brought them to me. Then left me to sleep instead of waking me like he'd promised. My damn heart melted. I'd given his noggin a solid beating last night, and instead of retaliating, he'd taken the time to ensure my comfort before retiring to the bedroom.

Emotion gripped my chest until it damn near cracked.

My whole life, *no one* had ever cared about me enough to make sure I was comfortable. I'd seen television shows where parents scooped their kids up and carried them to bed, tucking them in, kissing them goodnight. I'd never experienced that. And what few men I'd dated, none had ever done anything quite like this. It was a small action—a pillow and a blanket—yet it nearly broke me.

I placed a hand on my chest and stepped back.

It's only a blanket, I told myself. But deep down, I knew it was more than that. Gabriel cared. And I had no idea how to react to that. I'd never been in love, and what few relationships I'd had, they'd been quick and shallow. Flings, mostly.

A piece of paper caught my eye. It sat on the living room table, beneath a mug of water. Those hadn't been there when I'd fallen asleep. I plucked both up and read the paper.

Don't be mad. You needed more than an hour's sleep. I trust you'll wake up if anyone comes barging in. Rest, I'll see you tonight.

He'd written me a *note*. And left me a glass of water.

I...wasn't sure I could handle this. To most people, these were small things. But to me, they were monumental.

I placed the mug back on the table, then hurried to my bag. I fished out my phone and groaned when I saw the time. Three p.m. I'd slept for ten freaking hours! Damn blackout curtains.

Shaking off the remnants of sleep and all my conflicted emotions, I dialed Lucy's number. She was the only one I trusted to help me make sense of this chaos, being that Sam was her mate, and she'd gone through all this before.

As her phone rang, my gaze traveled back to the bedroom. I stared at Gabriel, his blanketed figure a dark silhouette against the bed.

"Auntie Maddie!" my niece Annabelle chirped when she answered the phone.

"Hi, sweetie. How are you?"

"Great! We miss you. When are you coming to visit?"

A smile curled my lips. "Soon. I have something I'm working on. But once that's done, I'll be there right away. I miss you guys too. How's your brother?"

Annabelle blew a charming raspberry, one that reminded me she was only five.

"Where's your mom?" I asked. "I need to speak to her."

Movement rustled across the line before I heard a bellowing, "*Mommy! It's Auntie Maddie!*"

I pulled the phone away from my ear with a wince. The girl had a set of lungs on her, that was for sure. Laughter grew louder as someone approached, then took the phone.

"Hey, girl," Lucy said as a greeting, her voice a soothing balm to my rattled nerves.

I collapsed onto the worn sofa and sighed. "I need your help."

"What's wrong?" she demanded, her alpha werewolf voice coming out. We'd only met five years ago, but in that time, Lucy had taken up the mantle of big sister with pride. I knew without a doubt that she'd kill anyone who messed with me. It'd overwhelmed me at first, but I'd loved every minute of it.

Staring at Gabriel, I started at the beginning and explained everything. From Gabriel saving my life at the bar a few nights ago, to the bounty and my friends hunting him, to me kidnapping him. After I got it all out, I briefly paused, then ended with, "He's my mate."

Lucy gasped. "Gabriel? Like the Vampire King, Gabriel? Vlad's best friend, Gabriel? *That* Gabriel?"

"Yeah, him," I said.

Lucy whistled under her breath. "You certainly don't do things small, do you?"

I chuckled. She wasn't wrong. When I'd first gone in search of family, I'd come across our psychotic half-sister, Olivia, who'd been hell bent on murdering Lucy. It was actually how we'd met. But I'd chosen to side with Lucy. She'd seemed the saner one of the two. Soon after, I'd joined the Academy and become a vampire slayer. And now my mate was the Vampire King. So yeah, she was right. I didn't do anything small.

"Tell me about the mating bond," she urged. "What makes you think that's what this is?"

I paused for a moment, giving myself a chance to come up with the right words. "I can't really explain how I know. I just do. When he's around, I feel... complete. But also terrified."

"Terrified?" Lucy repeated. "Of what?"

Oh boy, talk about stripping me bare and going right to the crux of the problem. "Of him leaving. Of him dying. Of not being with him. But also terrified to be *with* him. He's a vampire, for crying out loud. And I'm a werewolf. I mean, who does that? Who pairs a vampire and werewolf together?"

"Fate," Lucy whispered.

I waved a dismissive hand. Fate could kiss my ass for all I cared.

"What else are you afraid of?"

A shaky breath slipped past my lips. "Of failing him."

Lucy fell silent.

"We...we kissed already," I admitted. I'd conveniently left that part out of the story earlier.

She gasped. "You have? Tell me about that, and don't leave out any details!"

I chuckled. Right now, she sounded exactly like what I'd expect from a big sister. "It was perfect. That was the moment I figured out he was my mate."

"Yeah..." Lucy murmured. "I remember my first kiss with Sam. It's like all the pieces of your life finally come together."

I nodded, relating so completely to what she'd said that it shook me.

"But here's the thing," Lucy said. "The bond is merely the start of what you two can have. It doesn't guarantee a perfect relationship. It doesn't simply hand you a happily ever after. You have to work at it every single day. It's like a marriage."

I winced. "And if I don't want to work at it?"

Lucy laughed softly. "Oh, sweetie. You can pretend you don't. You can tell yourself that until you're blue in the face. But I know you. I know your dreams and desires. You, yourself, have told me that all you've ever wanted in life is a family. Someone to call your own. Well, here's your chance. Gabriel isn't perfect. But he's perfect *for you*. Fate doesn't get these things wrong."

Her words rocked me to the core. "What if it doesn't work out?"

"Oh, honey..." Compassion warmed her words. "You can't think like that. If you go in expecting failure, then you'll fail. Give Gabriel a chance to show you what it means to have a mate."

I gulped. "And in the meantime?"

"In the meantime, work the case. Find out who accused Gabriel of murder. Prove them wrong. If you can prove that he never murdered anyone, the Academy will absolve the bounty, right?"

"That's the hope. But how do I do that *and* keep him safe?"

"Well, that's the best part. You aren't alone anymore, remember? You have people who love you and would love to help."

"Lucy, I can't ask that of you. You have kids, and this could be dangerous."

"Not me, silly," she said, chuckling. "I'm talking about Anna and Vlad."

I froze.

"Vlad is Gabriel's best friend, and Anna loves you like her own sister. I promise they'll help you through this."

I heard her words, but still resisted the idea. I didn't want to drag anyone else into this. The more who knew, the greater the risk to Gabriel's life. But Lucy was right. I wasn't alone anymore. And I *did* need help. I couldn't be in two places at once.

"Would you like me to call her for you?" Lucy offered.

I bit my lip to keep from shouting *no*, then nodded.

"Maddie?" Lucy prodded.

Right. She couldn't see me. I had to speak. "Yes, sorry. Yes, please call Anna. But make sure she knows I won't hurt him. The three of them had plans to meet at the fundraiser last night, so I assume they already know he's missing. And I don't want them to make any assumptions. I—"

"Sweetie," Lucy interrupted. "Everything is going to be okay. Anna and Vlad have faced their own issues in the past. They know how complicated these sorts of things can get. If anyone is going to side with you, it'll be them. Heck, they might even talk some sense into your vampire."

Ha. Sure. I'd believe that when I saw it.

"Okay. Let's call them."

"How do you want to play this?" Lucy asked. "Do you want Anna to call you so you can tell her where you are? Or do you trust me to pass that information along?"

I considered my choices. Keeping Lucy in the dark could protect her. On the other hand, I had this crazed fear that if I *didn't* tell her, and someone went looking for her, she'd have no information to pass on. That could cause her a lot of trouble. I *never* wanted to be the reason anyone harmed her, the kids, or Sam.

"I'm going to give you the directions to pass along," I said. "If *anyone* comes looking for me and threatens to harm you unless you tell them where I am, give them the directions. Do you understand me? I don't want you playing alpha and trying to protect me. You have a family to think about."

"You're my family too, Maddie," Lucy murmured. "And don't worry about me. I know how to take care of myself. Trust me, if someone threatens me, they won't live to see the sunrise."

I knew Lucy could protect herself, I'd seen her do it. But she had kids now. People who depended on her. Doubtful anyone would attack her, though, considering her alpha status. Doing so would open a whole new can of worms. But I still didn't want her risking anything for my safety.

"Promise me," I told her.

"Fine, fine," Lucy said, even though I knew it was a lie. She'd fight to protect me. And so would Sam. Because that was what family did.

Sighing, I gave her the directions to the cabin.

"Anna will wake in about an hour," Lucy said. "Vlad won't wake till sunset."

I knew all that. Thanks to some ancient blood Anna had drunk years ago, she could wake before the others. She still couldn't walk in the sunlight though. It was the one thing she missed most from her human life.

"Do you need anything else?" Lucy asked.

I was about to say no, then stopped myself, laughing. "I need everything. Clothes for both me and Gabriel. Toiletries. Blood. Food. You name it."

Lucy joined in with my laughter. "You didn't pack anything at all?"

"I didn't even know we were coming here until I knocked him out," I confessed. "Didn't exactly have time to stop at a Target on the way."

Lucy choked on a laugh. "Okay, okay. I'll have Anna and Vlad bring you supplies."

Great, that'd keep me from having to go into town. I really hadn't wanted to leave Gabriel to do that.

"What else?" Lucy asked.

Again, I intended to say nothing, then stopped with a gasp. "Oh! I told Jaden there was a family emergency and you and the kids needed me. If she reaches out to you, I need you to continue that façade for me."

"I'll avoid any texts and calls from her," Lucy said.

"Good idea. Let me handle it. Thank you, Lucy. I don't know what I'd do without you."

She mimicked her daughter's raspberry, which made me laugh harder. I tamped it back, then glanced at Gabriel, but he hadn't so much as twitched. He truly was dead to the world.

"Keep me posted, alright?" Lucy requested.

"Thanks, Luce."

"And Maddie?"

I hummed a response.

"If you need us, we'll be there. The entire pack has your back. You know that, right?"

"But I'm not a member."

"Doesn't matter. We take care of our own."

Tears welled in my eyes. "Thank you." Geez, I was saying that a lot tonight.

"Love you," Lucy said.

"Love you too," I replied before disconnecting the call.

I plopped down on the couch, completely flustered. Even though Lucy had been in my life for five years, I still had a hard time believing I now had people who cared for me. It was difficult to retrain my brain and reprogram old habits. Before Lucy, I'd only had myself to rely on. But she was right. That *wasn't* my life anymore.

And it was time I started to accept that.

9

A<small>N</small> <small>ERRANT</small> <small>BEAM</small> <small>OF</small> <small>SUNLIGHT</small> <small>PIERCED</small> <small>THE</small> darkness and had my head jerking to the side. I glared at the offensive beam of light and pushed to my feet, stalking across the room to the window. The blanketing system I'd hung apparently had a chink in its armor, and the sun had exposed it. Thank goodness Gabriel wasn't in any danger, considering he was still tucked beneath the fireproof blanket in the bedroom, dead to the world. That didn't stop me from grabbing the hammer and driving another nail into the wall, though, snuffing the rogue beam of light. I'd never played bodyguard before, and death by sunlight would be an embarrassing addition to any resume.

I ran my hand down the blanket's edge, inspecting the improved seal against the wall, then nodded to myself. When I turned away from the window, my gaze snagged on the bedroom and Gabriel. Daytime vampire viewing wasn't a typical experience for me, and admittedly, it gave me the heebie-jeebies. People moved more than they thought when sleeping. Their bodies twitched, their breathing grew erratic, their eyes darted back and forth beneath their lids while dreaming. Not Gabriel, though. He was as still as the grave, and it was as creepy as a clown in a storm drain.

Just thinking about entering the room made all my little hairs stand on end. But I had no choice. The room had its own window, and I needed to check it too.

Resigned, I poked my head in. Darkness engulfed the entire room. Not a single beam of light penetrated the gloom. But that didn't mean it couldn't still happen. And considering this window's proximity to him, I needed to check the blankets.

I tiptoed into the room, my eyes constantly sneaking glances at the prone form in the bed. I had to get a grip and get over this fear of mine. He was only *temporarily* dead. In a few hours, he'd be up and about, and the world would make sense again. Well, until sunrise, at least.

After a thorough inspection of the window, a few more hammer taps, and a nod of approval, I retreated into the living room. I appreciated Anna's plight a little more now. It'd only been an hour since I'd woken, and already I was itching for some vitamin D.

I crept toward the door. I needed to patrol the property, which I'd intended to do tonight. But honestly, I would prefer to do it now while it was still light out. I hadn't had a chance to do it last night, and I knew I wouldn't be able to relax until I'd established a perimeter.

I bit my lip and glanced over my shoulder at Gabriel.

He was perfectly secure in his vampire cocoon, and I had no intentions of leaving the property. I'd know it the second someone approached. I could even patrol in wolf form to speed up the process. I didn't love the idea of leaving Gabriel alone, but I also didn't love the idea of sitting here in the dark, wondering what was happening outside. Knowledge is power, right?

"I'll make it snappy," I whispered, not that Gabriel could hear me—I didn't think. But it made me feel better to say the words aloud. "An hour tops. You'll be fine. I won't let anyone hurt you."

I cracked open the door and slipped outside, immediately sealing the door shut behind me. The sunlight hit me like a welcome punch in the face. I groaned and raised a hand to shield my eyes. The mid-February forest was more stark than lush, the trees bare of leaves, and their skeletal branches swaying in the chill breeze. But it still felt good to get outside. The scent of earth woke my senses and stirred my wolf, urging me to shift.

I gave into the irresistible need, and quickly disrobed before letting my wolf take over. My body suddenly twisted, reshaping itself into a form that came to me like second nature now, thanks to my many years of practice. Bones cracked, muscles reformed, and fur spread down my skin in a flowing ripple.

I'd been a werewolf for six years, so shifting didn't cause me much physical pain anymore. But in the beginning, it'd been agonizing. I'd never heard anything quite so harrowing as the sound of every bone in my body snapping. My late half-sister, Olivia, had promised me the pain would one day ebb, and she'd been right—as much as I hated to admit it.

Now on four legs, I shook out my fur and stretched, which was my favorite part of this entire process. Stretching in human form didn't compare to stretching in wolf form. Then I kicked off the porch and strode into the woods, disappearing into the underbrush.

I needed to make this quick. I didn't feel comfortable leaving Gabriel so vulnerable, even for a short period of time. There were too many things that could go wrong. The logical part of my brain assured me that no one would even think to come look for us here, but the other, irrational part of my brain laughed. It promised me that everything that could go wrong eventually would. It even went so far as to show me an image of the cabin burning to the ground with Gabriel trapped inside.

Needless to say, I needed to hurry.

The cabin sat nestled in a patch of seven acres, complete with its own pond, and apparently, some feathery squatters. I came across a pair of geese squabbling over something and quickly took my leave when they started giving me the evil eye. My last showdown with a goose hadn't ended well. Never underestimate the savage fury of a waterfowl. They put werewolves to shame.

I was on the final leg of my patrol, the cabin in sight, when the sound of an approaching car stopped me in my tracks. Dead-end roads did not invite casual traffic. If someone was on it, they were here for a reason.

Gnashing my teeth, I made a sprint for it, racing through the trees like a scene from a car commercial. The sound of tires rolling over gravel spiked my anxiety. Who the hell had found us? I'd been so careful! With the sun still sitting high in the sky, I knew it wasn't vampires. But a dark thought began to form.

Was it Chris? Had he somehow tracked Gabriel here?

In full panic mode, I reached the front porch and spotted my discarded clothes. The car had taken the last bend. I had a minute at most.

Instigating the change, I gasped as tears pricked my eyes.

It hurt this time. I'd forced it, and now I was paying the price. But I couldn't have time for a breather. The second the cool breeze hit my dewy skin, I scrambled into my clothes in time for a familiar car to pull in and park next to mine.

Jaden's cherry-red SUV. Oh boy.

Had she come on her own? Had the guys tagged along?

I stepped off the porch and peered down the road. The dust had settled, and I could now confirm she'd come alone. A small measure of relief loosened my muscles, but I instantly tensed the second the driver's side door opened and Jaden stepped out. She met my gaze with a furious glare, one that had me wincing and stepping back.

"What the hell, Maddie!" she shouted.

Oof. This was not going to be a fun chat.

Jaden slammed her door shut and stormed over, fists balled at her sides. She clenched her jaw so tight, I worried she might crack a tooth.

"*This* is your family emergency?" she hollered. "Are you kidding me?"

I bit my lip, almost afraid to respond for fear of upsetting her further.

"You had us worried sick!" she continued, her heated words like little daggers. "Chris, Josh, and I had no idea what was wrong. You had us thinking the worst! That the kids were sick, or someone had died. But this whole time, you've been here?" Her eyes scanned the front of her cabin. "Why are you even here? What are you doing? Did you seriously break into my cabin?"

Ah, well that was one question I could answer. "Spare key?"

Her eyes narrowed as they darted back to me. "Spare key? That's your explanation?"

I winced. "I'm sorry, Jaden. I—"

"You what?" she spat, her words sizzling with anger. She marched a couple steps closer. "You have no idea how worried we were. Josh couldn't reach Sam. You weren't answering my calls. Are Lucy and the kids here with you?"

"No," I quickly replied.

She blinked. "No? Then where are they?"

"At home, I imagine." I wouldn't lie about that again. "They're fine, I promise. Nothing's wrong with either of the kids."

"So you lied," Jaden accused—rightfully so.

I ducked my head, avoiding eye contact.

"I can't believe this. What the hell are you doing that's so important? *More* important than helping Chris with his bounty? You bailed!"

I had. And for good reason. I couldn't tell Jaden about that. If I told her Gabriel was inside her cabin, she'd try to stake him, no questions asked. And I refused to let that happen. The last thing I wanted was to hurt her, but I couldn't let her see or touch Gabriel.

"I wish you hadn't come," I told her.

Her temper flared and she threw her arms in the air. "I wish I hadn't *had* to come! I had to track your cell phone like you were some common criminal."

Ouch. That hurt. Yet another thing I hadn't taken into consideration. Man, this whole situation had really thrown me off my groove.

"And then to find you here..." She fell quiet and frowned. "Are you alone? Is someone here with you?" Her eyes scanned the perimeter, seeing only my car.

Fuck. What could I even say to that? If I said yes, she'd insist on introductions. If I said no, she'd want to know why I was here alone. And I had no idea what to say. I hated lying to her, because Jaden was my best friend. My ride or die. I hated doing this to her, hated that I couldn't be completely honest.

Her eyes widened. "Someone else *is* here, aren't they?" When I didn't respond, she gave a bitter laugh. "Are you seriously using my cabin for hook ups?"

I sputtered a nonsensical response.

She ran a hand over her tight curls and spun

away from me, pressing her hands on the hood of her car. I considered her question and wondered if that was the angle to take. To convince her I'd brought someone here. It wouldn't be a lie—I *had* brought someone here. But not for the reason she believed.

Jaden gave another bitter laugh, then spun back to face me. "Unbelievable. You bailed on us so you could bring some guy here and bang him?"

I swallowed. That...wasn't the impression I wanted to make.

"Who is it, Maddie?" she demanded.

Oh boy. I didn't have an answer for that one.

"Is it Garrick?" I made a face, one that had Jaden sucking in a sharp breath. "Oh my god, it *is*, isn't it?"

Garrick was another slayer, and my personal archnemesis. The man was arrogant and ignorant—an interesting combination—and the one person I loathed the most in the world. I wouldn't touch him with a ten-foot pole.

"That explains everything," Jaden continued, seemingly unaware that I hadn't confirmed or denied anything. "I always wondered about you two. The way you fight and bicker. The way you stare daggers at him. I knew—I *knew*—there had to be something else there. People don't hate each other the way you two do, not without reason. You and Garrick?"

I tamped back the urge to vomit at the suggestion. If I didn't say a word, it wasn't lying, right? Not that that made me feel any better. It made me sick to know Jaden thought I was capable of such a thing. Sleeping with Garrick rated somewhere alongside robbing a bank or mugging an elderly lady.

"God, Maddie." Jaden ran a hand down her face. "What is going on with you?"

"I don't know," I croaked—and wasn't that the truth. I had no idea how to handle this mess with Gabriel, or what was going on inside my head and heart. For the first time since Jaden arrived, I could give an honest answer and it loosened something in my chest.

She took a step forward.

I jumped into her path. "What are you doing?"

She lifted a brow and eyed me. "Going inside? To say hi to Garrick?"

"No!" I shouted, then flinched and glanced back at the cabin. I couldn't let her inside.

"Why on earth not? It's *my* cabin," she stated.

"He...he doesn't know you're here." Another half-truth. Garrick wasn't here, but Gabriel was, and I couldn't let Jaden know that. "I want it to be a secret." Another truth. "I *need* this to be a secret."

Her other brow winged up. "You're ashamed?"

"No," I immediately said. "More like... unclear about the boundaries and what's happening. Confused. *Very* confused. And upset."

"Upset?" she repeated. "Did he hurt you?"

"Oh, no." If anything, I'd been the one to hurt him. "I'm upset because I don't know what to make of this." The instant I started talking, I felt all the words come rushing out of me. Jaden was my best friend, and I didn't realize how badly I wanted to discuss all this with her. Lucy was great, I loved her to death, but it was different hashing these things out with your bestie as opposed to your sister. "We aren't supposed to be together. He's...him. And I'm me. And he's..."

"Loathsome?" Jaden supplied.

I almost laughed. She was speaking of Garrick, but it fit for Gabriel as well. Other slayers would certainly consider him loathsome.

"We're almost enemies," I said. "Oil and vinegar." Vampires and werewolves. A king and a slayer.

Jaden cocked her head and regarded me. "Have you slept with him?"

"No," I admitted, shaking my head. "No, I haven't done that."

Her mouth parted softly in surprise. "But you brought him here?"

I nodded. "To be alone." To protect him. From her. From Chris. From Josh. From the Academy. "To see what this is between us. I'm confused. So I needed to get away from the city and give myself time to figure all this out."

She gave a sage nod. "I can understand that." Then she glared at me. "What I don't understand is how you can lie to me and turn your back on us, the people who matter most to you."

Oof. Low blow.

"I'm so sorry," I sputtered. "I didn't know how to tell you about this. About what's going on. What could I have even said to make you understand?"

"This sounds serious," Jaden commented.

I merely nodded. I shot another glance back at the cabin, then faced Jaden. "I know I lied. And I really am sorry. Technically, I broke into your cabin, and I'm sorry for that too. I hope you can forgive me." I blew out a heavy breath and dragged my hands down my face. "Jaden, I'm so lost. And confused."

Sympathy softened Jaden's face and she wound her arms around me, pulling me in for a hug. "It'll be okay. You'll figure this out, and then you'll come home, and everything will be fine."

"Can you tell Josh and Chris I'm sorry? I never should have said there was a family emergency. And I never should have bailed like I did. I promised I'd help Chris, but I think this has to take precedence for me. I didn't know how to tell you guys about this."

She rubbed my back, then pulled away. "I'll tell them. But they need to hear it from you."

"I know. But I need some time to work all this out. A few days. A week at most."

Jaden offered me a wan smile. It wasn't the same as before, and that broke my heart. Hopefully, I'd gain her trust back. Though that didn't seem likely, considering I was still sort of lying to her. It wasn't Garrick inside that cabin. And the truth made this so much worse.

"How's everything going? You know, with the bounty?" I asked, trying so hard to sound casual.

Jaden sighed. "Not well. Ironically, you weren't the only one to vanish. The king did last night too."

My gut twisted.

"According to our sources, the king never showed up at the fundraiser event. And from what we've been able to suss out, not even his men know where he's gone, which is quite alarming."

I feigned surprise. "Gone?"

She nodded. "No one knows a thing. At least not

that we've heard. Chris is checking with a few more sources to see if there are any leads to chase, but I won't know anything more until I get back to Jackson." She eyed me. "You could come too, you know. You don't have to hide Garrick from us. I'll make sure Josh keeps his comments to himself, and Chris doesn't mind Garrick so much. I'm sure he'd understand."

"Thanks." But no way in hell was that happening. "But I need to stay here. And take the time to sort everything out."

She hummed something quietly, then nodded. "Well, now's as good a time as any. If Chris can't find any more leads, we may have to press pause on this bounty until the king resurfaces." Then she scowled and wagged a finger in my face. "But no more lying. Got me?"

I bobbed my head, hating myself a little more. The only lie I'd told had been about the family emergency, but I knew my friends would see this entire situation as a massive betrayal. The optimist in me wanted to believe everything would be okay, but the realist feared this would be the end of our friendships.

"I'll head out," Jaden said. "Keep me updated. I want to know what happens with you two, 'kay?"

I gave another jerky nod, silently hoping she didn't run into Garrick anytime soon, and blow my cover.

Jaden shot me a thumbs up, then climbed back into the car. With a quick wave, she reversed and drove off. I watched until her car was little more than a dot on the horizon, all the while wondering what the hell I was going to do.

I STEPPED BACK INSIDE THE CABIN, CAREFUL NOT
to let any light stray beyond the welcome mat, and
closed the door behind me. The silence was
welcome, but the anxiety gnawing away at the pit of
my stomach wasn't. I could only imagine what Jaden
would tell Chris and Josh, and I could quite easily
picture their stunned expressions. The thought of me
and Garrick together was about as appealing as a root
canal with no anesthetic. The guy's rap sheet with
other slayers was as long as my arm. Guess he liked

to snipe bounties from other slayers, which was absolutely despicable.

The thought of him touching me made me want to yack. It sent a shiver down my spine, and not in a "falling for the bad boy" kind of way. No, that honor belonged to Gabriel. He had a way of making me feel things I didn't know were possible—things I'd honestly thought I *couldn't* feel. Growing up as a foster kid, I'd often wondered if there was something wrong with me. If there was a reason no one wanted me. Those kind of toxic thoughts stick with a person and mess them up. So, yeah, maybe I was a little twisted up inside, but with good reason.

Sighing, I strode into the living room and melted onto the couch. I'd done my perimeter sweep and now all that remained was waiting for Sleeping Beauty—aka Gabriel—to wake up. Then came the imminent arrival of Anna and Vlad. Right on cue, my phone pinged with a message from my sister, giving me the Draculas estimated arrival time. According to Lucy, it would be between seven and seven-thirty.

A fresh wave of anxiety surged through me at the thought.

Right now, it was only me and Gabriel here. I liked it that way. It felt safe here. Cozy. Like the cabin belonged to just the two of us. Anna and Vlad's presence would change that. Someone knew where we were now. Three someones if I counted Lucy. Six if I counted Jaden, Chris, and Josh. So much for the covert operation.

Lying flat on the couch, I stared up at the ceiling, my mind a whirl of how to burn time till sundown. I refused to sleep—I'd rested long enough, thanks to Gabriel not waking me. And the cabin's entertainment options were severely lacking. No TV, no internet, no gaming system. Maybe a movie on my phone? But no, one look at the battery killed that idea. Plus, there was the whole "tracking me here" problem. If Jaden had done it, someone else could too.

Ugh.

I needed to do the responsible thing and turn it off.

I was ninety-nine percent sure no one but Lucy, Anna, and Vlad knew I was with the king, but I couldn't risk that one percent. It was silly to go through all the trouble of abducting Gabriel only to expose our location by using my phone to watch a movie.

After sending Lucy one final text informing her that I was going dark, I powered down my cell. It didn't take long for the withdrawal to set in. Phantom vibrations pulsated against my bottom, since I always carried my phone in my back pocket, and I itched to check my notifications. Clearly, I had an addiction.

I rose from the couch and discarded my phone in the kitchen. Out of sight, out of mind, right? When Anna and Vlad left, I'd have them take it with them. Gabriel's too. Best to get rid of both of them. Call me paranoid, but better safe than sorry.

Amidst my phone detox, I was at a loss for what to do next. Succumbing to boredom, I raided Jaden's cupboards and drawers, going through all her personal items in search of *anything* to distract myself. I struck gold when I discovered a stash of books. I was so relieved, I could have kissed the spin of the first one I grabbed.

I withdrew a thriller-esque looking novel, then sat on the loveseat and tucked myself beneath the blanket Gabriel had draped over me. I cracked the cover and before I knew it, a few hours had passed. I'd reached the book's halfway mark when I *felt* something—a charge that swept through the cabin.

I closed the book, untucked my legs, and glanced at the clock. Quarter to six. The sun had officially set, and my vampire was awake. I could feel it. A part of me wanted to dash into the room and see him, but I ordered that needy part of me to calm the eff-train down. He didn't need to know how eager I was for his company.

The shadows moved and suddenly Gabriel stood in the bedroom doorway, his stormy gray eyes locked on me. In the darkness, they almost seemed to glow. Fuck, that was unnerving.

"Hey," I murmured, placing my book down on the coffee table. I rose to my feet and smoothed my clothes. "Sleep well?"

He managed a grin, the tips of his fangs peeking out at me from behind those lips of his. My gaze dipped and I stared at his mouth, remembering exactly how it'd felt when pressed against mine.

"Like the dead," he said, his attempt at macabre humor bringing a reluctant smile to my face.

"Har, har," I replied.

He winked, then studied the living room. "Any trouble today?"

"Nothing I couldn't handle."

His eyes narrowed and his nostrils flared, as though scenting the air. "What happened?"

I waved off his concern, then returned to my seat on the couch and pulled the blanket back over my legs. With the sun setting, the temperature inside had plummeted, and my warm-blooded werewolf body was feeling it.

"One of my friends tracked my phone here." I gave him a quick rundown, avoiding all mention of her being a slayer or her connection to all this. "She was worried, since I'd vanished and came to make sure I was alright. I convinced her I was and off she went." Okay, so I'd glossed over quite a few details.

Gabriel cocked his head as he regarded me, then he strode into the room with his hands clasped behind his back. "You know, being that you're a werewolf, I'm shocked that you think you can lie to me."

I stiffened.

He shot me a glance over his shoulder, one brow raised in a silent challenge. "I'm sure you know the tells. Elevated heart rate, pupil dilation, quickening of breath, those sorts of things. Then, of course, there're the tells. People playing with their hair, for instance."

He paused long enough for me to realize that I had a lock of hair twisted around my finger. Stunned, I dropped my hand to my lap and held his stare. I'd never thought of myself as a bad liar before. Not that I was lying, per se.

"So, shall we try this again? I'll ask what happened, and you'll say…"

I counted to ten in my head before replying, "I'm telling the truth. A friend tracked my phone here. We spoke. She left. The end." I simply wasn't being as forthcoming with the details as he would have liked.

Amusement flared in his eyes.

"I don't need to share every detail of my life with you," I countered, then decided to change the subject. "Anna and Vlad are dropping by tonight."

I almost laughed when his expression shifted into something far more comical. "I have so many questions," he muttered. "But let's start with, you know Anna and Vlad?"

Ah, he hadn't known that. My lips curved into a smug smile. "Yep, I do."

He blinked, clearly taken aback by this. We'd never actually had the opportunity to learn much about each other.

Maybe it was time we started. And this information didn't cost me anything to share. "Anna is best friends with my sister, Lucy."

This time, his face went blank. "Lucy."

I nodded.

"Lucy Williams is *your* sister? When we spoke of

your sisters on Valentine's night, you never mentioned that. You said your sister was dead."

"I said *one* of my sisters was dead. That sister is not Lucy."

Gabriel turned and stared off into space. Lucy had once told me about her trip to England. She'd briefly mentioned meeting Gabriel, though it hadn't sounded as though the two had established much of a relationship. He'd only come in at the end, when he and Anna found her half dead. According to her, she'd been too busy turning into a werewolf to establish a friendship with him at the time. But he'd been there, and he'd seen the aftermath.

The realization dawned. *That* was how he knew about changed wolves. He'd seen it happen before.

"Lucy wasn't the one to change you then," he concluded, clearly remembering our conversation from the night we'd met.

"No. A different sister kindly volunteered for that job."

"I see." He turned away from the covered window. "So, through Lucy, you know Vlad and Anna."

"Anna mostly," I said honestly. "I've met Vlad, but I get the sense that few truly *know* him."

A grin broke out on Gabriel's face. "You'd be right."

"Anna, however, is like a sister to Lucy, so I made the effort to get to know her."

Gabriel frowned. "Anna and Lucy have been friends nearly their entire lives. Wouldn't that mean you've known Anna just as long?"

Ah. Personal life questions. This thread wasn't my favorite to discuss, but I'd practically walked into this one with open arms. To answer or dodge? That was the question. Opening up about my past was usually a no-go area filled with emotional landmines. I debated ignoring his question. I wasn't sure I was ready to explore our emotional wounds yet, which my upbringing fell under.

"Maddie?" he murmured.

He closed the distance between us and crouched, lowering himself to my level. He lifted his hand and touched my cheek with his cool fingers. I almost nuzzled him. Only a mental slap at the last second stopped me from seeking that comfort from him.

"There's pain in your eyes," he continued, his thumb smoothing my skin.

I averted my gaze. I hadn't meant for him to see that.

"Don't hide," he said. "Not from me." He tipped my chin up until our eyes met. "You can tell me anything."

Except, I couldn't. I certainly couldn't tell him my best friends were the ones hunting him. But maybe...maybe I could tell him this. It wasn't like I kept my upbringing a secret, I simply chose carefully who I shared it with. And Gabriel *was* my mate, after all.

I swiped my tongue across my lips to dampen them, completely aware of how he tracked the movement. A flash of our shared kiss rose to mind, but I pushed it aside. Now wasn't the time for that.

Instead, I found myself spilling the tea. "I grew up in the foster system. My biological father—whom I share with Lucy—abandoned me at six months old on the steps of a church when he realized I wasn't born a werewolf." I waved a hand. "He'd abandoned Lucy too. But she'd had her mother and a wonderful stepfather. I, unfortunately, had neither. My mother had died a few days after giving birth to me. Postpartum complications, I guess. My father had initially taken me in, but when I'd showed no signs of shifting, he'd tossed me to the wolves, metaphorically speaking. I grew up without a family." I shrugged. "I only met Lucy a little more than five years ago."

His silence and unwavering stare made my eyes burn with unshed tears. I quickly blinked them back.

"And your other sister?" he asked softly. "The one who died?"

"Olivia," I murmured. "Like Lucy, she had parents who raised her in a real home. She was the one who'd turned me. She's dead now, though. Family squabbles."

"That's a pretty serious squabble," Gabriel commented.

I nodded but didn't elaborate. I didn't feel the desire to get into all that with him. Olivia was dead. That was all that mattered.

"I'm sorry," he said, "for your upbringing. I, myself, know how abandonment feels."

My eyes widened. "You do?"

"Vampires can't conceive," he told me. "And my vampire mother, Queen Genevieve, was a fair bit older than me. She'd found me in an abbey where I was training to become a monk. My human mother left me there when I was five. She actually believed she was serving a higher calling by giving me up. My upbringing wasn't the same as yours, but my mother did abandon me. The queen found me when I was thirteen. She and her husband raised me until they felt I'd matured enough. Then they turned me and made me their second. The 'spare,' so to speak. They hadn't intended for me to rule, but..." He shrugged, as though to say, "what can you do?"

I knew what had happened to the queen. Anna had told me that story *many* times, always with more elaborations than her previous telling. I knew that Gabriel had saved Anna and Vlad's lives by stepping in and staging a coup. Then they'd petitioned the council for permission for him to take the throne instead of his older brother, who they'd felt wasn't the right choice for a ruler.

My heart broke for him. His story was far more tragic than mine. Yes, we'd both lost our mothers, and I'd grown up alone. But he'd grown up alongside a psycho queen, who he'd then killed. That had to have fucked him up a little.

"Parents, huh?" I said, attempting for a bit of levity. "Can't live with them. Can't live without them. Or so they say. I really have no idea."

The sorrow on Gabriel's face melted into a smile, one that made me all glowy inside. "You have family now, though."

"I do." My smile softened. "Lucy and Sam and their kids."

"Yes, Vlad mentioned them to me."

"Lucy told me that you and Vlad are best friends."

He chuckled. "Well, we are now. We weren't when we first met."

"Yes, Anna mentioned that."

"I imagine she did." He shook his head, still laughing. "After all that bloody nonsense, Vlad returned home with Anna. He and I remained in contact and then continued to see each other over the years. I visit whenever I have some free time— which admittedly isn't often. But Vlad and I have grown rather close."

"That must be nice," I teased, "to still make friends at your age."

Gabriel jerked back with an incredulous expression. "How old do you think I am?"

"Oh..." I tapped a finger against my mouth. "Hmm. A couple hundred at least, for sure. It shows here, and here." I touched his face, tracing the creases at the corners of his eyes. The second we connected, my breath caught, and a tingle spread through my fingers. I shouldn't have done that. I quickly dropped my hands. But Gabriel clasped them and brought them back to his face, pressing my palms against his cheeks, then sliding them around his neck.

"I was born in 1849," he told me, his voice taking on a husky note.

"So, an old man," I joked.

"Extremely old," he agreed.

"And you look it." No way in hell. He looked spry and utterly delicious.

He didn't say anything, and instead, just held my gaze. Once more, I licked my lips. It was unavoidable when this close to him. He brought out *all* the lip-licking tendencies.

Out of the blue, he said, "I haven't kissed you since Valentine's day."

I blinked, not entirely sure where he was going with this. We hadn't kissed again because that would complicate matters.

"So?" I asked.

"So, I would love to kiss you again." His eyes flicked to my mouth. "And again. And again."

My breath hitched. I wanted to scream *yes* and claim his mouth right here and now. But of course, fate intervened—as it always seemed to do lately, the nosey bitch—and someone knocked on the front door.

I shot the clock a startled glance and sighed.

Seven p.m. on the button. Vlad and Anna were here.

Worst. Timing. Ever.

I scrambled for the door, my face a fiery testament to my embarrassment. No time to dwell on what could've happened without that timely knock. Gabriel's magnetism was hard to ignore, and I suspected he could have had me on my back within ten minutes. Would it have been fun? Sure. But it seemed like dangerous ground to venture toward.

Clearing my throat, I yanked open the door to a moonless night. Two shadows lurked on the unlit porch, their figures swathed in darkness. The meek cabin light hit them, revealing Anna and Vlad's pale faces.

Great. Three vampires in one place. My pulse shifted into high gear when I realized they outnumbered me. My fingers twitched involuntarily, eager to grip a stake. I reminded myself that these were my friends. No one wanted to hurt me here. But five years of vampire hunting had left its mark. Before these guys, the only vamps I'd met were those with contracts on them. And those nights always ended with a body bag. Not how I wanted tonight to end.

Vlad's lips quirked, as though he sensed exactly what I was thinking. As far as I knew, vampires couldn't read minds. But after learning Gabriel had the superpower compulsion—something the Academy claimed didn't exist—I had my doubts. Anna had once let it slip that Vlad had a second power, common among older vamps. He could shapeshift, which, as a werewolf, I found fascinating. As for his second power? Anna always dodged that question whenever I asked.

And speaking of Anna, she was a social media celebrity with the ability to talk to animals. That was one skill I wouldn't mind having. She could even communicate with werewolves while they were in wolf form. A handy trick, for sure.

"Anna, Vlad," I greeted. "Please, come in." I'd learned this lesson already and wouldn't soon forget.

With a happy smile, Anna practically skipped inside, but Vlad played it cool, taking his time. His cautious steps brought him flush with me, and he shot me another inscrutable look. I never knew what the man was thinking.

"Madison," he said, his voice inhumanly deep. He had this thing about using my full first name. I think he enjoyed how much it irked me.

"Nice digs!" Anna chirped. She studied the interior with an appraising air, then zeroed in on Gabriel and sat next to him. Head cocked, she grinned at her king. "What trouble have you gotten yourself into now?"

Gabriel rolled his eyes, but there was no mistaking the smirk tugging at the corner of his lips.

Vlad passed me and joined the other two in the living room. His gaze slid to Gabriel, and the barest flicker of concern crossed his usually impassive face. "Murder charges, Gabriel?"

Gabriel waved a regally dismissive hand. "*One* murder charge, and need I remind everyone that it's fake? Let's get our facts straight."

Vlad's nose wrinkled. "The Academy seems to think otherwise."

"Do you know something?" I demanded.

Anna and Vlad turned to face me as one. Anna's smile never wavered. I'd always thought she was cool —for a bloodsucker.

"Only what you told Lucy," Anna said.

Disappointment soured my stomach. I'd hoped for more. So much more. It would have been nice if they'd swooped in with all the solutions.

"Let's not worry about all that right now," Anna said. "Maddie, come help me unload all the supplies we brought you."

I quirked a brow. Seriously? Why hadn't they brought in the supplies in the first place?

Anna tossed a comment over her shoulder at Gabriel. "Bet you're thirsty, huh?"

"A spot of something to drink would be nice," he retorted. "Someone nicked me away last night before I could grab a bite."

Vlad laughed, the deep sound contrasting with Anna's light giggle. "We're aware. Believe me, that isn't something we're going to let you live down anytime soon. To think you let a lone werewolf kidnap you."

"Eh, maybe I *let* her kidnap me," Gabriel teased, his gaze locking with mine.

"You keep telling yourself that," I retorted.

Anna chuckled as she strode toward me. Without asking, she took my hand and hauled me outside. A cool breeze caressed my face as we headed for the car, and the smell of snow hung heavily in the air. It rarely snowed in Mississippi, but I looked forward to those moments. There was something so magical about the white, fluffy flakes that fell from the sky.

"Okay, talk," Anna ordered the second we reached the car. She whirled me around and pressed my back against the passenger side door, caging me in.

My wolf came out to play with a low, menacing growl. But Anna didn't cower. Instead, she merely rolled her eyes. "Please. Our niece is more frightening than you. Now, talk. I want details."

"About what? I told Lucy everything."

"Sure, but I want to hear it all from you, face to face."

So she could decide whether or not I was lying. Fine. Sighing, I started from the beginning and recapped everything—minus any emotional gushing about Gabriel's and my mating bond. Vampires could hear as well as werewolves, and I'd bet Gabriel and Vlad were all ears right now. Therefore, I wouldn't be waxing poetic about how his kiss turned me to mush anytime soon. No need to feed Gabriel's ego.

When I finished, Anna peered into my eyes for a few moments. Likely waiting to see if my pupils dilated or if I blinked. Finally, she grinned and scooped me into a hug.

"Whoa," I said, my hands gripping her arms in an attempt to extricate myself. I didn't *do* hugs. Probably because I'd never received any physical form of love as a child. So shows of affection were foreign to me, and they made me super uncomfortable.

"I'm so happy about this!" she whispered in my ear.

"You...are? I wouldn't think a bounty on Gabriel's head would be cause for celebration."

She scoffed, then pulled away from me. "Oh, who cares about all that? I'm talking about you and Gabriel being mates!"

She squealed.

Literally squealed.

I resisted sticking my fingers in my ears.

"It's crazy to think that fate chose you two. I

mean, Gabriel is my king and my husband's best friend, and you're my best friend's long lost sister. The odds are..."

"Baffling," I responded. "But that doesn't matter. Fate may have decided to put us together, but that doesn't mean we *have* to be. We need to focus on clearing his name. That's all that matters."

For a moment, her expression fell. Then she gave a sly smile. "Sure. Whatever you say."

She said it like she was placating me. But come on. Did she really expect me to unpack my emotional baggage when Gabriel and Vlad could hear every word we said?

"Anna—"

"Hey, don't worry about it. We can focus on the bounty, if that's what you want." Then she winked. "We can figure the rest out later. When you're ready."

"There won't be a later!" I whisper-hissed. "I can *choose* not to be with him."

She blinked. "Why would you do that?"

Exasperation had me pinching the bridge of my nose. "Can we focus on the bounty, please?"

This time, she wasn't as confident when she said, "Sure. But let's bring in the supplies first."

Thank goodness. This was the last conversation I wanted to have right now.

Anna popped open the trunk of their car and bags spilled out. Cursing, we caught them before they dropped to the ground. I fumbled with what appeared to be a bag of clothes, then grabbed a few boxes of food and tote bags teeming with what looked like books and board games. Tucked into the back corner was a plastic crate full of bottled blood. And next to that sat an oversized messenger bag.

"Grab it all," Anna said.

I stared at the massive pile and let loose a low whistle. "You did all this today?"

She laughed. "Hun, I have people who do this stuff for me. I can't go out in the sunlight remember?"

Right. Duh. I really needed to readjust my perspective. I was so used to being able to come and go as I pleased that I'd never really given much thought to how vampires lived their lives.

"Come here." Anna motioned me over, then started hooking bags on my forearms. When I couldn't hold any more, she pulled out the bottled blood crate, messenger bag, and the few last remaining bags and piled them in her own arms. She caught my gaze and snickered. "One trip, or we bring shame to the family."

I blinked. What on earth did that even mean?

Anna led us back into the cabin. "A little help would be nice, boys."

I grunted my agreement. It wasn't that the bags were too heavy for me, but they were certainly awkward, and the handles was digging into my forearms.

Vlad and Gabriel took one look at us, then laughed and came to our rescue.

Anna began distributing the goods. New phones. A laptop for me. A box full of bottled blood for Gabriel. Mountains upon mountains of clothes. It was like some kind of tech-infused, vampire Costco haul.

Anna handed me a new phone, identical to my old one. "Lucy mentioned that you needed to go dark. But I don't love the idea of you two being without a means of communication. So we grabbed you each a new cell phone, and Maddie, a new laptop. I gave strict instructions to make sure that they're untraceable. I'm told the tech guy also included a mobile hotspot for you, which will let you connect to the internet, even out here. The account isn't in your name or ours, so it should be secure enough for you to use it."

She fished a piece of paper out. "The tech guy jotted down some notes about the apps he downloaded onto the laptop to help keep the device secure. It's all gibberish to me. Hopefully you know how to use a Mac?"

I did not, but I was sure I could figure it out.

"We'll take your old phones. Best not to have them, just in case."

"Where will you take them?"

Anna smirked. "With us. Maybe someone will show up, and we can get some answers."

Wouldn't that be nice? I wouldn't mind some answers right about now. I grabbed my phone and handed it over to Anna, before turning to Gabriel. "What about yours?"

He shook his head. "Don't have one, luv."

Anna stared at him as though he'd grown a second head. "Seriously? How do you...even function?"

Yeah, I had the same questions.

He shrugged, looking mildly amused. "I hate social media. And if anyone needs to contact me, there's an appropriate chain of communication they have to follow. If I had a cell phone, it would never stop."

Anna shot Vlad a stunned look. "How did I not know this about him? He's a psycho! No cell phone? Seriously?"

"If you lived my life," Gabriel said, "you'd probably forgo all means of communication as well."

"No, no, no," she chanted. "I'd simply keep my phone number a secret and only give it out to people I trusted."

"Doesn't work," he said. "I've tried. My number always gets out somehow. It's just easier to go without."

I stared at the device in my hand, dumbstruck. I could never go without. My phone was like another limb. I took it everywhere.

"Okay, but then how do *you* reach people you want to talk to? Or visit?"

"I don't," he said. "I have an assistant who does it for me."

Anna turned to Vlad as though looking for confirmation. He nodded. "Brenda and I are well acquainted."

"*Brenda*?" Anna repeated, her brows slowly rising. "Her name is Brenda, huh? And you two are well acquainted? Exactly *how* well acquainted?"

Oh, no. Abort, Vlad. Abandon ship. Tuck tail and run. I knew from experience with Lucy and Sam that mates could sometimes get a wee bit jealous. And that question was certainly a trap.

Vlad smiled. Then he leaned in and pressed a kiss to her temple. I watched his lips move, but I couldn't hear his whispered words. Whatever he'd said, though, did the job. Because a look of utter adoration crossed Anna's face. He'd diffused the situation within seconds. I almost applauded him.

"I still can't fathom living my life without my phone," Anna murmured. Then she held up the one she'd gotten him. "Do you want this?"

He shook his head, but I stepped in. "Yes. Take it."

Everyone's gazes darted to me.

"Some of the best slayers in the country are hunting you. If something happens and we're separated, you need a way to contact me. Or Anna and Vlad."

"Maddie—"

"No arguments, Gabriel," I said. "I won't bend on this. Your life is in *danger*. And you not having a means of communication is reckless. Give the number to me, Anna, and Vlad, and no one else. We certainly aren't going to give your number out."

"Bossy." Anna grinned, clearly enjoying the show. Then she took Gabriel's hand and slapped the cell phone into it.

He stared down at the device, a gamut of emotions playing out on his face—defiance, irritation, then finally, resignation.

"You don't have to use it," I told him. "But I need you to carry it with you at all times."

"And protective," Anna said. "I like it."

Gabriel chuckled. "I may like it a little bit too. Why do you think I decided to stick around?"

I rolled my eyes, then slipped my phone into my back pocket. I'd set it up later to my liking, after Anna and Vlad left.

"Maddie, your clothes and toiletries are in the red and yellow bags. Gabriel, yours are in the green and black." Anna pointed at each as she spoke. "There's enough blood to last you about a week. If Maddie's still holding you prisoner by then, we'll bring more."

"I'm hardly holding him prisoner!" I snapped.

Gabriel faced me, a twinkle in his eye. "You lured me away, knocked me out cold and dragged me here without my permission. That feels a bit 'hostage-y'."

"Like you're complaining," I grumbled, crossing my arms over my chest.

"Oh, I'm not complaining in the least," he said. "It's not every day someone you fancy kidnaps you. I want to explore that a bit more before returning to my mundane life."

My jaw dropped at his confession.

Anna tried to stifle her laughter. "You two are something else, and I'm excited to see how this unfolds."

"There's nothing to unfold," I insisted.

"Ooh, denial. The first stage of love," Anna said.

"As entertaining as this is," Vlad said, drawing the focus to him. "Perhaps we should get down to business. All teasing aside, there's a very real contract on Gabriel's life. I, for one, would like to fix that."

Heat blasted my cheeks. I nodded and gestured for everyone to sit. The couch could fit three of us, if we didn't mind half-sitting on each other's laps. Personally, I opted for the chair, and watched as Anna centered herself on the loveseat, with Vlad and Gabriel on either side of her.

It was like a bizarre sitcom set. Starring a hunk vampire heartthrob, his two best friends, and me, the overwhelmed werewolf.

Just another day in my oddball life.

12

"Alright," I murmured, not knowing where to begin. Tapping my fingers against my knees, I glanced at the trio of vampires who seemed perfectly content with me taking the wheel. Great. Because I was a pro at this sort of thing. "Gabriel, earlier you mentioned that you have a list of enemies longer than most."

He gave a succinct nod. "There are many who'd fancy a shot at replacing me."

Okay, that gave us a place to start at least. "Can you make a list?"

"You want me to make a list of everyone who wants me dead?"

"Is that a problem?" I asked.

He rubbed his jaw. "It'd be a long list, Maddie."

"That's fine. It'll give us a place to start. We could use it to start crossing off names."

"And how do we cross them off?" Anna asked.

Um. Good question. I was more of a Buffy than a Sherlock Holmes. I never investigated these sorts of matters. Hell, I didn't even read or watch mysteries. My preference ran more toward the "explosions and car chases" type of entertainment.

"Well..." I pursed my lips. "We could check his list against, I don't know, whoever's currently in town? Or see if any have been in contact with the Academy recently?" Oy. I frowned. "Or maybe see if anyone's done anything sketchy lately? Sent Gabriel hate mail?" People did that when they had a grudge, didn't they? Or was that stalking?

Dead silence from the vampire squad.

I tossed my hands in the air. "I don't know, guys. This isn't my wheelhouse. I just want to keep Gabriel alive. Undead. Whatever. My entire strategy until now consisted of getting him out of town, and I nailed that. Job well done, me. So if someone else has a brilliant plan, *please*, speak up."

"If I may…?" Vlad piped in, one eyebrow arching in question.

Relief flooded me. "By all means."

He gave a nod, stood, and began pacing the small living room. I didn't know Vlad all that well, but he looked deep in thought. Something was definitely turning in that vampiric brain of his.

Thank all things garlicky and yummy.

I had no issues handing over the reins to someone more competent.

"The Academy should have all the answers we need," Vlad said. "They received the complaint. They ran the investigation. They put the hit on Gabriel. Rather than us guessing and piecing things together, we could go right to the source."

The relief I'd felt earlier instantly curdled. "You want to go to the Academy? And do what? Tell them we have Gabriel?"

"No, of course not." He stopped pacing and pivoted to face me, his dark eyes probing. "You're correct that our main goal is to keep Gabriel safe. Alerting the Academy to his whereabouts would be counterproductive. However, you are a slayer and have connections we don't. Perhaps you could tell us a little about the organization?"

I shot Gabriel a glance. "Weren't you involved in the Academy's creation?"

"Not as much as I would've liked," he admitted. "I got the pitch, then a report from your government once they green-lit the legislation. I may be a king, but your country's government and legal systems are out of my hands. I can lobby for changes in laws affecting vampires, but my proposals are often nixed. Before the Academy came into being, we had our own vampire cops. Similar to sheriffs. But once we went public with our existence, your government decided our system wasn't cutting it."

Anna snorted. "That's an understatement."

Vlad patted her shoulder reassuringly.

"Once the Academy was born, the sheriffs were no longer needed. Any vampire choosing to live here must abide by local laws or suffer the consequences."

That made sense.

"So, Maddie, give us the inside scoop," Anna prodded. "Take us through the process."

"I don't have all the details," I admitted with chagrin. "We get a rundown when we join, but they don't fill us in on the finer details. As far as I know, the Academy has three divisions. Grievance, Investigations, and Reparations. Someone wronged by a vampire files a complaint with Grievances. If it ticks all the right boxes, the report is then passed to Investigations. They do their thing and issue a verdict. If it's guilty, the case goes to Reparations, who then decide the penalty. As a slayer, I only handle the death sentence cases."

"Who's in charge of these departments?" Anna asked.

"The council."

Her eyes narrowed. "And who or what is the council?"

Crap, I knew that question was coming. It was one I didn't have an answer to. I'd heard of the council, obviously, but I'd never met them. Nor had anyone else I knew. The council was this mysterious group that called all the shots, and that was all we knew.

When I didn't answer, Anna tilted her head. "Who do *you* report to?"

I shook my head. "I don't report to anyone."

Now her eyes widened. "You don't have a boss? Someone to keep tabs on you?"

"Nope. Why?"

"Who reins the slayers in if they lose control? Who issues the contracts? Who ensures that you follow all the laws?"

"The contracts come from Vera. She's the office

administrator. She receives the contract, then assigns it to an available slayer."

"Who gives her the contract?" Vlad asked.

I shrugged. "I assume from Reparations. As for how she assigns the contracts, I don't know. She has a system to keep it fair, but I don't know it."

"You've never met her in person?" Anna asked.

"No."

"And you've never met the council?" Vlad questioned.

My eyes bounced between them, suddenly feeling like I was the one in the hot seat. "No."

"So, you're handed a random assignment from some woman, then you go and slay yourself a vampire?" Anna demanded, baffled.

My annoyance flared. "She isn't random. She's Vera. And she receives the contract from Reparations."

"Or so you believe," Anna retorted.

I exhaled heavily. "Do you have a point?"

"Have you ever stopped to hear the vampire's side of the story?" Anna inquired.

"No. That's not my job."

"Right. So you're blindly following the orders of someone you've never met in person."

A slow realization dawned on me, and I bristled,

my defenses slamming into place. "Vera would *never* falsify an assignment. Nor would she send us after innocent vampires."

"How do you know that?" Anna shot back. "You never ask questions. The only reason you hesitated this time was because the hit was for someone you know. Your mate. Did your slayer buddies even consider his innocence? Or are they also blindly hunting him, ready to drive a stake through his chest because *Vera* says so?"

I scoffed. "That's *not* how any of this works. The Academy is a trusted entity that shields humanity from murderous vampires."

"Is that the company line?" Anna pushed. "Look at the facts, Maddie. Someone has supposedly accused Gabriel of murder, right?"

"Right," I grudgingly admitted.

"But who accused him?"

"I. Don't. Know," I gritted out.

"In the human legal system, the accused can face their accuser. So why doesn't the Academy? Someone makes an accusation, and they launch an investigation. We established that, right?"

I nodded.

She turned to face Gabriel. "Were you ever notified of your investigation?"

"No," he offered softly, his eyes on me.

Anna bulldozed ahead. "So, the Academy issued their verdict and deemed him guilty. Then they dispatched their slayers." She threw him another telling glance. "Were you notified of *that*?"

"No," he murmured again, clearly content to let Anna take the lead.

Anna lifted her hands. "All I'm saying is there are some problems with this system you so blindly trust. I get that it's your job, and it's the first place you've ever felt truly home. But Maddie, open your eyes. Something's fishy here."

Rage flared within me. "Look, every bloodsucker I've taken out was a total psycho. The last one I dusted had his fangs buried in his next victim's throat when I found him. If I hadn't been there to save her, he would have bled her dry."

"You're one hundred percent sure of that?" Anna challenged.

"Of course! I caught them in a back alley. He had pinned her to a wall and was feeding off her like he hadn't eaten in a week."

"And you're sure she didn't sign up for that?" she asked.

My jaw dropped. "What?"

"Humans feed us. Sure, we can buy bottled

blood, but a lot of vamps prefer the 'farm-to-table' approach. It's legal, as long as the human consents. Did you check with her before you staked her dinner date?"

I stared at Anna, baffled. Of course I hadn't stopped to question him. I'd found him sucking the life from another innocent woman. I hadn't been there to give him a warning.

"Well, how do *you* know she *did* consent?" I countered.

Anna tipped her head. "That's exactly my point. We *don't* know. Your Investigations team decided he did it. Your Reparations folks decided his fate. And Vera put you on the case. But can we say, beyond a shadow of a doubt, that he was guilty?"

"Anna—"

"Gabriel's fed off humans before. So has Vlad. Heck, I've even done it once. We aren't murderers."

"The vamp I slayed was a—"

"You don't *know* if the vamp you killed was guilty. You don't *know*," she emphasized. "You never saw the reports. The Academy never gave him a trial. Someone dropped his name, and the next thing you know, you've got a contract. Maybe he *was* a murderer. The point is, *maybe* isn't reason enough to put a vampire in the ground.

"I admit, there are quite a few of us in the vamp community with concerns about the Academy. In the human legal system, a jury has to be sure beyond a reasonable doubt to call someone guilty. They need evidence. Witnesses. The accused gets to tell their side. Your Academy? Skips all that. Vampire versus human? It's curtains for the vamp at the slightest hiccup."

"We're not here to critique the Academy," I growled. "We're here to help Gabriel and figure out how to fix this mess."

Anna's mouth twisted. "I think this conversation is immensely relevant, given that it's our king's neck on the line. But fine. You said Vera gets the contracts from Reparations." She turned toward Vlad, who stood by the window, his gaze riveted to Anna.

The instant her gaze left mine, I drew a deep breath and glanced at Gabriel. He lounged on the couch, his fingers braced beneath his chin and his expression deeply contemplative.

"We need to figure out what's happening behind the scenes," Anna said to Vlad. "I think our first step is arranging a chat with this Vera. Find out who her contact is within Reparations."

Vlad gave a severe nod. "From there, we can follow the trail until we find the culprit."

Anna flashed him a cheeky grin. "You're sexy when you think like me."

If Vlad were a human, he'd likely be blushing right about now. It took me a few more seconds to realize exactly what Anna had said. My eyes widened, and I jumped to my feet. "Wait, you guys are planning to handle this?"

"Do you see anyone else stepping up?"

I shook my head, my long blond hair spilling over my shoulders. "No. You can't *infiltrate* the Academy. You're vampires. If the council finds out, they'll kill you!"

"Oh, please," Anna scoffed. "We've tackled far more dangerous things. Overthrown governments, even."

From the corner of my eye, I caught Gabriel's wince, and blood heated to a boil. "If you're talking about the murder of Gabriel's mother, may I remind you whose company you're currently in?"

My biting words must have struck a chord within Anna, because she visibly deflated as she stared at Gabriel.

"I'm so sorry," she whispered. "That was totally out of line."

He waved her apology off, quick to forgive.

But back to the matter at hand... "The Academy won't take kindly to you two snooping around."

"Any organization afraid of people asking questions is exactly the sort of place that needs questioning," Anna replied. Something sparked in her eyes, and I remembered she'd been an amateur investigative journalist in her human days. Lucy had told me all about it, about how Anna had become famous. She'd run a vlog dedicated to finding the truth. That curiosity had brought about her death when she'd infiltrated a vamp club in search of an illegal blood bank.

"Anna, this could be risky," I said, my focus darting to Vlad. Surely he could reel her in a bit?

"Why?" she demanded. "We're simply asking a few questions."

"Yes, but if you're caught, the Academy might—" I fell silent, my eyes widening as I realized exactly what I'd been about to imply.

A smug smirk tugged on Anna's lips. "The Academy might, what? Put a price on our heads? Even though we haven't broken any laws?"

My heartbeat quickened.

"Looks like deep down, even you're not sure if your precious Academy is infallible." Before I could respond, Anna stood. She placed a sympathetic hand on my shoulder. "Be careful, you two. No opening the door to strangers, no answering the phone unless it's me or Vlad. Text me every night so I know you're safe. And call me if anything feels off."

I gave a weak smile. "Yes, Mom."

Her smile turned friendly. "That's my girl. Vlad and I will call you in a few nights with an update. Try not to kill each other while we're gone." Then she glanced at Gabriel. "And save the sex for after this mess is all sorted out. Don't mix business with pleasure."

"Anna," Vlad chided, sounding both amused and scolding.

"What?" She shrugged. "These types of situations can get messy, or so I've heard. I'm merely giving them fair warning."

"Alright, out," Gabriel said, pointing to the door. "Go."

She winked at him. "Yes, my liege." Then she vanished from sight.

Vlad was slower to leave, first clasping hands with Gabriel. "Stay safe, my friend."

"And you."

13

"So, WANNA HAVE SEX?"

I swear, I spun around so fast, I must have broken the sound barrier. "W-what?"

Gabriel turned to face me, his expression purely innocent. "I asked, do you want to play chess?"

When I didn't respond, he frowned, then pointed at one of the bags Anna had dumped on the floor. A bag of games, apparently. And sure enough, right on top, sat a chess set.

Sweet baby cheeses. My ears had totally punked me. What was the term for moments like this? A

Freudian slip? Anna's flirty farewell must've embedded itself deep for my brain to make that leap. The worst part was my damn body wanted to follow through on it.

"Right. Chess." I rubbed my brow. "Yeah, I suppose we could play a round after we tackle this mountain of bags. Think Anna brought us enough stuff?"

Clearly, my sarcasm wasn't lost on Gabriel. He chuckled, then reached for the crate of bottled blood. "She might have gone a tad over the top."

I appreciated the new laptop and cell phone. I definitely appreciated the bags of clothes and toiletries. Jaden kept her cabin sparse, understandably. She wanted nothing to do with this place and its haunting past. I, however, needed a toothbrush. Desperately. And while the king here didn't need to use the facilities for things like relieving bladders, I did. I only hoped Anna's helpers had thought to pack toilet paper. The half of a roll that had been here when we got here was dwindling fast.

Gabriel toted the crate of blood into the kitchen, then returned for the bags of food. I watched his muscles flex as he heaved the bags up. The whole scene felt a bit too domestic for my liking.

I snapped myself out of it, then found the toiletries bag and carried it to the bathroom. Relief had my legs uncrossing when I spotted the full pack of toilet paper. They'd also included soap, shampoo and conditioner, razors, and an assortment of feminine hygiene products. More than one woman needed. I made a mental note to store the stuff I wouldn't use. Once my life resumed normalcy, I'd donate it all to a women's shelter.

After happily stocking the bathroom, I returned to the living room and picked up the bags of clothes Anna brought us. Then I took a long look at the bedroom.

Gabriel didn't seem to have any problems with us sharing the room. But that was a hard no for me. And there was only one dresser. The thought of placing my folded clothes next to his was just too homey.

"What's wrong?" Gabriel asked.

He stood next to me, his own bags in hand.

"Where are we going to put all this stuff?" I asked, hefting the bags up so he could see the clothes.

"I'm sure there's plenty of room in the dresser. And whatever doesn't fit can go in the closet."

My mouth flattened. I considered leaving all the clothes in the bags and just ditching them in a corner of the living room. It wouldn't be much different than living out of a suitcase, right?

"Maddie," Gabriel said, his hand brushing my arm. "We can share a dresser without it meaning anything. It's just storage."

I took a shaky breath.

It wasn't that I had intimacy issues, per se. I wasn't *afraid* of commitment. I just lacked all experience with it. Any boyfriends I'd had, I'd always kept them at arm's length. Casual affairs had always seemed safer. Strangely, I probably wouldn't have minded sharing a dresser with any of them. But something about Gabriel terrified me. Maybe because I knew he was more than just a fling—or so destiny had decided.

In my mind, sharing a dresser with him felt like the equivalent of an engagement. An utterly irrational thought—I knew that. Yet, I couldn't stop myself from freaking the heck out.

"Why don't you let me handle this?" Gabriel offered when I didn't move.

I stood rooted to the spot, unable to step into the bedroom.

"I'll put the clothes away, then you won't have to worry about it."

Until I had to change my clothes.

Without a word, he took the bags from me and walked into the bedroom like he didn't have a care in the world. It wasn't until I heard him rummaging around that I realized he'd be handling my underwear—and my cheeks flushed.

To distract myself, I grabbed the bag stuffed with board games and pulled out the chess set. It was nothing fancy, but it would do the job.

"Ah," Gabriel said when he returned to the living room. "Brilliant. Have you ever played before?"

"A couple of times," I said with a shrug. "Not enough to really know the rules, though."

He sat opposite of me in the chair and quickly explained the rules, reminding me of the limited paths each piece could take. When he came to the queen and mentioned how she could do whatever she wanted, I grinned. This was a game I could get behind.

"Ready?" Gabriel asked.

I nodded, and after Gabriel moved his first pawn, I mimicked his move. He noticed and grinned. As I moved a third pawn, I asked, "So, who in your personal life wants to kill you?"

Gabriel blinked, pausing mid-reach for his knight. "Well, that's one way to set a mood."

"We need to discuss this," I replied, watching as

he finally moved his knight and captured one of my pawns. Huh. Okay, I was a man down.

I moved my bishop. "Well?"

He sighed and leaned back in his chair. "Off the top of my head, I can think of four."

Four? Wow. I couldn't think of a single person in my personal life who would want to kill me. Then again, I wasn't a vampire. Or a king. Or a couple hundred years old, plenty of time in which to amass enemies.

"Let's hear it."

Displeasure tightened his eyes. "There's Alexander, a rival vampire lord. He's loathed me and my family for a few decades now. Wants the throne for himself."

A power grab. Classic.

"Then there's Cecilia, a former lover."

Acid churned in my stomach as the image of him with a woman sprang to my mind. Not from jealousy, because I *wasn't* jealous. More like indigestion. Like the thought of him with someone else made me sick.

"There's Frederick, a member of my vampire council who does *not* like me. I can't imagine him going this far, but best to include his name than not."

"Okay, and number four?"

Gabriel released another sigh and met my gaze. Sadness dimmed his eyes—something I hadn't expected. "My father."

Alarm shot through me. "Your *father*?"

"How much do you know about my takeover?"

I moved my queen and snatched one of Gabriel's knights. The tightening of his mouth told me my move hadn't gone unnoticed. "Just what Anna's told me. But she likes to embellish."

That earned me a chuckle. "Allow me to tell you the proper story then." He captured my knight in retaliation.

"I'm sure you've heard of Petrik?"

I nodded. The vampire who'd attacked Anna and left her for dead in the alley behind some vamp club. The same place where Vlad had found her and turned her into a vampire. Petrik was also the source of the ancient blood that had given Anna the ability to wake hours before sunset.

"He thought he'd killed Anna. But when he learned that Vlad saved her and turned her into a vampire, he tried again. Nearly burned her alive."

I winced, even though I'd heard that part before. In great, gory detail.

"Sam and Lucy rode to her rescue and killed

Petrik. The most important thing you need to know about all this is that Petrik was the queen's lover."

"The queen, as in your mother?" I said, even though I already knew the answer.

He nodded.

"The woman married to your father?" I clarified.

Another nod.

Yikes. And here I'd thought my life was complicated.

"Adrian Roche is my father," Gabriel said. "Petrik was not."

"Oh damn."

He gave another nod. "Oh damn, indeed. When my mother learned of her lover's death, she set the inquisitors on Anna. The inquisitors are a special vampiric breed. They obeyed only my mother. One of them did a thorough dive into Anna's involvement in Petrik's death, which resulted in Anna and Vlad's arrest."

Wow. Talk about a soap opera.

"The inquisitor shipped them to England where they would face my mother's so-called justice. While imprisoned, their friends arranged their escape. My mother didn't take kindly to that. She issued a vampire-wide manhunt. And when that didn't work, she attacked businesses suspected of harboring them.

She also began"—Gabriel swallowed and shook his head—"taking vampires hostage to force their partners into aiding in the search."

Whoa.

"Obviously, I couldn't allow that to stand."

I nodded along with his story.

"Anna, Vlad, and their allies sought me out. Begged me to step in. To stop my mother. After seeing what she was capable of, and how little she cared about her people, I agreed. She wanted revenge, nothing more, and she didn't care if she had to torch the kingdom to get it. I, however, did care. Except, I wasn't the heir. My brother, Elias, was. Unfortunately, he was my mother's puppet. Whenever he opened his mouth, her words came out. We couldn't trust him with the throne. So we petitioned the vampire council to remove my mother from her seat and place me on the throne instead. They agreed to my request, and I removed my mother from power. But as we were escorting her to her prison cell, she attacked Anna. Staked her in the chest."

Ah yes, this part I'd heard many times. Her miraculous survival had entertained many over the years.

"It was only by blind luck that Anna survived.

My mother's actions forced my hand. I loved her. But she left me no choice."

"You killed her?" I whispered, completely invested in his story. I already knew the answer but couldn't resist asking.

He jerked a nod.

"Wow." It took me a moment to figure out how this related to our current problem, but eventually, the lightbulb lit. "So, you think your father wants revenge?"

"My father doted on my mother. He adored her. The feeling wasn't mutual, but that never seemed to bother him. I suspect he wants me dead as retribution for killing his wife."

It made sense. Except for one small thing, "Why now? Why wait five years?"

"I don't know," Gabriel admitted. "I've left European soil before. I've come to America numerous times during the past five years. He could have attempted this at any time."

"Maybe he's conflicted about killing his own son?" I mused. "Struggling with the decision?"

"It's possible. And five years in the eyes of a vampire is like a month to you."

Fair point. Eternity would give a person a slightly different perspective.

I reached for the new laptop Anna had given me and turned it on. It took longer than I would have liked to figure out the operating system. But eventually, I had Safari booted up and was searching for Adrian Roche online.

"From what I can see, he's still in England," I said. "There's been no mention of him jumping the pond."

"It would look highly suspicious for him to come here," Gabriel said. "The man hasn't stepped foot off England in centuries. To do so the moment there's a contract placed on my head would give him away."

That made sense. "Does he have connections here? Someone who could put his plan into motion?"

"Undoubtedly. My father never actually ruled. He was king in name only. But he has connections all over the world."

"And you're sure he wants you dead?" I asked, softening my words. It had to hurt, hearing that a parent wanted to kill you.

Gabriel lifted one shoulder in a half-shrug. "He seems the most obvious suspect to me."

I opened a memo app, then placed my fingers on the keyboard, ready to take notes. "Tell me everything about the others you mentioned. Cecilia, Frederick, and Alexander."

A dark chuckle slipped past his lips. "Of those three, I could see Cecilia being the one behind this. She's...clever."

I gritted my teeth as I jotted that note down. I didn't want to hear about his clever ex-lovers. I was quite happy imagining them as nothing more than faceless names. "And the others?"

"Nothing really to tell. They're just normal people. Vampires. Vlad and Anna can check them out." He repositioned himself and resumed our chess game. We'd lost track of it during his story. He moved a pawn and stole my rook.

"You're cheating," I grumped.

He shot me a wide stare. "You wound me with such accusations, madam!"

I snickered at his words, his accent adding a flare of drama to them.

"I'm the king of vampires," he continued. "The embodiment of honor."

I snorted. "Right. Vampire King, embodiment of honor, accused of murder, and currently on the lam."

"Touché," he said, a playful smile tugging at the corner of his lips.

I put the laptop aside and moved my remaining rook, capturing Gabriel's pawn, which somehow let him corner my king.

"Checkmate," he said, beaming.

"What?" I studied the board. "My queen's still in play. Surely, I have some moves left."

His smile widened, his fangs peeking out at me. "Oh? I think the only move she has left is to graciously admit defeat."

"Admit defeat?" I laughed, enjoying our banter. "Never. That sounds like something a vampire would do."

"Ouch, now that's cold," he said, feigning a hurt expression. When he popped that bottom lip out in a coy pout, I almost leaned in and kissed him. *Almost.*

"Just remember, Gabriel. The game's not over till the queen concedes, both on the board and off it."

Gabriel met my gaze and winked. "I am eagerly looking forward to that moment."

14

"You should rest," Gabriel suggested the moment we packed up the chess game. He still sat across from me, his elbows perched on his knees.

My gaze instantly shot to the bed, and I quickly shook my head. "I'm good."

"It's three in the morning," he stated, as though I wasn't fully aware of the time. Being that I was a vampire slayer, I kept odd hours. I usually went to bed at sunrise, after a night of slaying. I had a few more hours left in me before I'd need to crash. Except, in a few hours, Gabriel would succumb to the daylight. I wasn't thrilled about the idea of sleeping at the same time as him. What if someone found us? I'd slept harder than expected yesterday, and I didn't entirely trust myself to wake.

"You can take the bed," he said. "I'll nudge you before sunrise, if you'd like."

Which would give me three hours of sleep, thereabouts. Definitely not enough to be firing on all cylinders.

"Or...you could stay with me in there after sunrise," he murmured suggestively, leaning close. "Shouldn't a bodyguard get as close to the body she's protecting as possible? I'm confident you'd wake up if someone came barging in."

Stay with him? In bed? All day? While he was... dead? I shivered, and not with anticipation. The idea of sleeping in a bed with a man was nerve-wracking enough, but bunking with a "dead" vampire made the hairs on my arms stand up. I knew from Anna that they weren't *actually* dead. But it was hard to wrap my mind around it. She'd once told me to think of it like sleeping. Except they were completely unresponsive during the day. That sounded like dead to me.

"That's okay," I murmured. "I can take the couch."

An amused smile touched Gabriel's lips. "Why sleep on the cramped couch when you can sprawl in a big bed?"

Because on the couch, I didn't risk snuggling with a lifeless body. And according to Jaden, the only person I'd ever slept in the same bed with, I was a snuggler. Not even the pillow barrier had stopped me. I'd always found it a bit amusing, considering how uncomfortable hugs made me. I guess subconsciously, my body craved affection.

"I honestly don't mind sharing," he continued. "I won't notice you while I'm sleeping."

Kinda creepy, right? Who didn't notice when someone else was in bed with them? A "sleeping" vampire, that's who.

When I didn't respond, Gabriel reached out and laid a hand on top of mine. "Maddie, you need to rest."

"I will. Out here."

"So I'm banished to the bedroom?"

I shrugged. "That's your call. I won't force you to stay in there. I didn't yesterday, did I?"

He sighed and leaned back, his hand sliding away from mine. I immediately missed his touch.

"You realize I can't take advantage of you, right?" he said, chuckling. "The moment the sun rises—"

"You die, I know."

Understanding flickered in his eyes, then something darker, almost painful. "So, that's what it is. You're disgusted by the thought of sharing a bed with a vampire."

He thought I was ashamed of him. That sucked to hear.

"No," I hurried to say. Then I dropped my gaze to the living room table. Maybe it was time for a little honesty. Sure, the idea of sharing a bed with a dead vampire was nerve-wracking, but it didn't frighten me near as much as simply sleeping next to a man.

"No?"

I released a long breath. Guess it was time to get a little real with him. The last thing I wanted was to hurt his feelings.

"I've...never *slept* in a bed with a man before." I snuck a peek at him, my mouth twisting at the sight of his arched brow.

"Never?"

I shook my head. "I've *shared* a bed with a man before, obviously." I tucked my hair behind my ears. "More than once, of course." I cleared my throat. "But I've never actually *slept* in one with a man. The only person I've slept next to is my friend Jaden."

His silence had me gnawing the inside of my lip.

When I finally braved a glance up, he was leaning back in his chair and smiling.

"That's almost...endearing," he said.

"Shut up. It is not. I'm a grown-ass woman."

"You are. And you aren't any less of one simply because you haven't slept in the same bed with a man. I find it a bit charming. Almost innocent."

To that, I laughed. "Believe me, there's nothing innocent about what I do when I *am* in bed with a man."

Darkness flashed in his eyes, but he blinked it away a second later. After a moment's pause, he cleared his throat and rose from his chair, carrying the chess box across the room to the pile of games.

"Well, the offer is there if you decide you're not comfortable out here. In the meantime, I suppose I'll hang out in the bedroom and wait for sunrise. You really should rest, though."

I gave a polite nod and watched as he strode out of sight. Once again, he left the bedroom door open, leaving me to stare at the bed. It *did* look comfortable. And he was right about one thing. When the sun rose, he wouldn't even be aware of me. And I *did* need more rest than the three hours that remained until sunrise.

Was I being needlessly stubborn?

Surely, I could take a few additional hours to rest. No one outside our circle knew we were here. Anna and Vlad had taken my old cell phone with them, to keep anyone from tracking us that way. Sure, Gabriel's guards had access to his wardrobe, so they *could* track him by scent. But if they found us, Gabriel would theoretically be safe. It was their job to protect him. If anything, they'd simply off me and retrieve their king.

Why, in the name of all things sweet and delicious, did that comfort me?

I shook my head and stared at my new laptop. It'd be a small miracle if his guards found him. We'd driven thirty minutes outside Jackson to get here. I couldn't imagine they'd be able to track his scent among the countless vehicles that used the roads I'd taken. And if they started canvassing the nearby towns, we hadn't stepped foot in the one closest to us.

We were safe here.

Enough that I could rest.

Just because I was an anxious ball of nerves didn't mean I should neglect my own mental and physical health. I needed to be in peak condition for the moment something did happen.

Biting my lip, I pushed to my feet and tiptoed toward the bedroom.

Gabriel stood with his back to me, facing the window. He'd untacked the two bottom corners and folded the blanket up, revealing the lower half. I saw nothing but swaying trees and shadows in the wintry night.

"I can trust you, right?" I asked from the doorway.

Gabriel didn't so much as stiffen, meaning he'd heard me approaching. He'd likely kept his back to me purposely. To make me feel safe.

"I'm probably the one guy you can trust most in this world," he replied, his voice soft yet husky in the silent confines of the bedroom.

"Because you're my mate?"

"That." He finally turned, the bedroom light refracting in his eyes. "And I fancy myself an honorable bloke."

"Been there, heard that," I admitted. "Seems like every foster dad I had fed me that same line. That I could trust them. That they were good guys. Nice guys. That they only wanted what was best for me."

I caught the slow tightening of Gabriel's shoulders. "Did they live up to their word?"

"Not a single one," I whispered, skipping the details. He didn't need to know about the few who'd tried to climb into bed with me—likely the crux of my trust issues. Or the ones who'd completely neglected and ignored me, there only to collect a meal ticket. Or the abusive ones who'd enjoyed causing pain. The foster system had amazing people in it. But it also had the worst. And I'd always seemed to land the bad apples. Just my luck, I suppose.

If I were human, I might've missed the telltale signs of Gabriel gritting his teeth, or his clenched fists. But my werewolf senses missed nothing. The fact that he was seething with anger knowing some of what I'd been through encouraged me to take a chance of him.

In Lucy's words, fate didn't screw these things up. It'd paired us together for a reason, right? Trusting him was easier said than done, but I wanted to overcome this stumbling block. He made me *want* to work on my personal demons.

Clearing my throat, I braved another step into the room. "If I do this, I need to be clear about something right from the start."

He tilted his head in response.

"There will not—nor will there *ever* be—any blood sharing between us."

His eyes widened. "You associate sleeping in the same bed with blood sharing?"

"I'm not sure what kind of late-night shenanigans vampires get up to," I confessed. "You know, other than...doing the do."

That made him smirk. "What, according to you, is 'doing the do'?"

I rolled my eyes. "Oh, please. We both know I'm talking about sex."

Gabriel chuckled as he strode toward me. He kept his steps slow and purposeful, as though afraid I'd bolt given the first chance. He wasn't wrong. My whole body was ready to dart back into the living room.

"I've never taken blood from anyone without consent," he assured me. "And I'm not about to start now. I swear, I don't wake up ravenous. Well, not for blood anyway. I can't guarantee I won't wake up with a different kind of appetite."

This time, I laughed, finding the topic of sex far less intimidating than the idea of sleeping together or sharing blood. Plus, I'd wake up long before him, which would keep me safe from his other "hunger."

"And no cuddling," I said.

"Ah, well that's unfortunate."

I bit back a laugh. He looked thoroughly

disappointed. Like a puppy who'd lost its favorite toy.

"Go on then," he said, jerking his chin to the bed. "I'll be a few hours yet, so you might as well get comfortable."

Right. Between the bed and the couch, the latter was a no-brainer. I'd slept on the couch yesterday and my back had been complaining ever since, reminding me I wasn't eighteen anymore. Twenty-seven wasn't old by any means, but right now, my back disagreed with that assessment.

"Fine," I said, sighing.

Gabriel's mouth twitched, evidently amused by my reluctance. Hell, he probably was.

I marched to the dresser and yanked open the drawers. Gabriel had placed his things in the bottom and mine in the top. I rifled through my new clothes and pulled out what Anna had brought me for pajamas. As I held up the tiniest pair of shorts I'd ever laid eyes on, I realized she and I had a wildly different idea of sleepwear. In the winter, I usually wore thick sweats. In the summer, I went naked. For some reason, these silky short shorts seemed worse than naked. In these, I would *feel* nude. The hem would barely conceal the curve of my ass cheeks, let alone anything else.

I cursed, then dug around for a top. Of course, all I found were skimpy tank tops with the thinnest straps known to man.

"Oh, this isn't happening," I grumbled.

"What's wrong?"

I spun around and tucked the questionable attire behind my back. "Nothing. Who said anything was wrong?"

Gabriel frowned for a moment, then understanding dawned. "Ah, yes. The, uh, pajamas Anna packed for you."

"She hates me, doesn't she?"

"No," he said, chuckling. "That's Anna's idea of a joke, I believe."

"I hardly find this funny."

"And that's probably what Anna finds most amusing," he said.

Growling, I stomped into the living room and snatched my new cell phone. I took a photo of the outfit and fired it off to Anna, peppering the message with more disgruntled emojis than a person could count. The laughing emoji she sent back did little to soothe my temper.

"Relax, luv," Gabriel said. "I've seen many women in many states of undress."

Okay, I didn't need to know that. Jealousy and

anger were a combustible combo.

"Let's refrain from rehashing your previous conquests," I grumbled.

I whirled around in time to catch the surprised expression he wore before I strode into the bathroom to change.

Many women in many states of undress, I mouthed as I stared at my reflection in the mirror.

Fine. If he could pretend to be mature about this, then so could I.

I wrenched off my clothes, took care of my bodily needs, brushed my teeth, then slid into the smallest, skimpiest pajamas ever. The shorts stopped just shy of being decent. And the top...well, it left nothing to the imagination.

Revenge was the only thing on my mind as I wrenched open the bathroom door and stormed toward the bedroom.

Gabriel stood on the threshold but froze at the sight of me. His face morphed into a blank expression, a master poker expression. But my heightened senses picked up on *exactly* what he felt. The scent of arousal and desire perfumed the air. He didn't move, but I caught the slight tic at his temple as he clenched and unclenched his jaw.

"Right. Well, goodnight," I muttered, slowly pulling back the bedspread.

Gabriel relaxed his jaw long enough for him to wish me a gruff goodnight. Then he tore out of the room like his pants were on fire. Hell, maybe they were.

Suddenly, I wasn't so angry anymore.

Maybe instead of exacting revenge, I'd send Anna a thank you note.

15

I STIRRED, SLEEP SLOWLY RECEDING AS awareness crept through my body. I blinked open my eyes, no longer surprised to find myself surrounded by darkness. What time was it? Was it still early morning?

I reached for my phone to check the time, when something stopped me. A hard, unyielding surface beneath me. No...not a surface. A person.

Oh great googly moogly.

A jolt of panic shot through me, kick-starting my heart into overdrive. My grogginess vanished in the blink of an eye. Just like that, I was wide awake, and shocked to find myself draped across Gabriel's unmoving form. My head rested snugly in the curve of his shoulder, my arm flung across the solid expanse of his chest. Pressure snaked around my waist, and I choked when I realized it was his arm wrapped tightly around me.

I racked my brain, trying to remember when I'd moved from my side of the bed to snuggle with Gabriel, but nothing came up. Even worse, given the possessive way his arm curled around me, he'd been awake when he'd done so. He couldn't move during his daytime slumber, meaning he'd *allowed* me to cuddle into him.

Mortification heated my face. I'd been so adamant—no cuddling!—and here I'd already broken my own rule. I couldn't even pretend it hadn't happened either. His blasted arm assured me he'd been a willing participant.

What a rookie mistake. Jaden had warned me I was a snuggler. For some reason, I'd thought I could control myself. Guess not. My body must have a mind of its own while I'm sleeping, my subconscious taking full control of me.

Quietly growling, I detached myself from Gabriel's embrace, a chill creeping in as I put more distance between us. He lay perfectly still, oblivious to my hasty retreat.

Small mercies.

I grabbed my phone and scrambled out of bed, my feet hitting the cold wooden floor with a quiet thud. I wrenched open the dresser drawers and pulled out the first outfit I could find, then rushed out of the bedroom and into the bathroom. I shut the door with a click that echoed in the unnerving quiet, then stared at myself in the mirror, my hands gripping the edge of the sink.

I should've known better. Should've slept on the couch. What was a little discomfort compared to *this*? Now I had to endure his smug face when he woke tonight. He'd surely rub it in too, after our discussion last night.

Closing my eyes, I drew in a slow breath and centered my thoughts.

Okay. This wasn't the end of the world.

If he teased me, I'd throat punch him.

Except, I *wouldn't*. I never wanted to hurt him again.

Ugh, what a complicated mess this had become. Every bone in my body wanted to call Lucy and talk to her about all this. She'd gone through something similar when she and Sam first mated. He'd been all for it, and she'd run away as fast as her feet could carry her.

I didn't have that option, thanks to the bounty on Gabriel's head.

Okay. It was really simple. No. More. Cuddling.

No touching, no kissing, no thinking sexy thoughts. Nada.

I almost snorted at myself. Deep down, I knew those were empty orders. If I was being honest with myself, I'd admit that I *liked* touching him. I just didn't *want* to like touching him, which was a whole different problem.

Deciding to stop wallowing, I relieved myself, then hopped in the shower. After a quick scrub down, I dressed and ventured out into the living room. Glancing at the clock, I saw that it was three p.m.

Holy shit.

I'd slept so long. Longer than I'd ever slept in my whole life. I wasn't someone who managed twelve hours of rest a night. My sleep had always been erratic and disrupted. But not this time. I couldn't remember waking once through the night.

I cursed out loud.

Had I slept so well because I was with Gabriel?

"Ugh!"

I snatched my jacket off the back of the couch and stormed outside into the blinding sun. I shielded my eyes, then sat on the porch and took a series of calming breaths.

"This really isn't the end of the world," I told myself. "Things could be worse."

A twig snapped in the distance.

My attention shot in that direction, and I scanned the bare trees. I stiffened, every instinct screaming at me to be on high alert. It was likely just an animal—those did live in the woods, after all. But that snap had sounded too loud for a small woodland creature.

Another sound rose to my ears. The rustling of fallen leaves. Closer this time. Slow and deliberate. As though something was trying to *avoid* making noise. My breath hitched, and my pulse pounded in my ears. I tried to calm myself. If there was something out there hunting us, they might hear my body's reactions and know I was onto them.

The forest went silent.

I strained my ears, listening.

When a bunny came darting through the trees, I almost laughed. Relief had every muscle in my body going slack. All that over a damn bunny.

A fleeting shadow whipped through the trees.

I gasped and shot to my feet.

That was no animal. The shadow had been tall and moved far too fast for anything natural. Something was definitely out there. Something more dangerous than a harmless bunny.

Fear gnawed at my insides.

If someone *was* in those woods, they were after Gabriel. Meaning they'd somehow tracked him here.

A second shadow whipped by, keeping its distance. Two of them? I listened closely, catching the sound of their movement. Definitely two. They were in sync with one another, but on opposite sides of the woods. It took a moment for me to realize their tactic. They wanted to lure me away from the cabin. They must have suspected Gabriel was inside. And vulnerable.

I gritted my teeth and stood my ground.

If they wanted to fight, they'd have to come to me. No way in hell I'd abandon my post. I was the only thing that stood between them and Gabriel.

I fished my phone out of my pocket and brought up Anna's contact information. Then I typed out the fastest text message ever. Calling her was pointless. It'd be an hour before she woke for the day. And a few more hours after that until Vlad and Gabriel woke.

I dialed Lucy, then Sam, dismayed when neither answered. Just my luck. I fired off a text message, telling her to phone me back ASAP.

I debated phoning Jaden. But I had no idea *what* was out there. It couldn't be vampires since the sun was up, and every werewolf in the state belonged to Lucy's pack. She was diligent about that. So what else could it be? These two moved too fast to be human. Bringing in Jaden not only risked Gabriel's life, but also risked exposing her to more of the paranormal. Neither option sat well with me.

I was officially on my own.

Resolved, I quickly stripped and let my wolf take over. My form shifted until I stood on four paws, and the world became a blaze of smells and sounds heightened by my wolf's senses.

I breathed in the cool air and picked out the two foreign scents. I'd never smelled anything quite like them before. They smelled earthy. Almost bitter. And a hint of something strange clung to them. Something almost...

Magical.

A pair of figures came together and emerged from the tree line. Shock ripped through me at the sight of their bald heads, glowing eyes, and tattooed skin. But now I knew *exactly* what they were.

Witches.

I'd never met one before, but Chris had once. He'd told me about the intricate tattoos they burned into their flesh. According to him, they used them as conduits to siphon power from their revered gods. The only other thing I knew about them was that they were an elusive breed. Isolated. And rarely interacted with other paranormals, believing themselves superior. That had been enough to convince me to keep my distance from them.

And now I stood before two.

Someone had hired them to find Gabriel—that I knew without a doubt. I'd made life a little difficult for his enemy. So they'd taken matters into their own hands.

The witches wore long, billowing robes that floated around their bodies. Their faces were pale, even in the mid-afternoon light, their eyes burning with a strange, otherworldly glow. They seemed out of this world. Alien, almost.

I was so out of my element here.

The Academy had trained me to fight vampires. Not witches. I didn't even know how to protect myself from them let alone protect my defenseless mate. I wouldn't let that stop me from trying though.

I growled a low, guttural sound, warning them to

keep their distance. And if they didn't, well, my teeth and claws were ready.

The taller of the two raised a hand toward me, fingers splayed. Words spilled from her lips in a language I didn't recognize, and from her palm came a glowing green light. It expanded. Growing. And before I had a chance to duck, the power slammed into me and flung me across the yard. Pain erupted within my body as I skidded backward, my claws leaving furrows in the earth.

I shrugged it off and jumped back into the action as the second witch bolted for the cabin door. She hit the brakes when she saw me barreling towards her. This time, I was ready when she raised her hand and started mumbling. I needed to get to her before she finished casting the spell.

My claws tore into the soil as I raced toward her. When the glowing orb exploded from her hand, I dropped. Power whipped over me, missing me by a hair. Ozone crackled as it swooshed by, and the scent of burning fur filled my nose. So maybe not quite missing me.

I scrambled to my feet and sprung at the witch. Her eyes widened and she raised her hands again.

Oh no, you don't.

I knew their tricks now. And knew I needed to keep them from completing their spells.

When I was less than a foot away, fire spewed from her hands. She was trying to keep me at a distance. Smart. But she didn't understand how desperate I was to protect Gabriel.

I weathered the attack, my jaw tightening when the fire blazed across my side. Digging my claws into the ground, I lunged. I didn't know the first thing about magic and spells. But I knew how to fight. And I knew few creatures—if any—could survive decapitation. It was a form of death I was intimately familiar with. I used it for vampires too.

Midair, I opened my mouth. We collided, my weight riding her down to the ground. Her shriek ended with a gurgle when my mouth closed around her throat, ending her life.

The other witch cried out, her fury igniting the air around me with magic.

I hopped off the dead witch and turned to the second one. Power crushed me, forcing me to the ground. I slogged to my feet, pushing myself inch by inch across the yard. The witch screamed her rage at me, her face mottling with color. She thrust both hands in my direction, fire and ice flying at me.

Pain ripped through me, and the air was thick

with the smell of blood, ash, and burned fur. I wasn't sure how much of it belonged to me. I only knew every step was pure torment.

"How are you still alive!" she wailed, her eyes narrowing as she shot another spell at me.

It slammed into my chest with an agony I'd never experienced before. I collapsed, my wolf form retreating. I'd never had that happen before. Never been hurt so badly that I'd been forced back into human form.

I lay on the ground, staring at the sky above, the trees swimming in my vision. I could barely breathe. Whatever that witch had hit me with, it'd hurt like a mother.

A shadow passed over me and I blinked, now staring up at her.

She leered at me, her face a menacing mask of violence. The other witch, the one I'd killed, must have been important to her.

"I'm going to kill you," she seethed. "And then I'm going to kill the vampire you're trying so desperately to protect."

She meant for her words to hurt me, but instead, they empowered me. She lifted her hand, magic coalescing in her palm. The words came next, the odd, guttural chant. Before she could finish it, I summoned every last bit of strength I possessed and surged upward. I gripped her head, one hand on either side. Right as I started to twist, she pressed her glowing hand against me.

Excruciating heat ripped through me. I screamed as wave after wave of power burned me from the inside out. I couldn't let myself die yet though. Not without taking her out first. I would die protecting Gabriel, and I was okay with that.

With a last surge of strength, I snapped her neck like a twig and watched her body fall to the ground. Strangely, my last thought was how stupid I'd been to stress over waking in bed with Gabriel this afternoon. If I'd known it was going to be our one and only time, I might have cherished it more. Odd the things we think about in the face of death.

I swayed, then crumpled to the ground, lost to the darkness.

16

EVERY INCH OF MY BODY ACHED, AND FOR THE life of me, I couldn't remember why. All I remembered was pain. *So* much pain. Slowly, my memories started to resurface, and I recalled everything.

The witches. The fight. Death.

Being that I was a slayer, I obviously had experience killing. But never anything like this. I'd never faced off against magic before. Those witches had not only conjured actual magic right in front of me, but tried to kill me with it too. I remembered the smell of my burned fur and the feel of my insides set aflame. When the second witch hit me with that final spell, I'd honestly thought I was as good as dead. Hell, I could have sworn I'd seen the Grim Reaper himself, looming over me, ready to drag me into the beyond.

I never wanted to feel anything like that again.

Movement came from my right. I gasped and struggled to sit up. If there was another witch, I had to move. I couldn't lay here and—

"Shh, luv," came a soft but strained voice. A cool and soothing hand brushed a stray lock of hair away from my face. "You're alright. Relax."

"Gabriel?" His name came out hoarse, barely more than a raspy whisper. My throat felt blistered. Like I'd gulped down a boiling mug of water. But I was so relieved. He was okay, thank goodness.

"It's me. I'm here," he said. He cupped my cheek, and I leaned into him, taking the comfort he offered. "How do you feel? Are you okay?"

He sounded concerned. For me. And I wasn't too sure how to handle that.

Sure, I had people who cared about me, but it wasn't the same as *Gabriel* caring about me. It was different with him. Deeper. And far more intense. It made the walls I'd built around my heart crack and shudder.

I attempted to sit up again. A fresh wave of pain flared through me, and I winced, my vision blurring. Gabriel instantly reached for me, but I held up a hand.

"I'm okay," I panted, trying to alleviate his concern.

"You're not okay," he chastised softly, his firm hands guiding me back down. "You're injured. You need to rest. Quit pushing yourself."

I blinked, my vision slowly clearing. I leaned my head back against a pillow and took stock of my situation. Gabriel must have brought me inside, seeing as how I was lying on a bed instead of outside in the cold. He'd dressed me in one of the skimpy pajama sets Anna had brought me. That made sense, considering I would have been naked when he found me. Interestingly, that didn't bother me now like it might have earlier today. Strange how near-death experiences could put things into perspective for a girl.

My gaze took in the bedroom. He'd kept the lights dim, likely so I could rest. Even so, I could see the tense set of his jaw and the tightness around his eyes. He was genuinely concerned about me. Why did that make me want to cry? I wasn't a child anymore, so I shouldn't still crave affection. But seeing him like this hit me in all the feels.

A faint gust of chilled air pulled my gaze to the window. He'd uncovered it and cracked it open. Likely so he could keep an ear out for any more danger while tending to me.

Thoughtful.

"Can you tell me what happened?" Gabriel asked. He eased onto the bed, the mattress dipping beneath his weight.

I slowly repositioned myself. It really did feel like someone had raked me over burning coals.

"I woke up and stepped outside. I was sitting on the porch when I heard movement." I recapped everything else, describing the witches in great detail. "I texted Anna and Lucy before the witches attacked me. Did either of them call? Or text? Anything?"

Gabriel's jaw was so tight I thought his fangs might snap off. "Lucy did. I told her what I could. She wants you to call her as soon as you're ready. I haven't heard anything from Vlad or Anna. And I've been calling since I found you."

That didn't bode well.

I bit the inside of my cheek. Anna woke hours before other vampires. She should have been able to reach out to me at some point.

"Don't worry about any of that right now," Gabriel said. "Vlad and Anna know how to handle themselves. They probably can't communicate right now. I'm sure they're fine, and they'll reach out to us when they can."

Glad someone was optimistic here, because I sure wasn't. "Has anything happened since sundown?" I asked. "Any strange noises?"

"No," he said. "Admittedly, I've been a bit busy tending to you. But I haven't heard anything peculiar."

"Okay," I whispered.

That was good. It wouldn't last. But for now, I'd take the win. The even bigger win was that I'd killed the two witches before they could report back to *whomever* that they'd located Gabriel. Granted, just because I hadn't seen or heard them call anyone didn't mean they hadn't. For all I knew, they could have sent a message telepathically. Or perhaps they phoned someone before closing in on the cabin. However, seeing as how no one else had attacked us, it seemed the odds were in our favor. For now, anyway. Eventually, the person who hired the witches would figure out they were dead. But I could worry about that later.

The bad news was that if they'd been able to find us once, they'd be able to do so again. I had no idea what magic could do. Had no idea if there were any limitations. But it seemed wise to assume they'd find us again. Which meant we were no longer safe here. Then again, we wouldn't be safe anywhere. Wherever we went, they'd find us.

I needed to get my ass out of bed. Because I refused to let this happen again. Now that I knew the extents Gabriel's enemy would go to, I could better prepare for it. Thankfully, I learned fast.

Gabriel smoothed a cool cloth over my forehead.

I gently pushed his hand away. "I don't need a nursemaid." What I needed were weapons. Ones suitable for killing witches. And every other supernatural breed out there, because who knew what'd come for us next.

"I'm not playing nursemaid," Gabriel shot back, irritation bleeding into his tone.

I stilled on the bed, a bit shocked by his response.

"You almost died, Maddie. When I found you"— he shuddered, his eyes slipping closed—"you were barely breathing. I couldn't hear your heartbeat. Do you know what that means?"

Yup. It meant I'd been knocking on heaven's door.

"You aren't as invincible as you think," he continued.

I was about to tell him to back off, to remind him I'd survived worse—not that I could think of anything specific at this particular moment. But the words died when I caught his expression. The look in his eyes, the hard set of his jaw... He looked scared. Gabriel. The man who'd barely batted an eyelash when I'd told him there was a bounty on his head. I'd shaken the unshakeable Vampire King. Me.

I slowly sat up, ignoring the sharp protest in my body. Gabriel's hands hovered uncertainly, as though he wanted nothing more than to help me, but wasn't sure I would accept the assistance. If I wasn't in so much pain, I might have laughed. He clearly wanted to take care of me. And I was being a stubborn little brat.

This afternoon's events made me realize there were far more frightening things than liking a guy. I wasn't sure if it was the witches nearly killing me or what, but the walls around my heart seemed smaller somehow. Like Gabriel had chipped his way past my defenses.

He truly cared about me. It was time I stopped running from him.

I cupped his face and stroked his cheek with my thumb. "I'm okay," I said, softer this time, hoping to reassure him.

He covered my hand with his. "I hate that I wasn't there to help you."

"There wasn't much you could have done. The sun was up."

He cursed under his breath. "I hate this. I hate knowing that you're in danger because of me, and there's nothing I can do to help during the day. I should have stayed with my guards. Then you'd be safe. You wouldn't have had to face those witches. You wouldn't have nearly died. This is the reason I employ both humans and vampires. That way, I'm never vulnerable."

"Until we know for sure who's behind the bounty, we can't trust anyone. For all we know, the person responsible is a member of your guard."

Gabriel scoffed, then lowered our hands and cradled mine in his lap. "My guards have full access to me twenty-four-seven. If one of them wanted me dead, I'd be dead."

"That's not a convincing argument, Gabriel," I said, terrified by the thought of one of his own betraying him. "Until we know without any doubt who's organizing all of this, we need to keep our group small. I'm not willing to risk your safety."

He shot me a glare. "But I'm supposed to be okay with *you* risking yours? Did you hear me when I said you almost died?"

"I heard you," I said. "Believe me, I know exactly how close I came to death. Besides, we aren't alone. We have Vlad and Anna."

"Except they're missing."

"We don't know that." When Gabriel turned away from me, I grabbed both his hands and squeezed. "Hey. Listen to me. Everything is going to be okay. Like you said, Anna and Vlad will call when they get a chance. And we'll find the person responsible and put an end to all of this."

Gabriel shook his head. "I ought to leave right now."

"But you won't," I murmured.

His gaze snapped to mine. "What gives you that impression?"

I couldn't help but offer a small smile. "Because I'm not leaving. And you won't leave me."

His glare deepened.

"Don't worry, Gabe. I can take care of myself. I've been doing it my entire life. I simply never considered that they'd send witches. Now that I know, I can prepare better."

His scowl faded and he grinned, which left me blinking.

"What?"

"You called me Gabe," he said.

"Okay, and?"

"You've never called me that before. Always Gabriel. And always with such derision in your voice."

"Well, I can go back to Gabriel"—I growled his name—"if you prefer."

"Don't you dare." He studied my face. "Are you really okay? Don't lie to me, please."

It was the please that did me in. "I'm sore. It feels like those witches set my insides on fire. Even breathing hurts. But I'll be fine. I heal really fast. Perks of being a werewolf."

His expression darkened with my words.

"Thank you, though," I said. "For being here. For taking care of me."

For a long moment, he didn't speak. He stared at me with that intense gaze of his, as though he was trying to see through me, maybe figure out what made me tick. It'd be awhile before he solved that riddle. Heck, I hadn't even figured that one out yet.

Finally, he nodded. "Always, Maddie. I hope you realize that."

Always. It terrified me to think of us being together like that, but at the same time, I wanted to hold him to that promise.

I immediately thought back to our first kiss in the bar. The way he'd possessed my mouth made me hunger for more. I inched closer until our lips were barely a hair's breadth apart. I hesitated for a fraction of a second, then brushed my mouth against his.

Gabriel responded instantly, his lips moving gently against mine. His hands fell to my waist, but there was a carefulness to his touch, a restraint that spoke of his concern for my injuries. His thoughtfulness stirred something within me, and warmth spread from my lips down through my entire body. It chased away the lingering pain from the witches' attack and made me feel...safe. Protected. Wanted. Things I'd never quite felt before.

I parted my mouth, deepening the kiss. He slid his tongue along mine, and I sucked in a sharp breath. This kiss felt different than our first. He wasn't possessing me, likely for fear of hurting me, but it felt deeper. Softer. And I practically heard the rest of my barriers come crashing down.

I gave myself over to him. He explored my

mouth, but his hands never strayed from my sides. I barely felt the pain anymore. Wonderful thing, endorphins. Sadly, I knew it wouldn't last. But I was willing to experiment, to see how long he could keep me blissfully numb.

When we finally broke apart, Gabriel stared at me with such intensity, my breath caught. His lips were slightly parted, and even though he didn't *need* air, his chest rose and fell rapidly.

Neither of us spoke. We didn't need to. We were both intimately aware of the change that was occurring. Something had changed. Something that both excited and terrified me. For the first time, I saw Gabriel not only as a vampire or the king, but as *more*.

Gabriel leaned in and kissed me again. Slow, tender. I slid my arms around his neck and speared my fingers into his dark hair, committing the silken feel to memory. When we parted, he leaned his forehead against mine and rested his hand on my chest, right above my heartbeat.

"There it is," he whispered. "Its rhythm is nice and strong now."

"Guess your kisses can bring a girl back to life," I teased.

His shoulders shook with weak laughter. "That's not funny."

"Then why are you laughing?"

Still chuckling, he leaned back and cupped my cheeks. He placed a featherlight kiss on my brow, the tip of my nose, then another on my mouth. "When I found you out there, and I couldn't hear your heartbeat, I reckon mine stopped."

"You don't have a heartbeat," I reminded him.

He rolled his eyes. "Figuratively stopped. I don't fancy experiencing that again."

I didn't make any promises, since neither of us had any idea what the future had in store for us. Instead, I smiled, still blissfully numb from his kisses. "I'm still here. Guess whoever's behind all this will have to try a little harder."

His face fell. "That's what I'm afraid of."

"Hey, no more worrying. You don't need any more wrinkles."

Gabriel choked out an unexpected laugh. He barely looked a day older than twenty-five. Wrinkles were the least of his problems. Of the two of us, I was the one with that little problem. And I was trying very hard not to focus on that.

We were heading down a path that made very little sense logically. He was an eternal vampire. I was a mortal werewolf. He still had quite a few years on me, but appearance wise, not so much.

Give me a few more years and I might start looking like his older sister.

Soon his cool aunt.

Then his mother.

How could fate pair us together knowing at one point he'd have to say goodbye?

The question made my head—and heart—ache, so I pushed it aside. No point in borrowing tomorrow's problems when we already had enough on our plates today. I had to keep him alive and put an end to this mess before we could even think about "tomorrow."

I leaned back against the pillows and let my body relax. Then I patted the bed next to me.

Gabriel's gaze shot from my hand to my face. "You're serious?"

I couldn't blame him for questioning me. I'd made such a big deal out of sharing a bed with him this morning. And then freaked out when I'd woken in his arms this afternoon. But nearly dying had put a few things in perspective for me. Like, why was I stressing out over the little things? It was a bed, not a wedding ring.

When I didn't yell, "*psych!*" Gabriel crawled in

next to me. I curled into his side, exactly as I had this morning, and rested my head on the curve of his shoulder.

"Hmm. I'm experiencing a touch déjà vu," he teased.

I swatted his side, then closed my eyes. Hopefully a night of rest would cure my ails. I needed to be back on my feet tomorrow.

I WOKE A FEW MINUTES BEFORE SUNRISE. IT WAS like some internal alarm went off inside me, telling me I *had* to get up now. My body begged for more rest, but the cold grip of reality reared its ugly head. We were at our most vulnerable during the day. And today would be even worse, thanks to my injuries. I could already tell I was in no condition to keep watch, but the sun gave us no choice.

"You're awake," Gabriel said.

He strode in from the living room, a glass of

water in hand. He passed it over, then sat next to me on the bed, his gaze raking me over.

"You don't look any better."

Nor did I feel any better. But I needed to keep that to myself. The last thing I wanted was to worry Gabriel.

"I'm okay," I said for the umpteenth time as I took the glass from him. I took a sip, my eyes closing as my throat reveled in the cool liquid. "Anything happen overnight?"

"Nothing," Gabriel assured me. "Everything's quiet."

"Anything from Anna or Vlad?"

He nodded, and relief nearly had me dropping the glass. "They rang while you were sleeping."

"What happened?"

Gabriel sighed, then held up my phone. "Your text never went through. Apparently our service is dodgy out here."

"You've got to be kidding me," I griped.

"Calls are coming and going no problem, but texts are hit and miss. We sent about ten texts to each other to test the network. I only received two, they received three."

"Ugh." That was inconvenient. "But at least we

know they're okay. Why didn't they answer when you called them?"

"They had their phones on silent because they were in the middle of questioning someone. Anna was quite beside herself that she wasn't here for you. She apologized over and over."

I sat up, then instantly regretted it. Pain ripped through my entire body, and I choked on my breath, the glass slipping from my fingers. Gabriel snatched it out of the air before it shattered on the floor, placed it on the nightstand next to me, then cupped my cheeks.

"Breathe," he murmured. "Just breathe. It'll pass."

I bit back a whimper and nodded. It *did* pass. But if felt like it'd taken eighty-four years to do so.

"Are you okay?" Gabriel asked, combing the hair back from my face. He leaned in and pressed a gentle kiss against my forehead.

I released a shuddering breath and nodded. "I'll need to be more careful for a day or two, but I'm fine."

He studied me but chose not to comment. We both knew my injuries put me at a huge disadvantage.

"The sun's almost up," I rasped. "You need to get into bed."

A hint of panic flared in Gabriel's eyes. "I expect you to be at my side when the sun sets tonight. Please, don't make me go looking for you again."

"I didn't make you do anything last night," I teased, hoping to add a little levity to the conversation.

He scowled. "You know what I mean. Also, Anna and Vlad are coming tonight. They need to chat with you about what they've learned." Before I could ask, he shook his head. "They didn't tell me anything yet. They said they'd wait until they saw us together in person."

Disappointment flared within me. I wanted to know *now*. I didn't want to wait until tonight to hear what they'd learned.

"Please, please, please be careful today," Gabriel said, leaning forward until our brows touched. "I don't want a repeat of last night."

"You and me both," I murmured.

"And brush your teeth," he teased.

I swatted his shoulder and closed my mouth.

Chuckling, Gabriel kissed me, then stretched out in bed. The instant the sun rose, it was like the encroaching light sucked the very life out of him. His body went unnaturally still, and his essence vanished from the room.

I wasn't sure I'd ever be able to get used to that. Or the ache that bloomed within me when he was gone.

As much as I hated the thought of moving, I knew I had to get out of bed. If I stayed with him, I'd fall back asleep, and I refused to let that happen. Gabriel had kept watch all night to let me rest. I would do the same now.

I slowly slipped out from under the covers, wincing as pain flared through my body. I placed my feet on the cold wooden floor, then paused for breath and waited for the cabin to stop spinning. Once it did, I rose on shaky legs and made my way to the bathroom to tend to my needs, achingly aware of every step I took.

After, I grabbed the couch blanket, wrapped it around my shoulders, then stepped out onto the porch, my eyes scanning the forest that lay beyond. The trees were still, the fallen foliage rustling gently in the morning breeze, but I couldn't let the tranquility lull me into a false sense of security.

I returned inside, then went through my morning routine, lamenting the whole time about how slow I was. Fifteen minutes later, I returned to the porch with a mug of coffee in hand. The morning air was still brisk, but I reveled in the chill. After yesterday, I was lucky to be alive, and I didn't want to take anything for granted ever again.

Thankfully, Gabriel had handled the bodies. I wasn't sure what he'd done with them, but they weren't cluttering the yard anymore, and that was all that mattered.

I drained my coffee, then placed the empty mug on a small table situated between two chairs. My wolf kept pawing at the front of my mind, begging me to let her free. Guess she was feeling a little anxious after yesterday, too. After a moment's consideration, I agreed. My senses were a bit sharper in wolf form, and I would need every advantage today.

I stripped, then shifted. Every second of it was pure torment, thanks to my injuries, but eventually, I stood on four legs. With a small whine, I stretched out every limb, then trotted into the woods in preparation for a long day of patrolling.

～

IT WASN'T UNTIL THE SUN HAD FULLY DIPPED below the horizon that I let myself relax. I'd remained in wolf form all day to patrol the grounds, only stopping once to eat. Call me obsessive, but I hadn't been able to focus on anything else beyond keeping watch all day. The memory of those witches would likely haunt me the rest of my life, and I *never* wanted to run into one again. At least I could relax a little when Anna and Vlad arrived. Maybe take a small nap. After they filled us in on everything they'd learned, of course.

I loped through the woods, my heart thudding in sync with my paws against the earth. It was only now that I remembered Gabriel's request that I be by his side when he woke. Hopefully, I made it back in time.

Once I reached the porch, I shifted back into my human form, a whimper escaping my lips as the transformation ignited a fresh wave of pain. I tried to focus on anything else, but I might have cried out once or twice.

I'd barely finished dressing when the cabin door flew open, revealing a wild-eyed Gabriel. He was by my side in an instant, his gaze frantically scanning me for new injuries.

"Are you okay?" he demanded, his hands curling around my arms.

"I'm fine," I managed to choke out, attempting to

pull away. His grip only tightened, his eyes never straying from mine.

"You're hurt," he said, his voice barely above a whisper. It sounded more like an accusation than a question.

I stared up at him and saw the panic within. He looked to be on the verge of losing control, likely because I hadn't been at his side when he'd woken. He'd probably heard me cry out too.

"I swear, Gabriel. I'm fine," I assured him, offering him a small smile. "I was shifting back, and it's not as easy to do that when you're injured. But I'm—"

With a growl that sounded more relieved than angry, he swooped down and kissed me. His lips were demanding, fierce, possessive. When I didn't pull away, his arms came around me in a gentle hold, as though trying to convince himself I truly was okay. He deepened the kiss, and the second our tongues touched, a different heat flared through me. One that chased away the constant pain. I practically sagged against him, feeding off the relief his touch offered.

Gabriel broke the kiss, and I sucked in a ragged breath, trying to calm my pulse. My body screamed in protest, but at least it was for a different reason this time. It wanted to ride him like a pogo stick. The idea was rather enticing, but unfortunately unrealistic, since Anna and Vlad would be here within the hour. I didn't want to rush our first time. Time to clamp my thighs together and force myself to wait.

"Sorry luv," Gabriel murmured. "I might have gone a bit mad when you weren't there when I woke up. Then I heard you cry out. I didn't think. I just reacted."

"It's okay," I said. "I'm sorry I didn't make it back in time. I'm not moving as quickly as I'm used to."

He nodded, then pulled me in for the gentlest hug ever. I wrapped my arms around him and rested my head against his chest.

"Have you been patrolling all day?"

"Yeah. No unwanted visitors, thankfully."

Gabriel sighed. "You haven't had a bit of rest, have you?"

"I'll rest once Anna and Vlad get here."

Gabriel slid an arm around my waist and guided me toward the front door. "Come on, luv. I'll fetch you something to eat."

I brushed his concern aside, then laughed when my stomach chose that moment to audibly announce its displeasure with me. Werewolves ate a fair bit more food than humans, and my belly wasn't happy that I'd ignored it all day.

Gabriel seated me at the kitchen table, then did a quick loop around the small cabin, opening all the windows so we could hear outside. He returned to the kitchen, then started perusing cupboards. I was about to tell him that I didn't need anything fancy—a peanut butter and jelly sandwich would suffice—when he started pulling out a random assortment of ingredients. He moved with precision, chopping vegetables and adding spices into the bubbling broth. Every now and then, he'd lean over the pot and inhale deeply, as though testing the aroma. I marveled at the contradiction of it all—this powerful king delicately stirring a pot of homemade vegetable soup for me.

"You cook?" I asked, riveted by the sight of him. "Even though you don't eat?"

"Only for those I fancy," he responded, shooting me a quick glance. "I learned when I lived in the abbey. Soup was one of the simplest dishes to prepare. I've perfected it throughout the years. It's been a long time since I've had anyone to cook for, though. I don't socialize with humans, or werewolves for that matter, too often."

Before I could reply, he was at my side with a

steaming bowl of soup cupped between his palms. He set it on the kitchen table in front of me, then folded a cloth napkin beside it.

"Careful, it's hot," he warned, sitting next to me.

I scooped up a spoonful of soup, then blew on it to cool it off. The second I took my first sip, flavors exploded in my mouth, and I gave a satisfied hum.

"This is amazing," I moaned, my eyes fluttering shut. It probably didn't help matters that I was starving and would have eaten a raw rabbit at this point. But the soup really was quite remarkable.

"I'm chuffed you like it," he said, his gaze never leaving mine.

I devoured three whole bowls—and laughed every time Gabriel's eyes widened when I asked for another. Seeing as how he didn't hang out with werewolves, this would be his first time witnessing our unending appetites.

"Where do you keep it all?" he asked, watching me with a baffled expression.

"We have incredibly high metabolisms," I told him. "It's why we run warm and burn off drugs incredibly quickly. Alcohol too."

"So, what you're saying is we'll need to hire a chef," Gabriel teased.

I ignored that little comment and chose instead

to grab a glass of water. I really didn't want to think about the future right now. Not when we didn't even know what the present held in store for us.

I'd drained my second glass of water when a light knock echoed through the cabin.

"It's Vlad and Anna," Gabriel said, not that he'd needed to tell me that. I could smell them.

Neither waited for an invitation today—it wasn't needed—and they opened the door and stepped inside. Gabriel and I joined them in the living room, and though he had to slow his pace down for me. Vlad and Anna noticed, and both wore a frown as I gingerly seated myself on the couch. No one sat near me, likely for fear of hurting me.

"Guys, I'm fine," I said preemptively. "Sit."

"Gabriel mentioned witches?" Anna asked, ignoring my invitation to take a seat.

"Murderous witches," I said, because that seemed equally important.

"I've never faced witches before." She shuddered. "And from what Vlad's told me, I don't ever want to. Kudos to you for surviving."

Yeah, well, I had a lot to live for right now. But I didn't say that aloud.

Settling back against the cushions, I glanced first at Vlad, then Anna. "Gabriel said you've found something?" I was hoping for a name. If we could find out who was engineering all this, we could put an end to the bounty.

Vlad nodded, his usually stoic face holding a somber expression. He shared a weighted glance with Anna before reaching into his pocket, extracting a manila envelope, and handing it to me.

I opened it and pulled out a document almost identical to the one Chris had shown us at the coffee shop. Had that really only been a few days ago? It felt like my entire world had changed since then.

"That's the bounty on Gabriel's head," Vlad informed me, as though I needed the reminder.

"Hmm. A rather good likeness," Gabriel joked, studying the portrait of himself.

"Where'd you get this?" I asked.

Anna plopped down onto the couch next to me. "We got this copy from that Vera woman you mentioned. Turns out she's a nice lady. I didn't get the feeling she was behind this at all."

"Thank goodness."

"She's just doing her job, from what I gathered. So we followed the chain of command to the person who issues her the bounties. A gentleman by the name of Liam."

I'd never heard that name before.

"Liam was also a decent fellow. He gave us the name of *his* boss. A woman named Claire. Now Claire wasn't quite as nice," Anna said. "She screamed. A lot."

I shivered. That didn't sound good at all. "Tell me you didn't kill her."

"Nah. She's still alive. However, it turns out Ms. Claire has been 'selling her services' to anyone who can pay enough. She works in Reparations and is the person who issues the bounties to those beneath her. It's quite the chain, actually."

"Did you find out who paid Claire?" I asked.

"Unfortunately, no." Anna sighed and leaned back next to me. "According to Claire, it's an entirely anonymous system. In her words, 'for this exact reason.' I didn't like her."

Yes, I got that feeling.

"Here's the kicker, though." Anna turned her head and stared at me. "Claire isn't the only one doing this."

My eyes sank shut. This was my worst-case scenario. "Then there's corruption within the Academy?"

"I'm afraid so," came Vlad's solemn voice.

18

A HEAVY SILENCE SPREAD THROUGH THE CABIN, one punctuated by the soft sounds of my breath. Anna plonked down next to me on the edge of the couch, her usually cheerful demeanor replaced by a tense frown. Vlad leaned against the wall, arms folded, and eyes thoughtful. Gabriel sat on my other side, the picture of calm, though the furrow in his brow suggested otherwise.

As for me... my whole world had fallen apart.

For five years, the Academy had been my everything. My job. My purpose.

It'd all started when my half-sister, Olivia, turned me into a werewolf. She'd wanted me to join her crew, a notion I'd found appealing until I'd met them. I'd quickly decided their lifestyle of murder and mayhem wasn't for me. Ironic, considering where I ended up. And it was all thanks to a chance encounter with a bloodthirsty vampire feasting on what I'd assumed was an innocent woman. One decapitated vampire later, and I was the newest recruit at the Academy, slaying vampires and feeling, for once, like I actually mattered.

It'd felt like kismet. My true place in life. It was where I'd met Jaden, Josh, and Chris. We hadn't gotten along at first. We'd been a wee bit competitive with each other. But that'd all settled once we realized we were stronger together. Over the years, our bond grew into what it was today.

And now, the ugly truth was out. The Academy, my sanctuary, was playing a deadly game with innocent vampires. I felt sick. I'd slayed a lot of vampires, and now I wondered how many were truly guilty? They'd turned me into a murderer. The exact thing I hadn't wanted to become.

I breathed deeply, hoping to settle my stomach before the soup made an encore appearance.

How many innocents had I killed? How many

had I stolen from partners? How many mating bonds had I destroyed?

The vampire from the club who'd attacked me the night Gabriel and I had met. Had she been right to hunt me down? Every vampire kill I'd ever made played through my mind like a movie on rewind. How many had actually been guilty?

"Bathroom break," I mumbled, my hand darting to my mouth.

I stumbled out of the living room and into the bathroom. I faced the mirror and stared at my reflection. Pale, waxy, lifeless. Shadows darkened the undersides of my eyes and my cheeks were hollow. At least my outsides matched my insides now, because I felt like complete shit.

I splashed my face with cold water, but it did nothing to cool the guilt ripping through me.

I had to tell Jaden, Josh, and Chris right away. They had the right to know. *Everyone* did. I couldn't sit on this information. Sure, we'd probably killed quite a few guilty vampires, but that didn't justify us slaying a single innocent.

A soft knock rapped against the bathroom door.

"Maddie?" Gabriel murmured, his voice muffled. "Are you okay?"

"I'll be right out," I said.

I closed my eyes and drew in a slow breath. I counted to eight, then released it. I repeated that five more times until my heartbeat finally calmed and my stomach settled. Only then did I open the door and venture back into the living room.

Three pairs of vampiric eyes followed me, each too soft and sympathetic for my liking.

"Sorry about that," I muttered.

"You have nothing to apologize for," Gabriel said. "I'd imagine this information is a little jarring."

A little. More like an existential crisis. I loved my job, but playing judge, jury, and executioner to innocents? That wasn't in the handbook. The Academy's council had to know about this, right? Were they ignorant, or worse, complicit?

I sat back down on the couch, between Gabriel and Anna. Gabriel took my hand and gave it a squeeze.

"Okay. So the Academy's corrupted, and we still don't know who's behind Gabriel's bounty."

"Well, I wouldn't say the entire Academy is rotten," Anna commented. "More like a couple bad apples spoiling the bunch. From what we gathered, they've got this anonymous bounty drop system in place. Someone, no names mentioned, plops in a bounty, and then those on the inside pass it onto a slayer. Claire told us she had no idea who'd placed the bounty, but the client was specific. They wanted the 'best'. Now, any clue who Vera handed over the contract to? She wouldn't give us that information no matter how hard we pressed."

"And we pressed hard," Vlad confirmed.

Oh, thank goodness. At least there was some honor among thieves. It would have killed me if Vera had given Chris's name to Anna and Vlad, especially before I had a chance to explain things. What if they'd gone after Chris tonight while I was here with Gabriel? I never would have forgiven myself.

"Maddie?" Gabriel asked, his arm snaking around my waist. "Did you hear Anna?"

"Right." I cleared my throat. "I'm not going to lie to you guys. Yes, I know the slayer that holds Gabriel's contract. No, I'm not going to give you his name."

"Maddie—"

"No, Anna. I refuse to see any more innocent blood spilled. There's no reason for me to give you their name. I will reach out to them myself and explain the situation. Hopefully, once I talk to them, they'll refuse the contract."

"But then the Academy will reach out to the next best slayer," Anna countered.

"Yes, and that's me."

All three jerked as though shocked by that information.

I rolled my eyes. "Okay, yes, I got my ass handed to me by a couple of witches. But I've never fought them before. And considering I'm still standing and they aren't, I think I did a damn good job." I lifted a hand when Gabriel opened his mouth to speak. "I won't betray one of my fellow slayers. I'll speak to them first and inform them of the situation. Once they drop the contract, the Academy will theoretically try to reach out to me. Since I don't have my old phone, that'll delay things a bit. There's a rule that they have to give me forty-eight hours to respond before they can move to the next slayer. That gives us some time to figure out our next move."

"So, we have at least two days to figure all this out before the Academy involves another slayer?"

I nodded.

"How do we find out who's behind Gabriel's contract?" I asked.

Anna sighed and leaned back against the couch. "Unfortunately, in this situation, the only thing I can think of is waiting for the next attack."

Oh, I didn't like the sound of that at all.

"When they attack, we incapacitate them, then

we question them and find out who they're working for."

So many things could go wrong with that plan. Number one, I didn't want to face witches again. I wasn't sure I'd survive. And number two, what if they also didn't know the name of the person behind all this? This faceless person was pissing me off.

"I think it's Adrian Roche," I said. "The night before last, Gabriel gave me a list of names of people who might want him dead—Cecilia, Alexander, Frederick, and Adrian."

Vlad straightened and locked eyes with Gabriel. "Cecilia Moreau?"

Gabriel nodded.

"Why would Cecilia want you dead?"

"Apparently she's a former lover he pissed off," I informed Vlad, unable to keep the displeasure out of my voice.

Anna scoffed, then reached behind me and clocked Gabriel upside the head. "You slept with *Cecilia?*"

Gabriel didn't offer any comment, just rubbed his poor head.

My gaze leapt between the three of them. Vlad seemed perturbed, Anna pissed, and Gabriel ashamed.

"Okay, what's the deal with this Cecilia? Gabriel said she's cunning but didn't offer much else. Is she gonna be a problem?"

Maybe she was a bigger problem than I'd initially estimated. I'd leaned toward the father because revenge had seemed the more plausible reason to want to kill someone. But jealousy had kept me from inquiring further about this Cecilia.

"I can't believe you, Gabriel!" Anna groaned, then rose to her feet. "When did this happen?"

"A few years ago," he said. "We were both in a rough spot and sought comfort in each other."

"You sought comfort. From Cecilia. Are you out of your mind?"

Okay, this was getting interesting. I definitely needed the backstory.

Vlad grunted his own displeasure, then strode over to Anna, resting a comforting hand on her shoulder. "If Cecilia is the one behind this, I'm surprised it took her this long to retaliate."

"Alright." I held up my hands. "I need the full story. Right now, please."

Gabriel flinched, which only piqued my curiosity further.

"Cecilia was one of Camilla's best friends," she said. "The two women had known each

292

other for a long time, but when Camilla moved to the States, the two drifted apart. Cecilia preferred France to America, so she refused to travel. But they loved each other dearly, regardless."

That told me absolutely nothing.

My attention darted between the three vampires. Gabriel strode to the window and stared outside, his back to me. That made me frown.

I turned back to Anna. "I'm sorry, who's Camilla?"

The house fell into a startled silence. Anna and Vlad stared at me, shock rounding their eyes.

"Who's Camilla?" Anna asked.

I lifted a brow. Had I spoken in a different language?

Before I could so much as blink, Anna stormed across the room and swatted Gabriel a second time, clearly not caring that he was her king. Guess they were that good of friends.

"You didn't tell her about Camilla?" Anna shouted. "Gabriel, that's...low."

Unease twisted my stomach. Another woman. Whose name also started with a C. I was sensing a pattern here. And now I was bracing myself for a possible parade of ex-lovers.

"It didn't seem relevant," Gabriel said, his voice softer, sadder.

"I could just...." Anna held up her hands, as if she were visualizing strangling him. Then she growled a series of choice words too mature for young ears. Hell, even my ears. "Well, are you going to tell her who Camilla is or should I?"

"Who Camilla *was*," Gabriel murmured.

Oh. I definitely picked up on the sadness that time. Heard it deep in his voice. Saw it in his stooped shoulders and bowed head.

Camilla was obviously no longer in the picture. I could do the math. But who had she been before she died?

Gabriel turned to face me. Then he said four words I never expected to hear. "Camilla was my mate."

19

His...mate?

Had I heard him correctly?

I stared at Gabriel, utterly floored. When no one said a word, I slowly shook my head. "*I'm* your mate."

"You are," he assured me, moving to sit on the coffee table in front of me. He took my hands and squeezed them. "*You* are my mate."

That did very little to help clear this matter up.

Seeing my puzzled expression, Gabriel smiled, then dropped his gaze to our joined hands. "Camilla was my mate before you. But she died. And when a mate dies, it severs the bond, leaving way for a new connection to develop. Fate rewires the cosmos to choose a new partner."

"Not always," Anna countered. "But in this case, yes."

"You had another mate?" I asked. It wasn't the cosmos that needed rewiring—it was my brain. I couldn't wrap my head around this at all. "Why didn't you tell me?"

"Because she's gone," Gabriel said simply and with very little emotion. "And to be perfectly honest, she and I never really connected."

I pulled a hand away from him and rubbed my brow. My head hurt, and I just needed someone— *anyone*—to speak clearly. "Someone explain this to me using small words, please."

"Camilla came into my life when I first became a vampire," Gabriel said. "It's a volatile time when you first transition. I had Adrian and Genevieve to guide me. Then I met Camilla. We knew there was something between us. Something my mother didn't approve of. Camilla recognized this. But instead of sticking around to fight for us and change my mother's mind, she bailed and moved here, to the States. We didn't see or speak to each other for a hundred and fifty years. It was only six years ago that she tried to reconnect with me."

Six years ago. A timeframe I was becoming intimately familiar with. "That's when your mother arrested Anna and Vlad, and dragged them to England."

He nodded. "Camilla was one of their allies I told you about. She and a few of her friends arranged Anna and Vlad's escape. Then she sought me out and asked me to arrange a coup. During the conflict, Camilla...died saving my life. My mother's people killed her."

I couldn't help the gasp that escaped my throat. His *mother* was responsible for killing his mate? Damn, that was terrible. If I'd ever thought my life hard, it was nothing compared to his. How could a mother do something like that to their child? To cause them that much pain?

"But Maddie, Camilla and I were never truly a couple," he continued. "Not really. There was some excitement when we met, but we never connected. Not like you and I have. What we share feels infinitely stronger." The sincerity in his gaze warmed something in my chest and eased a bit of the hurt.

"Then why hide her?" I asked.

He ran a hand through his dark hair, the action

betraying his emotions. "I was afraid it would upset you." His gaze found mine again, holding it captive. "The first night we met, you ran."

My gut twisted. I had. He'd kissed me, and I'd tucked tail and disappeared. Just like Camilla. I knew better now.

"The only reason we're together now is because my life is in danger. You didn't come back because you wanted me. You came back out of obligation."

Oh. Ouch.

"So, I told myself I wouldn't do anything to spook you. I refused to give you any reason to pull away. I feared bringing up Camilla would do exactly that. I'm sorry. I should have told you earlier."

Yes, he should have. But I suppose I could understand his reasoning. I didn't condone it, though. I guess I wasn't the only one nervous about this developing relationship. We both had our own issues we had to work through. Mine was intimacy. His was trust. Perhaps, we could work on these wounds of ours together.

"How about this," I said. "Let's agree to be open and honest with each other about everything from here on out. We disclose it all, even if we're afraid it might hurt the other person. I can't promise I won't run again. In case you haven't noticed, I have some problems with intimacy."

"Who? You?" Gabriel teased.

I rolled my eyes. "But I can promise to try not to spook so easily. So long as you're honest with me about everything."

A relieved smile curved his lips. "Agreed. But just so you know, if you run again, I will find you."

"Uh, okay?"

"Not find you in a creepy way," he said, laughing. "Find you so we can talk things out. If you ever want to leave, that's fine. But let's talk first. Don't immediately run. Don't hide. Deal?" He extended his hand.

I stared at it, almost afraid it might bite me. It seemed only fair that he asked something in return from me.

So, I bit the bullet and slid my hand into his. His fingers closed around mine, but instead of pumping it in a handshake, he placed them together, against his heart.

"Good," he said, quickly lifting my hand to his mouth to kiss it. "Then let's move on. Because we still have a lot to figure out."

Right.

The whole *who's trying to kill him* problem. I

shot Anna and Vlad a quick glance. Anna watched us unabashedly, her amused expression taunting me. Vlad, however, stared out the window, as though content to ignore us while we hashed out our issues.

"I personally believe Maddie is correct. Adrian has motive, resources, and utter contempt for Gabriel," Vlad said, his cool voice resonating through the cabin. He still didn't bother to look at us. Clearly, he'd been busy thinking this whole time. At least one of us had stayed on task. "Hiring witches, though. That's an interesting move. Witches aren't well liked in England."

"Or here, for that matter," I grumbled.

"Cecilia is troublesome, but I don't believe she'd ever try to kill you, Gabriel," Vlad continued. "As for Alexander and Frederick... Frederick I could see. He never agreed with the way you usurped the throne. But Alexander is too cowardly to do something like this."

Vlad finally turned away from the window. "What happened with Cecilia? We may need more details."

"It's nothing," Gabriel replied. "We spent an evening together on the first anniversary of Camilla's passing. Afterward, she pushed for more, and I rejected her."

Oof. Okay. So that wasn't great.

"Would rejection be enough of a reason for her to want you dead?"

Anna laughed. "I've only met Cecilia once, but I'd say yes."

"However, Adrian seems the more logical choice," Vlad said. "Last I heard, Cecilia has taken a new lover. I doubt she's angry enough with Gabriel to kill him if she's moved on."

"Whereas Adrian still refuses to speak to me," Gabriel added. "Last I heard from Elias, my father won't even speak my name."

"The man worshipped your mother," Vlad said. "He didn't care that she had lovers. He had his own. But the two still adored one another."

Gabriel winced. "I remember things differently, but that's irrelevant. The question becomes, how do we figure out for sure who's behind all this?"

"You mentioned Elias," Vlad said. "Would he help you? He could perhaps interrogate your father?"

"Oh boy," I murmured. "How about we avoid any interrogation tactics for now? If Adrian realizes we're onto him, he'll step up his efforts. And thank you, but I'm really not ready to play another game of cat and mouse with witches."

"Yes, and that's something else we need to discuss," Anna chimed in.

"Agreed. Witches are notoriously merciless and brutal," Vlad said. "I've heard some rather chilling stories. Their loyalty is to themselves and their sisters. They could just as easily turn on Adrian."

Interesting. "Are all witches female?"

"No, there are males too, but they're fundamentally weaker. Some men amass enough power to cast a spell or two, but nothing nearly as powerful as their female counterparts. Women rule the society, and they kill any man who dares to question their authority."

Yikes. And I'd killed two. "So, how much danger am I in? I'm assuming the coven"—I looked to Vlad to see if I'd used the right word—"won't be happy with me?"

He nodded. "You'd be right, I'm afraid."

Oh joy. Like I didn't have enough problems as it was.

"If they learn you killed two of their sisters—"

"Don't you mean *when*?" I asked. "I can't imagine they won't figure it out. If those two witches could track us here, then wouldn't their sisters be able to as well? And when they get here and find their sisters bodies in the woods..." Kaboom. I acted out my head exploding.

"You didn't burn their corpses?" Vlad demanded.

"I didn't do anything," I said. "I was too busy trying not to die."

"I buried them," Gabriel said.

Vlad shook his head. "We'll need to take care of that immediately."

"Won't they be able to smell that we've cremated their sisters?"

"Witch senses are akin to a human's," Vlad said. "As long as they don't catch us red-handed burning their bodies, we should be fine. But to be safe, Anna and I will take their remains with us tonight and burn them elsewhere."

"We will?" Anna said, looking a little green around the edges.

"We have some sheets you can use," I offered.

Anna rolled her eyes. "Gee, thanks."

"In the meantime, Maddie, you must be on your guard at all times," Vlad stated.

"Are they gonna unleash the entire coven on me?"

"Undoubtedly."

Gabriel surged to his feet with a snarl. "Let them try. If they so much as touch her—"

"You can't start a war with the witches, Gabriel," Anna said.

"Watch me," he snapped. He lowered his head and stared down at me. "*No one* is going to harm you. Not while I'm here. If the witches want you, they'll have to go through me first. And believe me, I'll make them regret it."

The depth of emotion I found in his eyes made my heart clench in response. His gaze burned into me, full of protective fury and deep, terrifying resolve. It was the gaze of a predator, a vampire ready to fight for his mate against any threat. But the protectiveness in his voice lent me a strange sense of calm. We were in this together. It wasn't just me against a coven of witches.

I settled against Gabriel's side, resting my head on his hip. "You know, a mere five days ago, my life was normal. Or as normal as a vampire slaying werewolf's life can be. Now, I have a mate, discovered that the Academy I pledged myself to has lost its way, and am blacklisted by a coven of alarmingly dangerous witches."

Not to mention, I'd kept secrets from my friends, which was something I'd never thought I'd do.

Anna chuckled. "Oh, I know this story. I remember the day I went from a mere human wannabe journalist to a vampire. Nothing's been the same since." She reached out and clutched Vlad's hand. "But I wouldn't change anything that happened. Not for the world."

"Neither would I," Vlad added. "Every challenge we've faced, every danger we've encountered, merely brought us closer together. I wouldn't exchange any of those hardships if it meant losing what we have now."

Vlad and Anna shared a tender glance, one that sparked a surprising twinge of envy in me. They were so secure in their love for one another, so assured of their bond. I knew from Anna's stories that it'd taken time, and as Vlad had said, many hardships. But here they stood, stronger than ever, side-by-side.

I never thought I'd find something like that. The one person in life chosen to be with you. Or, in Gabriel's case, the second. And now that I saw it was possible, I *wanted* that.

Hard to believe that less than a week ago, I'd run from Gabriel after we'd shared our first kiss. And now, here I was, thinking about spending forever at his side.

"Well then," I said, lifting my head from Gabriel's hip. "Bring on the witches, and the Academy's corruption, and"—I paused and glanced up at Gabriel, catching the hint of a smile on his lips —"us. Bring it all on. I'm ready."

As Gabriel sat beside me, he slipped his arm around my waist, his fingers pressing against my side. "No matter what happens, we'll face it together. And we'll come out the other side stronger for it."

"If we survive it," I teased, hoping to add a little humor to the conversation.

My joke fell unsurprisingly short.

Anna, however, snorted.

I smirked at her, my heart feeling strangely light despite the grave circumstances. Maybe it was the realization that, despite everything, I wasn't alone. I had people who would stand with me, no matter what happened.

So, yes. Bring on the crazy.

I was ready.

20

I watched through the window as Anna, Vlad, and Gabriel vanished into the woods to retrieve the bodies of the two witches. They'd all insisted I stay inside and rest. My body was feeling better, thankfully. Food always seemed to help, and Gabriel's soup had worked like a charm.

After caring for the bodies, Vlad and Anna took off, and Gabriel returned inside, heading right for the shower.

"To wash the stink of dead witch off," he'd said.

I, however, sat on the couch, my fingers absently

trailing the creases in the worn cushions as I listened to the sound of him in the damn shower.

I imagined Gabriel standing beneath the hot spray, water coursing down the muscled planes of his body, his dark hair slicked back. It evoked within me a need I hadn't felt in a *very* long time. Maybe I simply missed sex. Or maybe I craved something deeper from Gabriel. Either way, I was finding it a tad hard—ha!—to sit here and wait.

My gaze drifted to the bathroom door, the soft glow of the light spilling out from underneath it. I was a werewolf who'd never allowed herself the luxury of a deep relationship. Yet here I sat, contemplating jumping the bones of my destined mate.

A soft sigh escaped my lips. My life certainly had taken a drastic turn recently. There were still more challenges to face, and even more threats to overcome, but that didn't stop me from feeling drawn to Gabriel. Toward his strength and fierce protectiveness, toward the warmth in his steely gaze when he looked at me.

I debated going to him. Of stepping into the bathroom, stripping myself bare, and slipping into the shower with him. I pictured my mouth on his body, my tongue licking away the water droplets as I navigated my way south. I could imagine how he'd look, with his chiseled muscles and fine dusting of hair. How he'd look when I took him into my mouth.

The shower shut off, and I slowly rose to my feet. Heat flushed my cheeks and warmth spiraled through my center. There was no way I'd be able to hide my attraction to him. Vampires—and werewolves—had keen senses of smell. He'd know exactly where my mind had strayed the instant he opened the door.

A few moments later, the door creaked open, and there he stood with nothing more than a towel draped around his waist. Real life water clung to his chest and arms, emulating my fantasy. Steam emanated from the bathroom, swirling around him as he strode out, a second towel clutched in his hand as he rubbed his hair.

My heart pounded against my ribs as I watched, his entire body flexing with his movements. This was my first time seeing him without any clothes, and *fuuuuck*, he was downright gorgeous. The literal embodiment of a woman's fantasy.

His hand paused, and he lifted his head, his gaze seeking me out. The instant he saw me, his eyes widened.

"Maddie?" His voice was low and questioning.

There was so much I wanted to tell him, so much I wanted to know about him. But as I crossed the living room, I realized that right now, words weren't necessary. Sometimes we had to show people how we felt.

I came to a stop in front of him and touched his chest, my fingers tracing his abs. His eyes flicked to my lips, and an understanding passed between us.

"Are you sure?" he asked.

"Yes," I said. "I'm ready."

"And you're not too sore?"

Not for this. And even if I was, he'd make the pain go away. I didn't doubt that he would be a more-than-capable lover. The man practically oozed sex.

I trailed my fingers up his chest, along his neck, then plunged them into his wet hair. Heat still clung to his body, and I wanted to wrap myself around him. Without a word, I pulled his head down to mine, our lips meeting in a soft, tender kiss. One that showed him exactly how sure I was about this.

Our mouths parted, and Gabriel massaged my tongue with his. I couldn't help but give a soft moan. I had a feeling I would never tire of kissing this man.

His arms encircled me, pulling me flush against his damp body. I didn't complain. Nor did I complain when his hands swept down to my ass and lifted me until my center rested above his. I wrapped my legs around his hips and held tight, our gazes now level.

"Are you sure?" he asked again. "I know this has been a lot for you. And I know you said you're ready, but it's okay if you aren't. We can take this slow. There's no reason to—"

"Gabriel," I murmured, holding his stare.

"Hmm?"

I slid a hand between us and tugged on the towel. It came apart and slipped to the ground with a soft thump.

"Oops," I teased, grinning. "Look who's naked."

A wicked light glinted in his eyes, but he sobered a moment later. "I don't want to hurt you."

"You won't break me, I promise," I assured him.

As though that was the permission he needed, Gabriel unleashed himself on me. One hand left my ass and cupped my cheek as he thoroughly and expertly kissed me. The way he dominated my mouth and sucked on my tongue showed me that he'd been holding back. That, right there, nudged me toward the love category. But I couldn't focus on that now. Not with his tongue in my mouth and a hand cupping my ass. I'd almost forgotten how strong vampires were, but he reminded me as he carried me into the bedroom without so much as breaking our kiss.

We entered the bedroom, and Gabriel lowered me onto the bed, my head braced against the pillows. He worked fast, stripping me bare, discarding my clothes without a second thought. Then his naked body covered mine. God, the feel of him, of his weight pressing me into the mattress. I felt a small ache in my muscles, but a fresh rush of Gabriel-induced endorphins took care of that little nuisance.

His hands and tongue mapped every inch of my body with unending devotion, committing every one of my curves to his memory. His fingers traced a teasing path up the insides of my thigh, brushing tantalizingly against my core. Each caress had my hips bucking off the bed, pleading for an end to the exquisite torment. I arched into his touch, silently begging for more.

Clearly understanding my needs, Gabriel clasped my wrists and lifted them above my head, pinning them in place with one of his. His other hand ran tauntingly down my body, touching where he pleased when he pleased. I gasped when the hot heat of his mouth engulfed one nipple, then cried out when he did the same with the other. His slight push of my arms against the bed told me to leave them there, even after he released them.

His hands trailed down my sides, his lips coasting across my ribs to my navel, then farther south. He paused, his mouth hovering above me, and looked up at me. His intense gaze made me shudder, but it was the feel of his mouth coming down right between my legs that made me throw my head back with a sharp gasp.

If I'd thought his tongue wicked before, that was nothing compared to now.

Gabriel unleashed every ounce of talent he possessed, licking and sucking until blessed heat started spreading through my body. I fisted the pillows, squirming in perfect misery. Gabriel pressed a hand against my stomach to hold me down and keep me still. Pleasure blasted through me, and fireworks ignited behind my closed eyes. I cried out, my fingers tearing through the sheets.

I felt Gabriel move above me, but I couldn't focus on his actions, not until the bliss subsided. When it did, I opened my eyes to find him perched above me, his cock in hand.

"Would you like me to fetch a condom?" he murmured.

Vampires couldn't have children, so I wasn't

concerned about that. Nor could they catch diseases. Truly, there wasn't anything holding us back. So I shook my head.

Gabriel smiled, then guided himself forward. He didn't slide inside me, though. Not yet. Instead, he teased my entrance with his tip, coating himself in me. He tormented me, slowly, sensually. I wanted to hook my legs around him and force him inside, but I made myself wait.

He moved at a delightfully slow pace, gliding against me, his hand controlling his movements so perfectly. He lowered his head and kissed me again, our mouths locked as he continued his beautiful torture.

He drew back from the kiss and stared at me, his eyes hooded and mouth swollen.

"Maddie," he whispered. Then he tucked his head in the crook of my shoulder, and slowly entered me.

The moan that tore free of me was one I'd never heard myself make before. Then again, I'd never had anyone quite like Gabriel. He made me realize how empty my other affairs had been. They'd lacked *everything* that made this so wonderful. The connection between us was powerful and addicting.

I wanted to devour him more than any other man I'd been with.

He started moving within me, and my whole body quivered. This time, I did hook my legs around him, afraid to let him go. I wanted him to go faster, to flatten me against the bed and ride me until I screamed his name.

But Gabriel seemed to have other plans.

He moved slow and steady, his talented fingers finding their way between us to help me along. I gripped the pillows above my head and lifted my hips, allowing him to go deeper. Gabriel grunted, and his fangs scraped my throat.

A hint of fear cleared my mind. "No blood," I whispered.

"I know," he murmured, his lips soothing my skin. "I wouldn't without permission."

Oh god, that nearly finished me. There was something so erotic about knowing I held all the control, even though he was stronger and the one with all the power right now.

I released the pillow and curled my fingers into Gabriel's hair, reveling in the feel of him inside me. I dragged his mouth back to mine and whispered, "Harder, faster," before kissing him.

Gabriel obeyed and thrust into me with a

strength and speed that pinned my hips to the bed. I wrapped my arms around his neck and held on as he repositioned us, sitting me on top of him. At first, I thought he wanted me to ride him, but instead, he positioned himself on his knees, wrapping my legs around him. Then he gripped my hips and took my weight, holding me up as he slammed into me, over and over. He didn't once break rhythm, even when my inner walls clamped around him.

I cried out, my head falling back as I succumbed to the ecstasy he unleashed within me. Pleasure pulsed through me and spread through my whole body, stealing my senses. I trembled in his arms, unable to control myself. Distantly, I felt Gabriel rest his head against my shoulder as he groaned.

Finally, when the overwhelming pleasure passed, a happy numbness spread through me.

I speared my fingers through Gabriel's damp hair, combing it back from his cheeks, while I fought to catch my breath. My whole body felt limp and loose. And for the first time today, I didn't feel a speck of pain.

Tucking me close, Gabriel eased me back down onto the bed, then laid down beside me. I stretched my limbs, enjoying the sweet bliss, all the while knowing it wouldn't last. But that was okay, I had my own personal Vicodin. One touch and he'd send me to happy town again.

"Wow," I whispered.

Gabriel's shoulders shook with silent laughter. He pressed a kiss to my neck, then rose up to look at me, resting his head in his palm. "No regrets?"

I had to imagine that was a big fear for him, so I offered him a soft smile. "No regrets. Not now. Not ever."

Relief relaxed his face, and he leaned down for another kiss. When he pulled back, he had his own little smile. One that looked suspiciously mischievous.

"Wanna know a perk to being a vampire?" he asked.

I raised a brow.

"All I need is a little blood, and I'll be good to go again. In fact, we can go all night," he said, winking. "If you're up for it that is."

Both brows shot upward. "All night?"

"All. Night."

Shivers broke out across my body, and I trembled with anticipation. I reached for him, wondering how much my body could take.

"Sign me up."

21

I watched Gabriel sleep, memories of last night still fresh in my mind. Warmth lingered in my body, and every bit of me wanted more. Who would have thought the Vampire King, someone whose title equated power and strength, could be so tender and loving? The way he'd touched me, cared for me, had broken down the last of my remaining barriers. He'd stripped my heart bare. I only hoped he didn't break it, or I his. It was certainly scary to expose yourself to someone so completely. And I wasn't referring to stripping naked. He'd stripped *all* of me. He'd exposed all my vulnerabilities, my weaknesses, my wounds. But rather than run from them, he'd embraced them. He made me feel strong. Loved. And worthwhile.

It almost hurt to feel this way after years of believing I wasn't worth anyone's affection. He'd taken every last broken piece of me and built me back up until I was whole again.

It was rejuvenating. Addicting. And so very terrifying.

I couldn't lose him now. But this bounty threatened everything we'd begun to build together. It threatened our present and our future. I truly didn't know what our future would look like, considering he was immortal, and I wasn't, but I didn't want to worry about that.

Right now, I just wanted to focus on fixing this mess and figuring out if Adrian was the one behind all this. I wanted to pave the way for Gabriel and me to actually have a future together, whatever that might be.

I forced myself out of bed and dressed in one of Gabriel's shirts. I lifted my shoulders and buried my nose in it, committing his scent to memory. Then I made my way into the living room and settled onto the couch. My phone sat on the living room table, silent. The only person who had this number was Anna.

I had to imagine Jaden had been calling my old phone. She was probably losing her mind with worry. Or maybe not, considering she hadn't returned to the cabin to ensure I was alright. Her eventual arrival was inevitable, though. The second she grew tired of waiting for me to call, she'd drop by.

My mind circled back to last night's conversation. Vlad and Anna were certain the witches would attack again. And next time, their focus wouldn't only be on Gabriel, but also me. I'd killed two of their sisters. Their thirst for vengeance wouldn't fade anytime soon. And when they did attack, it would likely happen during the day, when they knew I'd be alone and at my most vulnerable. Remove me, the one person standing in their way, and they'd have unfettered access to Gabriel.

I glanced at the bedroom where Gabriel slept, a wave of worry washing over me.

I'd been lucky last time. I'd never survive a second battle with them, not without help. If they did send more witches, they'd likely send more than two. That was what I'd do anyway. Send my people with more reinforcements.

I needed help—as Gabriel had pointed out more than once. Daytime allies I could rely on.

Gabriel's guards were only an option once we vetted them. And who knew how long that would take. If we brought in his human guards, only for one of them to kill him while he slept, I'd never forgive myself. The risk was too great.

On the other hand, calling in my people was equally as risky. Regardless, I owed them an explanation. They had a right to know about the Academy. Once I filled them in, surely they'd realize Gabriel wasn't a threat anymore and side with me, right?

But what if they didn't?

Really, it boiled down to one issue—trust. Did I truly trust them enough to share this burden with them? Did I trust them to listen to, and believe, me? Most importantly, did I trust them with my mate's life? I absolutely trusted them. Deep down, I believed my friends would do the right thing. But what if I was wrong?

I dropped my head into my palms and heaved a heavy sigh.

What if they didn't believe me? What if they turned against me? What if they tried to kill Gabriel? What if they forced me to choose between them and him? What if it came to a fight? Could I kill them to protect him? What if, what if, what if... Countless questions invaded my mind until my damn head started to ache.

Ugh. Gabriel's cock had thoroughly distracted me last night, so much so that I hadn't even thought to bring all this up with him. I needed to speak with him first before I did anything. Guess that meant waiting until sunset.

In the meantime, I needed to do something physical. I couldn't sit here stewing in my thoughts all day. I decided to shift and spend the day patrolling the woods. There was a comfort in the familiar rhythm of it, in the sensation of the earth beneath my paws, and the scent of the withered forest around me.

Once the sun started dipping below the horizon, I made my way back to the cabin. My heart pounded in my chest as I shifted back into my human form and redressed in Gabriel's discarded shirt. My vampire would wake any moment now, and then we could chat.

I stepped into the silent cabin and headed for the bedroom where I leaned against the door frame, waiting for Gabriel to stir. Eventually, his eyes fluttered open, and he sat up with a small smile, not a hair out of place. I'd never understand that. I woke up looking like a swamp monster from the black lagoon, and he woke up looking like a damn model.

"Hi," I whispered, a shy grin curving my lips.

"Hey," he replied, his eyes drinking in my legs. Then he frowned. "What's wrong?"

"What makes you think something's wrong?"

"Because you aren't in bed with me right now," he said, cocking an eyebrow.

Fair enough. If it weren't for the conversation we were about to have, I probably would have crawled into bed with him the second he woke. Did he know me so well already?

"We need to talk," I said.

He was instantly alert, concern shining in his eyes. "Not exactly something a chap wants to hear after spending the night with his girl."

His girl... I smirked at that. Inching into the room, I eased onto the edge of the bed and took his hand in mine, tracing his palm lines. "I think it's time we bring in my friends."

He froze, every muscle tensing. "What?"

"My friends," I repeated.

"Yeah, I got that part. You mean your *slayer* friends?"

I nodded. "This cabin actually belongs to one. Her name is Jaden."

"Oh, bloody hell. We're squatting in a slayer's cabin?"

"Don't worry," I hurried to say. "She never uses it, so—"

"She's the one who came a few days ago, wasn't she? The friend you mentioned that dropped by. Blimey, that's why you didn't want to tell me anything about her."

I blew out a breath. "The thing is, since Jaden knows I'm here, so do Chris and Josh. It's only a matter of time before they come find me, seeing as how I no longer have my old cell phone for them to call."

Gabriel groaned, dragging his hands down his face. He was probably wishing this was all some sort of dream. "Maddie...."

"They need to know what's going on, Gabriel. It isn't fair to keep them in the dark. The Academy is important to them too. They also need to know the accusations against you are false. Hopefully, they'll believe me and stop hunting you."

Gabriel stared at me, dumbfounded. After a moment, he said, "Your *friends* are the ones who hold my contract?"

I nodded. "That's how I learned about it in the first place. My friend, Chris"—I stumbled over his name, regretting breaking the one rule I'd set for myself—"is the slayer Vera assigned to your case."

"Maddie," he repeated, clearly at a loss for words.

"I trust them, Gabriel. I trust that they'll side with me once they learn the truth."

"And if they don't? Do you realize what'll happen if they try to kill me?"

"I won't let that happen," I vowed.

"No, luv. *I* won't let that happen." Gabriel pushed the fireproof blanket off his legs and stood. "I've been telling you from the start I can protect myself. If your friends touch me, I won't hesitate to defend myself. Even violently, if necessary."

My throat tightened, but I nodded.

He lifted his hands, then dropped them to his side and turned away from me. "I don't like this."

"I know. But I have to tell them. I can't keep hiding all this from them. They're my family. They mean the world to me."

He whirled back around. "And if they make you choose? What happens then? What if they force you to pick between me and them?"

"Then I'll choose you," I said, hating the words even as I spoke them.

Gabriel's shoulders slumped and he shook his head. "Maddie, you just said they're your family."

"I did. And that's why I'm trusting them to make the right decision."

"You'd really choose me?" He sounded incredulous, his steely eyes searching mine for confirmation.

I remembered what he'd told me about Camilla. About how she hadn't stuck around to fight for him. How she'd abandoned him at the first sign of an inconvenience. I wouldn't make that same mistake. I knew what I had here. I refused to give that up.

"In a heartbeat," I told him.

For once, someone needed to choose him. And that someone was me.

A myriad of emotions flashed across his face—disbelief, surprise, relief.

"What we have is so new, and so fresh, but I won't lose you," I told him. I stood and took his hands, pressing them against my middle. "Gabe, I wouldn't do this if I didn't think I could trust them. And if they prove me wrong, if they try to harm you, I'll do what I must. I won't leave you. Ever. I promise."

I rose on my tiptoes and kissed him. He didn't immediately respond. I could only imagine how confused he must be. But the second I started to step back, he wrapped his arms around me and held me close, his mouth now devouring mine.

When we finally parted, he leaned his forehead against mine and whispered, "Okay. If this is something you have to do, I'll back you."

"Thank you."

Of course, now came the hard part. I stepped away from Gabriel and entered the living room. My cell sat on the coffee table. I eyeballed it like it was a rabid raccoon about to bite me.

"What's wrong?" Gabriel asked.

"Oh, working up the nerve to call her," I said, laughing nervously. "This isn't going to be an easy conversation to have."

Gabriel brushed a kiss across the top of my head. "I'll give you some privacy."

Or at least the semblance of it. I knew from personal experience that he could hear me from anywhere within the cabin.

Picking up my phone, I took a deep breath and dialed Jaden's number from memory. My heart stuttered every time the phone rang. I only hoped she picked up, which seemed unlikely, seeing as how she had class.

"Hello?" came her voice.

Right. I had a new number, so she wouldn't know it was me calling. For a moment, I didn't speak, afraid this conversation would ruin our relationship. I'd been desperate to protect both sides of this conflict in the beginning, but now, it seemed right to try to bring them together. I only hoped they were willing.

"Hello? Is someone there?" she asked when I didn't immediately respond.

I cleared my throat. "Hey."

She was silent for a moment. "Maddie? Is that you? Where are you calling me from?"

"Sorry, yeah, it's me. I had to get a new phone."

"And a new number?"

"Yeah. I'll explain later." I ran out of words then. Oh god, please don't let this be the biggest mistake of my life.

"Are you okay?" she asked.

"Yeah, yeah, I'm good. I'm okay."

Silence hung between us. I couldn't seem to get the words out.

"Did you need something? You sound strange," she said.

I closed my eyes and took a deep breath. It was now or never, right? "I, uh, need a favor."

Her chuckle only made me feel worse. "Another favor? Isn't it enough that I'm letting you use my cabin for some sexcapades?"

Heat scoured my cheeks. "A different favor."

"Okay. What's up?"

"Can you come to the cabin tonight? And bring the guys?"

"Uh, sure? You really want Josh and Chris to hang out with Garrett tonight?"

Oh shit. Garrett. I'd forgotten about that little tidbit. "No. Listen, Jaden. I...haven't been here with Garrett. I'm not sleeping with him. I would never."

"What? But you said—"

"No, you assumed. And I didn't correct you."

She blew out an exasperated breath, the sound harsh in my ears. "Wait, so you're not at my cabin with Garrett?"

"I'm at your cabin. I'm not with Garrett."

"Then what are you doing there?"

Fuck, the butterflies in my stomach had turned into full grown bats. "I think it'd be best if we discussed this in person. Bring the guys tonight, okay? Come around ten o'clock."

Ten p.m. would give me time to rally some reinforcements.

"Maddie...." Jaden sighed. "What's going on? You've been acting really weird since we went to Purgatory's Mark last week. Is everything okay?"

I decided to be honest with her about my emotional state. "No. It's not. But I'm trying to fix it all."

"What needs fixing?"

I pursed my lips, then said, "Tonight, okay? I really don't want to have this conversation over the phone."

"Okay, you're scaring me."

I winced. "I'm sorry."

"Fine. Tonight," Jaden said. "Chris, Josh, and I will be there with bells on."

"See you then."

I ended the call before Jaden could ask me any other questions, then I sat back and stared at the closest wall. Fuck, I hoped I hadn't just triggered the end of my relationship with my friends.

The worst-case scenario started playing through my mind. It was something I'd always done to help ease my anxiety. Focus on it, play it out to death in my head until it didn't hold any power over me. Then figure out what I would do in that scenario.

In this case, if Chris, Josh, and Jaden didn't believe me, if they attacked Gabriel, I'd do what I had to. Gabriel was innocent. If my friends chose to move forward with the bounty after hearing everything I had to say, then they weren't the people I thought they were.

The next worst-case scenario was them severing our friendship.

That one *hurt*. Even more than them choosing not to listen to me. But I would survive. I would. I had others in my life. I wouldn't be alone.

I truly hoped that one didn't come to pass, though. I loved Jaden, Josh, and Chris. I wanted them in my life. I just hoped they wanted me in theirs after all this.

On a last-minute whim, I phoned Lucy. After reassuring her that I was perfectly fine after the witches' attack, I asked her and Sam to come over tonight as well. Lastly, I texted Anna the same invitation. It made me feel better knowing they'd all be here. My support group.

I only hoped this didn't blow up in my face.

22

GABRIEL AND I SAT NEXT TO EACH OTHER ON THE couch. Neither of us spoke, the quiet before the storm. A lot rode on tonight, and we had no idea what to expect. I wanted to believe that my friends would side with me, but that little voice from earlier kept stepping on my thoughts, asking what if they didn't.

Every few minutes, I shot the clock a glare. Time was moving exceptionally slow. I expected Sam, Lucy, Anna, and Vlad any moment now. And my best friends in an hour.

As though sensing my apprehension, Gabriel pulled me close. I rested my head against his shoulder and took solace in his familiar scent. I'd changed out of his shirt and now wore a sports bra, tank top, and leggings. It was the best clothing I could find in the supplies Anna had brought. She'd packed me some fighting leathers, but I really didn't want to answer the door wearing them. It might give my friends the wrong idea.

I blew out a breath, then rubbed my palms on my thighs. They were so clammy. As was the rest of me. My body couldn't make up its mind. One moment I was hot, the next cold. Adrenaline had a way of messing with people's internal systems.

And I wasn't the only one struggling. When I last snuck a peek at Gabriel's face, he'd seemed miles away, his gaze distant.

"Hey, you okay?" I asked.

He jerked a sharp nod.

"Talk to me. What's going on in that brain of yours?"

He sighed, then repositioned himself, his thigh brushing mine. "I'm worried about tonight."

Yeah, me too.

"But not for the reasons you might think."

Okay, that made me stop. I lifted a brow, then turned to watch him.

"I'm worried about *you*," he said. "If the unimaginable happens, and you're forced to choose, and you choose me, you'll eventually come to resent me for it."

I snuggled against his shoulder.

"If they die tonight, you'll never forgive yourself. Or me. I can't see how this situation ends well for any of us."

I bit my lip and considered his words. After a moment, I said, "I refuse to believe that. My friends are good people. I think they'll be equally as upset about the Academy as I am. I know I've said this before, but I can't say it enough. Just because we slay vampires, doesn't mean we're murderers. Or at least, we weren't before all this. Now...."

Gabriel placed a kiss against the top of my head. "You could never be a murderer. They used you. It wasn't your fault."

I wasn't too sure about that. I'd followed the Academy blindly. I'd never questioned the process. I'd trusted them. The fault for that rested solely on me.

"No matter what happens tonight, we'll get through it," I said. "Even if it means the worst comes to pass. I can't guarantee it won't destroy me, but I would never blame you. I'm the one that called them here. I'm the one that hid all this from them in the first place. The only person to blame here is me."

"You were doing what you thought was best."

"Yeah, but you know what they say about good intentions."

Gabriel chuckled. "I do believe I've heard that one before."

A soft knock on the door interrupted our conversation. Gabriel's gaze darted to mine and he held it, a world of emotion shining within his eyes.

I kissed him softly. "We've got this."

His mouth curved into a weary smile. "Guess I'll just have to trust you."

"Good. Because I totally know what I'm doing," I said, with all the confidence of a five-year-old.

Another knock sounded.

Rising from the couch, I headed to the door and pulled it open, greeting Lucy with a massive grin. It'd been a few weeks since we'd last seen each other, and I'd missed her. Behind her lurked Sam.

Lucy slung a loose arm around my shoulders, knowing I didn't do well with hugs, then skipped into the living room.

Sam trailed inside next. Warmth radiated from his amber eyes and he nodded. "Maddie."

"Sam," I mimicked in a tone far deeper than my natural alto.

He smiled, then ruffled my hair, exactly as a big brother would. "Good to see you, kiddo."

Ugh, I hated when he called me that. But seeing as how he had four baby sisters, it made sense that he'd treat me as one of them.

"Thank you both for coming," I said. "I really appreciate it."

"Gabriel," Lucy said. "Long time no see."

"Welcome," he said, with a slight head bow. So formal. I could understand that, though, considering the last time they'd seen one another, Lucy had been transitioning into a werewolf. Now she was an alpha, and he was the king. Strange how things worked out.

Werewolves and vampires typically weren't friendly with each other. Bad blood and all that. But Lucy and Anna had been best friends long before they'd each joined the supernatural world. Nothing could ever destroy their bond. And because of it, sometimes vampires and werewolves had to play nice. Like right now.

"Hey, what about us?" came Anna's voice as she climbed onto the porch.

Vlad followed behind, hitting his FOB to lock the car doors. I laughed. We were in the middle of the country. Who out here would steal his car?

Anna entered immediately after Sam, her arms full of *more* bags. Dear lord, what had she brought us now? She thrust the bags in question into my arms, then dove for Lucy and hugged her. "Oh, girl. It's been too long!"

The two hugged and laughed while Vlad stepped inside and shook hands with Sam. Lucy had told me once that the two men used to hate each other. Apparently, they'd started feuding after some...inappropriate behavior. On both sides. I'd nearly busted a gut when Lucy first told me about how Sam had urinated all around Vlad's coffin. Punishment for some disparaging remarks Vlad had made against werewolves. According to Lucy and Anna, the guys had long since put aside their issues. And that was good. I highly doubted Jaden would appreciate anyone marking their territory inside her cabin.

"So, when's this all going down?" Lucy asked.

All eyes swung toward me. "I told them to be here at ten. That gives me an hour to prepare myself."

"What about us?" Anna asked. "What do you need us for?"

"Mostly, just support," I told her. "I don't want to bombard them with vampires the second they arrive. I'd actually prefer to speak with them alone outside first. Afterward, provided they're willing, I'd like to bring you all out and introduce you. I asked you guys here as backup, in case things go bad. Really bad."

Lucy closed the distance between us. She held my gaze as she asked. "And if they do? Then what?"

My chest tightened, but I nodded. "I'll handle it."

"And you're willing to do that?" she pressed. "Maddie, these are your best friends. You love them so much, you even introduced them to my brood."

"I know. But if they won't listen, if they still want to kill Gabriel, then what else can I do?"

Sympathy darkened Lucy's face and she pulled me in for a hug. "Whatever happens tonight, we're here for you, sweetie. We support you."

"Thank you," I rasped. "I need to make sure they see reason. That's all. I won't give up until they understand exactly what's going on."

Lucy nodded. Once she stepped away, Anna approached and pointed at the bags I held in my hand. "I brought you some gear," she said. "It's in the black bag."

I started shaking my head, but Anna shushed me. "Trust me, you're gonna love this contraption I had designed for you."

I peered into the bag and frowned. All I saw was leather.

"Put it on," Anna said.

Gabriel peered into the bag and whistled. "That's quite the rig you've brought."

Anna shrugged. "Consider it a gift." She plunged a hand into the black bag and pulled out a leather harness unlike anything I'd ever seen. There were so many straps, buckles, and slots. It almost looked like something someone would wear if they were into BDSM.

"What on earth...?" I mumbled.

"Gabriel, help me out," Anna said.

As the two worked together to strap me in, I quickly realized it was a harness.

"I custom ordered this," Anna continued. "It took a few days to put together, and it's untested, but it should work."

She yanked on a strap at my waist, securing it snuggly. Then she nodded to Vlad, who produced a large suitcase. He opened it up to reveal a silk-lined interior full of weapons.

The blood drained from my face. "I wasn't planning on going to war tonight," I commented dryly.

"I know. I started designing this after the witches attacked you. You need something more than a single stake. Gabriel is our king. We're trusting you with his life. Therefore, you get to be the next Rambo."

As though to prove her point, she withdrew five new stakes from the suitcase. She curled a lip as she handled them, but she slid them gently into their corresponding slots. Next came a pair of daggers, which she slid into the matching wrist sheaths. Then a sword, which slid perfectly into the sheath on my back. Last, she handed me a gun.

"You've trained with all these?"

"The stakes, daggers, and swords, yes. I'm not quite as proficient with guns, but I know how to handle them."

"Good. The stakes are for vampires. The daggers and sword are *silver*. Do you hear me, Maddie? No touching the blades without protection. Stick to the hilts. We loaded the gun with hollow-tipped bullets filled with mercury. That's for the witches. They're sensitive to it, much like how you are to silver. There's only one clip right now. So seven bullets. I have an order coming in, but they couldn't get it to me by tonight."

She patted a pouch on my side and unsnapped it. "The pouch has two pockets. One contains vials of holy water. The second mercury shavings."

Holy shit. I was a one-woman war machine right now.

"I asked around about witches. They have to finish their incantation to fully empower their spell. Take them out *before* they cast it. I don't care if that means shoving a handful of mercury shavings down their throat. Do whatever you have to do. Their magic is potent, as you know."

Yes, I was well experienced in that area.

"Anna," I murmured, flabbergasted by everything she'd done for me. "Thank you."

"You're welcome," she said. "Don't pull a stake on me, and we'll call us even."

I chuckled. "Of course."

I took three massive steps back, then practiced pulling the weapons, familiarizing myself with everything.

"Oh, I forgot to mention." Anna held her hands up as she approached, waiting for me to sheath the sword I'd been playing with. "There's an emergency escape strap. Pull this"—she tapped the one locked at my hips—"and the whole thing comes off. In case you need to shift."

"Wow," I breathed, mesmerized. I didn't pull it because it'd taken far too long to get on, but I committed that specific strap to memory, knowing there'd come a day when I'd need it.

Anna strolled to the couch and took a seat while I continued practicing, working on pulling the sword without slicing my neck or hair off.

"This might be a completely inappropriate time to say this," Gabriel said. He leaned against the nearest wall, watching me with what I would call a *heated expression*. "But you look hot in leather."

I snorted a laugh. "Completely inappropriate."

"Ah. Then I shan't tell you the things I want to do to you. Who knew I liked a woman in leather?"

I mean, didn't every man like that? I chuckled and continued practicing.

"So fuckin' hot," Gabriel muttered, his accent growing thicker.

I cocked my head. "Do you know how to fight?"

"I'm a vampire. Don't we all?"

Anna chimed in, "Camilla taught me. She said I was a hazard to everyone around us and she demanded to train me. And then I taught Lucy everything I knew."

I glanced at Sam and Vlad, but something told me they both were well-versed in violence.

"Who taught you?" I asked Gabriel.

"My folks insisted I learn," he said. "I started training about a year after my mother turned me. I became proficient within a few years, and since then, I've kept at it."

"We should have sparred," I said. "Probably would have been more entertaining than chess."

If I wasn't mistaken, heat flared in Gabriel's eyes. "Next time."

I shivered in anticipation. Was it weird that the thought of sparring with Gabriel turned me on? Probably. But I was a vampire slayer. I didn't shy away from violence.

"Get a room, you two," Lucy called to us from the kitchen.

I grinned and winked at Gabriel. "We already have one."

"Ah, yes!" Anna cried out, fist pumping the air. "I win. Fork it up, baby." She extended a hand toward Vlad.

Vlad scrutinized me. "She only said they had a room. She never suggested they—"

"Oh, they've slept together," Anna stated. "I can tell. Maddie's glowing."

"One"—I flicked up my index finger—"gross. And two, what are you guys talking about?"

"We made a bet," Anna said, beaming at Vlad. "I said you'd be knocking booties within three days. Vlad didn't believe me. He thought it'd be longer. He thought *someone* here might be smart enough to wait until the danger had passed." She shot Gabriel a telling look.

He feigned innocence. "Me? You expected *me* to be the mature and intelligent one?"

Anna wiggled her fingers and winked at her husband. "Come on, baby. Pay up. You owe me."

Vlad grumbled, then produced his wallet and pulled out a hundred-dollar bill. He slapped it into his wife's hand, all the while glowering at Gabriel.

"Thank you!" She leaned in and laid a loud kiss on his cheek. "And thank you, Maddie. This will go nicely with my collection."

"Collection?" I lifted an eyebrow. "Of hundred-dollar bills?"

She nodded. "Of all the bets I've won. Vlad always thinks he's right. I enjoy proving him wrong."

"I don't *think* I'm always right," he countered. "You just always want to bet over silly things."

"Sure, sure," she razzed her husband.

I shook my head and laughed. But before I could say another word, I caught the sound of tires rolling over gravel. My heart damn near stopped in my chest. I immediately hurried to Gabriel's side and took his hand.

My friends were here.

23

Gabriel squeezed my hand. "Are you ready for this?"

Hell no. But it was too late to back down now. "I'm going to step outside and speak with them on the porch."

"I don't like that," Gabriel said.

"It's okay. They won't hurt me," I replied. "Give me time to explain everything to them. Once I do, you guys can come out and join us."

Gabriel sighed, then released my hand and kissed me. "Good luck."

I gave them all my best smile, then stepped toward the door. When my hand touched the doorknob, I spared a quick glance at my new harness. Probably should have taken it off. And Anna had mentioned the quick release option. But if I waited any longer, Jaden might come storming inside.

Shrugging, I opened the door and slipped out into the cool night air. A chill prickled my skin, as though to remind me winter was still here.

I stood on the porch, bathed in the car's headlights. Whoever was driving killed the ignition, and the lights went dark. I blinked, relying on the porch light until my night vision returned.

Three doors opened and closed, then I listened to the sound of their approaching steps, their feet crunching over the gravel.

"Maddie?" Jaden called to me.

"Hi guys, thank you for coming."

The three came to a stop in front of me, each wearing matching confused expressions.

"Why are you out here?" Jaden said. "It's freaking cold. Let's go inside."

I stepped in front of the door to bar their way. "Uh, no. Let's chat out here first. Grab a seat."

"Here?" Chris said, laughing. "Are you out of your mind? It's freezing out."

"This won't take long," I said. "And I think there are some blankets out here we can use."

Josh scratched the back of his neck and glanced at Jaden, who shrugged.

They filed onto the porch and each took a seat, tucking themselves into Jaden's patio furniture. It wasn't anything grand, just three wicker chairs and a glass table. I remained standing, feeling as though I needed the room to pace, something I could hear Gabriel doing inside the cabin. Guess I wasn't the only one who needed to move when nervous.

"Who else is here?" Jaden asked, gesturing toward the other two cars.

"I'll get to that," I said.

"Nice rig," Chris said, leaning around to analyze the leather halter. "Where'd you get it?"

"A friend," was all I said.

"A friend? What friend?" Chris shot me an alarmed glance.

"I'll get to that too. Listen, guys, there's a reason I invited you here, and I need you to promise me you'll listen to everything I have to say before you react."

"Oh, this sounds serious," Jaden muttered.

I didn't disagree. Instead, I drew a deep breath and centered my thoughts. I needed to explain this just right, and truthfully, I had no idea where to begin. The beginning, obviously. But they didn't remember the beginning, or the night we'd partied at Purgatory's Mark. It'd all been wiped from their minds thanks to Gabriel compelling them to forget. Which made things a wee bit challenging.

"I met someone on Valentine's Day," I confessed. "A vampire."

Josh and Jaden shared a look, but Chris merely stared at me.

"We met at Purgatory's Mark. And I learned something interesting." I drew another deep breath and dove in headfirst. "The vampire I met is my mate."

Confusion wrinkled Jaden's brow. "What does that mean? Your mate?"

"It's like a soulmate," I told her. "Someone you're destined to be with."

Chris gave a disbelieving laugh. "That's a fantasy. Everyone knows soulmates aren't real."

"Oh, I don't know about that. I've always believed in soulmates," Jaden said. "Every little girl dreams about finding her prince charming and marrying him and—wait, you're saying you've married a vampire?"

All three gazes swung back to me. "Um. No, not

exactly. We aren't married. But we've accepted that we're mates."

"You keep throwing that word around," Josh said, "like it means something?"

"It means a great deal to vampires." And werewolves, but no matter what, I couldn't divulge that secret tonight. It wasn't only my secret to keep. Vampires had the advantage of being public. Werewolves didn't. "To vampires, there's no stronger bond. Your mate is the one person in the world you would die for. You need them as much as they need you."

"And you're saying this happened to you?" Chris leaned forward. "Maddie, you know how that sounds right? Why would a vampire bond with a human like that?"

Guilt shamed me. If I could tell them I was a werewolf, it might help them understand. "It happens," I said. Not that I could think of *any* human who'd mated with a vampire. But then again, I couldn't think of any werewolves who had either.

"And that's why you've been here?" Jaden said, starting to piece things together. "Is he inside right now? Is that why you told me you were here with Garrett? To hide that it was actually a vampire?"

"Garrett?" Chris admonished. "You and Garrett?"

"No!" I shook my head. "Jaden assumed I was here with Garrett, and I let her. I shouldn't have done that. And I apologize. I didn't know how to tell you about all this. I mean, I *never* expected to find a mate, let alone have it be a vampire."

Gabriel's grumblings in the living room almost made me laugh. But the seriousness of this situation sobered me quickly.

"Okay..." Jaden scratched her head. "But why hide this from us?"

And here came the even harder part. "The day at the coffee shop, when Chris told us about his new mark?"

They all nodded.

"You put a picture of the Vampire King down on the table."

They nodded again, clearly still not connecting the dots. Guess I'd have to spell it out.

"*He's* my mate."

Silence fell over us. The only sound was that of the wind breezing through the trees. I swallowed and forced myself to continue before they could react.

"I saw Gabriel's face on that bounty, and I lost it.

I knew something wasn't right. How could fate pair me with a murderer?"

"*Alleged*," came Gabriel's haughty reply from inside.

I bit my tongue to keep from responding to him. "I had to find out the truth. If he'd really killed someone. So, I tracked Gabriel down. And brought him here."

"The night we planned to meet up after scoping out the hotel," Jaden whispered, piecing things together. "You never showed."

"Because I was here, with him."

Something shifted in that second. Disbelief and anger washed over Chris's face.

"You have him? And you didn't tell us? Maddie!" He clutched the armrests, about to launch to his feet.

"Chris, stop," I said, holding up a hand. "I didn't tell you because I knew this was how you'd react. And I had to learn for myself what was going on." I placed a hand on his, then winced when he jerked it back. "Gabriel didn't murder anyone, you guys."

All three started shouting, and I couldn't make out what they were saying.

"Stop it!" I shouted, smacking the table so hard the glass shivered. "Listen to what I'm saying! This is important!"

Jaden was the first to settle down.

"I needed to figure out why on earth someone would accuse Gabriel of murder. So, I reached out to a few friends. They did some digging and learned something quite troubling."

Chris's eyes narrowed. "*More* troubling than you shacking up with a vampire?"

I ignored his snide remark and continued. "They found proof of corruption within the Academy. They spoke to Vera and Liam—"

"What?" Josh exclaimed. "Who spoke to them? What are you talking about?"

"Stop interrupting me, and you'll find out," I said simply.

Chris's face mottled. I knew going into this that he would be the hardest of the three to convince. He was so jaded against vampires.

"They questioned Vera, then followed the chain of command to a woman named Claire. When they interrogated her, they learned about a sect within the Academy that's taking payments in exchange for creating false bounties. They operate anonymously so Vlad and Anna weren't able to acquire any names. But it's happening and they're using us as weapons."

"This is bullshit," Chris snapped. "Who are these supposed friends of yours?"

I sighed. "Anna and Vlad. You know them as—"

"Dracula and his wife," Chris bit out. "More vampires. You've got to be kidding me. When did you start working with vampires, Maddie?"

"Why does it matter who I'm working with? All that matters is what we found out."

"It matters because they're *vampires*. My god, Maddie! How can you even trust them?" He shoved to his feet and started pacing the deck. "This is insane." He spun around to face me. "This is why you brought us here? To tell us that the Academy is supposedly corrupted? And that my mark, the king of the fucking vampires, is your mate or whatever? What do you want from us?"

Unsurprised by his vitriol, I rose to my feet and eased toward him, trying not to upset him further. "I want you to do what's right. Gabriel isn't guilty. You'd be killing an innocent vampire."

"There's no such thing," Chris snapped, spittle flying from his lips.

"Doesn't any of this bother you?" I asked. "Who's to say we haven't fulfilled a bunch of false contracts?"

"Let's get something straight," Chris snarled. "A vampire is a vampire. I don't care if the contract is false or not. They *all* deserve to die."

"Chris..." Jaden gasped. "You can't mean that."

He whirled around and glared at Jaden. "Of course I do! I thought you three felt the same way. Vampires are a plague on this world. They aren't *human!*"

I staggered back a step, his words piercing my heart. He didn't realize how hard that hit me—since I, too, wasn't human.

"Dude," Josh said. "It doesn't matter if they're human or not. We don't kill innocents. We protect them."

"I'm here to kill them all," Chris argued. He spun back to me and jabbed a finger in my direction. "And you. You're no better than them. I can't believe you would do this. Go behind our backs and steal my mark from me. I can't believe you would *work* with them."

"Chris—"

"Maddie, get inside," Gabriel's voice carried through the walls.

I ignored him. This was too important to run from. "Chris, you have to see how wrong this is. How slaying an innocent vampire is murder."

"We're *sanctioned*, Maddie. And that's all that matters."

"But it's a false contract!"

He stepped toward me, menace twisting his face. "I don't care."

My heart shattered.

"Dude, calm down," Josh said.

"Is he in there?" Chris demanded, jerking his chin toward the cabin. "Is this where you've been keeping him? Holed up inside while you scheme and plot?"

Chris tore toward the front door.

I reacted without a thought, leaping between him and the door as I pulled one of my daggers. Before Chris could so much as suck in a breath, I had the blade pressed to his throat.

"Maddie!" Jaden screamed. "What are you doing?"

Chris glared at me, his eyes shining with hate. "So, that's how it's gonna be, huh? You're going to choose *him* over me? One of your best friends?"

"You're forcing me to choose," I told him, my words low. "You're not thinking straight, Chris."

"Oh, I've never understood things better."

I wanted to cry. This couldn't be happening. I loved Chris like a brother. I truly hadn't believed one of my worst-case scenarios would play here tonight.

"Take another step, and I'll end you," I said, my

voice wavering. I hated this so much. Hated that I had a dagger to one of my best friends' throats.

"Maddie," Jaden cried.

"I'm so sorry," I told her without looking away from Chris. "But I won't let him harm Gabriel. I won't let any of you hurt him."

The door opened at my back. Fury flashed in Chris's glare, and I knew he was staring Gabriel down right this second.

"Chris," came Sam's voice from inside the cabin. "Back down, brother."

"Yeah, come on man," Josh said, clapping a hand on Chris's shoulder. "Think about this. If what Maddie is saying is true, we have no right to kill Gabriel."

"If what Maddie is saying is true," Chris scoffed. "So you believe this nonsense too?"

"It's worth looking into," Josh said. "I'd rather take the time to investigate it than kill an innocent."

Relief almost had me lowering my dagger, but then I saw the look on Chris's face. He wasn't convinced.

I leaned into my dagger, pushing Chris down the porch stairs and into the yard. "I think it's time you left," I told him.

His eyes hadn't once strayed from Gabriel. "I'm not going anywhere."

"Chris, you're outnumbered. Think about this. Do you truly think I'll let you do this?"

His gaze finally flicked to mine. "I can take you."

And there went the final pieces of my heart. "Guess we'll soon find out."

Rage transformed his face into something truly hideous. "The way I see it, you turned your back on us."

I lifted my chin, hating this so much. "Fine. Say you get past me. Do you think Gabriel will simply stand there and let you kill him?"

"Chris..." Jaden came up behind him and touched his shoulder. "Don't do this, please. Don't destroy the family we've built."

"I didn't," he snarled. "*She* did."

My eyes stung with unshed tears.

"She's the one holding a dagger to my throat. Or have you all conveniently forgotten that?"

"Please don't do this," I said. "I don't want to hurt you. Chris, you're like a brother to me."

He gave a disgruntled laugh but didn't respond to that.

"Go home," Josh said. "Think this through."

Chris finally tore his focus away from Gabriel

and me to stare at Josh and Jaden. "Screw you. Screw all of you." He took one step back, then another.

I let him. I didn't lower my guard though. Instead, I stepped back until I found myself pressed against Gabriel. He placed his hands on my hips in a silent show of support.

Chris shouted something incomprehensible, then turned on his heel and stalked to the car. Within seconds, he slid behind the wheel and peeled away from the cabin.

I heaved a relieved sigh and lowered my arm when I heard the car turn onto the main highway. My body started shaking, the adrenaline coursing through me.

"Well, that could have gone a little better," Lucy said, breaking the awkward silence.

Someone gave a breathy laugh, though I wasn't sure who.

"Maddie?" A gentle hand circled my arm.

I lifted my head and found Jaden standing in front of me. Even she looked a bit pale. I could only imagine she and Josh felt the same as me. Like our little family had just broken up.

Her gaze drifted to Gabriel at my back and her mouth pressed into a firm line. Then she extended a hand and said, "I'm Jaden. This is Josh."

Gabriel's hand slid into hers as he greeted her.

At least I still had them. A second later, Jaden's wrapped her arms around me. Without complaint, I sank into her hug, still trembling.

"I guess we should discuss this a little more," she said.

I nodded, about to lead her into the cabin, when I heard a snap in the woods.

Gabriel, Anna, Vlad, Lucy, Sam, and I all stiffened at the sound. The six of us jerked our heads simultaneously toward the trees.

Jaden and Josh stepped backward, their eyes on us.

When another twig snapped, the six of us stepped forward.

"Um, Maddie?" Jaden asked. "What's going on? You're all freaking me out."

"Someone's out there," I whispered.

"What?"

I lifted my chin and scented the air. But it wasn't until a small army of shadows stepped out of the trees that I realized exactly how fucked we were.

TIME SLOWED AS I WATCHED THE SHADOWS MOVE toward us, but it wasn't until they cleared the trees and stepped into the moonlight that I saw their faces. I took in our situation, counting. Six vampires, three witches, and a tenth figure in the back, cloaked in darkness. Preternatural light shone in the vampires' eyes, but the witches seemed to melt into the shadows, their forms barely visible.

"This isn't good," I muttered.

The approaching group sorely outnumbered us.

This was what we'd been waiting for. The second attack.

"Maddie?" Jaden whispered, her voice cracking. "What's going on?"

"They're here to kill me and Gabriel. I'll explain later." Assuming we had a later.

She gasped, and from the corner of my eye, I saw her grip Josh's arm. He pulled her close, whispering words of encouragement.

I glanced back at my friends. They were slayers, but they were human, which put them at a stark disadvantage.

"Josh, Jaden, take my car and go."

"What?" Jaden snapped.

"You aren't ready for this," I told them. "Go!"

"Fuck that noise," Jaden said. "We aren't abandoning you."

"Neither are we," Lucy murmured. "Not that anyone asked."

I might have cracked a smile at that if I wasn't busy trying not to shit my pants. With Josh and Jaden here, Sam, Lucy, and I couldn't shift. It was against the rules to reveal our existence to humans. But what did that *really* matter right now? The most important thing was making sure we all survived this fight. I needed Sam and Lucy at their strongest, and that was in their wolf forms. I would have to shift too, eventually—once I'd made use of all the weapons Anna had armed me with.

Lucy and Sam stood on either side of me. She lifted a brow and gestured toward my friends. I jerked a nod at my sister. If my friends were staying, then they were about to see something few humans ever saw.

Lucy and Sam immediately started stripping.

"What the...?" Jaden questioned.

"Josh, Jaden," I said, drawing their focus to me. "Vampires aren't the only supernatural thing in the world." I pointed at Lucy and Sam. "Werewolves." Then I pointed at the oncoming horde. "Witches."

Jaden stared at me, her mouth parted in disbelief. A disbelief that quickly turned to shock when Lucy and Sam shifted. Like me, they were fast. Thirty seconds at most. The cracking of their bones echoed through the night, but it was Jaden's erratic heartbeat that held my attention.

"It's okay," I told her. "They have full control over themselves, they won't hurt you." Then I gestured to the witches. "But they will."

I debated my options. Josh and Jaden weren't armed. Luckily, Anna had provided me with an arsenal. Between the two of them, Jaden was the better shot. I remembered our weapons training classes, and she'd always smoked me and Josh in target practice.

I drew my gun and handed it to her. "Mercury bullets. Toxic to witches." Then I handed one stake and one dagger to Josh and a stake to Jaden. I didn't need to explain those. That left me with the sword—handy for decapitation—two stakes, and a dagger. The silver wouldn't help much, but a blade was a blade. I only wished I had Sir-Stab-A-Lot, but I hadn't thought to bring him with me when I'd grabbed Gabriel.

"Give us the king, and we'll let most of you leave in peace," one witch said. She pointed a shadowy finger at me. "But not you. You die."

A low growl rumbled in Gabriel's chest. He stood at my side, ready to fight, his stance mirroring mine. I passed him my final dagger, while making a mental note to thank Anna for all these lovely weapons—provided we survived.

"Screw you," Anna called back.

"Witches use real magic," I said quickly, filling in Jaden and Josh as fast as I could. "Don't let them finish their incantations. And *do not* let them touch you. Keep one alive. We need to interrogate them."

The crackle of magic was the only warning the

witches gave before one flung a searing ball of flame at us. I cursed and dove to the side, pulling Gabriel with me. I knew exactly how painful their spells could be.

Two howls shattered the night, and I watched as Lucy and Sam leapt into the battle. Fear clogged my throat. They had kids. My niece and nephew. The thought of any harm coming to Lucy or Sam, or worse, losing them—I didn't know what I would do. But I couldn't let fear like that distract me. It would get me killed. Or worse, someone else I loved.

Anna and Vlad were a blur of movement, their vampiric speed a stark contrast to Sam and Lucy's brutal strength.

Together, the four of them engaged the vampires, working in tandem, as though they'd done this before. I rose and pulled Gabriel to his feet, a silent understanding passing between us. I would do anything to protect him, and I suspected he would do the same for me.

Sam and Lucy crashed into two of the vampires with bone-crushing force, their snarls echoing through the forest as teeth met flesh. The vampires hissed and struck back, their undead strength a formidable match for my sister and brother-in-law.

Gripping the hilt of my sword, I dove into the

fray, hurtling toward the nearest witch. Her glowing gaze locked onto mine, and I caught her sneer, her lips pulling back to reveal what looked like sharpened teeth. Jesus, witches were terrifying. She lifted her hand and started chanting, magic coalescing in her palm.

I remembered the advice I'd given Jaden and Josh. Don't let them finish the incantation. I forced my legs faster, panting for breath as I moved. I still wasn't at the top of my game, but I wouldn't let something as trivial as pain slow me down.

Unfortunately, I didn't make it in time.

The witch finished her incantation, and a massive blood-red orb streaked toward me. I feinted around it, but the damn orb tracked my movements. Agony erupted within me the second it struck my side. I cried out, but kept moving, locking the pain away in a special part of my brain. I could focus on it later. I had to remove this witch from the equation. And the two others.

Beside me, Gabriel clashed with one of the vampires. His fangs flashed in the moonlight before sinking into the vampire's neck. Blood sprayed, the scent perfuming the air.

My heart pounded in my chest, and with a burst of energy, I launched myself at the witch.

Her mouth moved as she chanted another incantation, but I reached her before she could finish. She backpedaled, fear alight in her eyes. I swiped with my sword and silenced her with a single deadly strike. Relief coursed through my veins, clashing with the adrenaline. But I couldn't relax. Not when I saw Jaden and Josh struggling with a witch.

Gunfire rang through the trees, but every bullet seemed to miss. Magic, I suspected.

Green power flooded the battleground, and I heard Jaden scream. The sound was unlike anything I'd ever heard her make before. Josh shouted her name, but he couldn't go to her, not until the witch was dead.

Jaden was down, her form prone in the grass.

I cursed, panic spreading through me when I saw a vampire spot her from across the field. His eyes gleamed with hunger, and he shot toward her.

Shit!

"Josh!" I shouted, but wasn't able to break free of the witch. He couldn't protect Jaden.

I whirled around to face Gabriel. I couldn't leave him to protect Jaden, but I couldn't abandon her, either. If someone didn't stop the vampire, he'd happily feed on her.

Gabriel spared a quick glance, then shouted, "Go!"

I didn't hesitate. Cursing, I hit the safety strap Anna had showed me and stripped off the harness. I didn't bother to remove my clothes—I didn't have time. Instead, I ran as fast as I could, then initiated the change mid-stride. I'd only attempted this once before—shifting mid-run—so I wasn't sure how successful I'd be. As long as I didn't trip over my own legs, I should be fine.

I felt my muscles contorting and bones snapping as I moved, but I ignored the rush of pain. I focused on my goal. Get to Jaden before that vampire did.

Once I was a few feet away, I leapt into the air and forced the rest of the change. I'd taken off on two feet but landed on four. As the vampire lunged at Jaden, I threw myself into him, our bodies colliding mid-air. The force sent us tumbling across the ground. The vampire let out a startled hiss, its fangs bared to strike. But I was faster, and my fangs were larger. With a powerful snap of my jaws, I sank my teeth into his throat and ripped it out.

The vampire struggled beneath me, clawing at my fur, but his movements grew weaker. Once he went limp, I finished the job, then scrambled off his corpse and returned to the battle.

Vlad, Anna, Lucy, and Sam had worked together in perfect synchronicity. The bodies of five vampires littered the ground. Now they'd paired off against the last two witches, Vlad and Anna assisting Josh with one, while Sam and Lucy fought the other.

I searched the field for Gabriel and found him on the other side of the field, fighting the tenth figure. The one who'd lingered at the back of the enemy's group. The figure moved with such terrifying precision, their strikes powerful and liquid fast.

Fear had me darting across the field. Gabriel fought hard, but his opponent seemed to be gaining the upper hand. I studied his enemy's movements. From what I could tell, he wasn't a vampire. And he didn't seem to be using magic.

What was he then?

Something powerful, that was for sure.

The figure lashed out at Gabriel again and again. Every blow seemed to suck more life out of him. His movements weren't as fluid anymore, his steps staggering. His opponent, a thing made of darkness itself, moved within the shadows, using them to take advantage of Gabriel's faltering.

The figure struck again, this time, vanishing and reappearing at Gabriel's side within the span of a breath. I sucked in a sharp breath as I ran. No one could move that fast. Not even vampires. What *was* he?

Another strike, one that slammed Gabriel into a tree. He slid to the ground, dazed.

The figure glanced my way, and I nearly fell over when I caught sight of his blood red eyes. They didn't glow like the witches' or vampires'. But they were ethereal, nonetheless. The creature grinned, its mouth splitting unnaturally wide. Then it lifted a hand, its fingers elongating into wicked scythe-like claws.

Terror coursed through me. I had to do something. I couldn't bear to watch this thing rip Gabriel apart. As the creature raised its hand for what was likely the killing blow, I didn't stop to think. I simply acted.

Running with all the strength I had left, I leapt forward, throwing myself between Gabriel and the creature. The claws meant for my mate hit me instead, sinking into my chest. A searing pain exploded within me, and I released a gasp, the blow forcing all the air from my body.

Time seemed to slow as wave after wave of pain poured through me. I'd made it in time, taken the blow meant for Gabriel, sacrificed myself for him.

"Maddie!" Gabriel shouted, pure agony ripping from his throat.

But I didn't fall. I couldn't. Not while the creature held me up by its claws. Instead of flinging me aside and finishing its task, the creature pulled me close to its face. Darkness clung to it, but I could see those red eyes. Somehow, they seemed to burn through my soul.

I knew then what it was. I'd never seen one before, but I'd heard of them.

"Demon," I rasped, blood trickling from my mouth.

Its mouth curved into another preternaturally terrifying grin. It held me close and cocked its head. Then it started to make a simple sound. Something akin to a heartbeat. It took me a few moments to realize it was echoing mine, its voice slowing along with my pulse.

Darkness creeped in at the edges of my vision. Distantly, I heard shouting. Snarling. Roaring. I saw people running toward us. Wolves lunging at the creature. I felt its claws rip clear of my chest. Felt myself tumble into someone's open arms. Heard so much yelling and crying.

I wanted to tell them everything would be okay. But I couldn't speak, couldn't see.

The darkness was different this time. More suffocating somehow. And behind it all, I saw a soft light edging toward me, welcoming me.

"Maddie," came a desperate voice. "Stay with me. Okay? Don't do this. I can't go through this again. Don't leave me."

I knew that voice. And I sensed his torment.

"Maddie?" he repeated, his chilled hands touching my face, gripping my hands, holding me close. "Stay with me. Stay with me."

"Gabriel—"

"*Do something!*" he shouted.

I tried to tell him it would be alright. But I couldn't form the words. I had no choice but to let the darkness take me away.

25

I swam through the murky darkness. Far ahead of me, a beacon of light shone like a lighthouse amidst a raging storm. Water lapped around me, trying to suck me under. It took so much strength to stay afloat. Strength I utterly lacked. My arms and legs were so heavy. It was impossible to move them. But if I didn't, I'd sink into the rough waters of oblivion.

I couldn't allow that.

I wasn't sure why, I just knew I had to get to the

light. There was someone there waiting for me. Someone who needed me.

I forced myself to move, begging my limbs to obey.

"Come on, Maddie, you can do this," a voice whispered. "Wake up, luv. Please wake up."

The waves grew stronger, ignorant to the voice's pleas. I flailed against them, but they won the battle and sucked me under. Back into the darkness.

A VOICE WHISPERED TO ME—FAMILIAR, STEADY.

I broke through the surface of the water with a soft gasp. Was it me, or was the lighthouse closer this time? Whispered voices echoed in my head, soft murmurs interspersed with bouts of silence. Among them, that familiar voice, steady and comforting, begging me to wake.

It was then that I noticed the waters had changed.

Grown calmer.

The chaotic undercurrent had vanished, replaced by a gentle, soothing tide. One that kept me afloat. A rhythmic beeping came to me, and I listened, letting it lull me into a sense of safety and comfort.

An image flashed across my mind of a man huddled by my side, his face worried and eyes tired. I tried to force myself to wake, desperate to anchor myself to him. But the harder I tried, the more exhausted I became, until I slipped back beneath the surface once again.

Those voices again. They were soft but insistent, and rested on the edge of my consciousness. I fought to open my eyes, but my lids felt weighted down, impossible to lift. Every time I tried, the water swept me under. I realized then that I couldn't fight it. I had to let the light come to me. I inhaled and exhaled, allowing my body to relax. The waves carried me across the sea until the warm light hit my face.

The water vanished then and something solid formed beneath me.

A bed, I realized.

Gone were the crashing waves and obscure darkness. In its place was the rhythmic beating of what I assumed was medical equipment, warm blankets, and a cool hand gripping mine.

"When is she going to wake up?" a harsh voice demanded.

"I don't know. Her body sustained a great deal of trauma, you know this. It takes time to heal from something like that. Even for a werewolf. We're lucky she's even alive. That thing nearly shredded her heart."

A frustrated growl reverberated through the room.

I knew that growl. I wanted to open my eyes and show him I would be fine, but my eyelids were still so heavy.

"Isn't there anything more we can do?"

"No. It's just a matter of waiting for her to wake up. But Gabriel, her stats are improving every single day."

"It's been three days," he snapped.

"I know. I know you're frustrated. I know you're scared. Try to hold on to the fact that she's improving. I'll come by and check on her later, okay?"

Another rumbling snarl. I listened to the retreating footsteps, almost about to drift back into unconsciousness, when I felt someone squeeze my hand.

"Time to wake up, luv," Gabriel murmured, his voice so weary. "I can't take much more of this, alright, Maddie? I need you to open your eyes, okay? Can you hear me?"

I could. I just couldn't find the strength to respond.

I needed to find it though. For him. It took every ounce of will I had left—which wasn't a lot—but eventually, my eyelids fluttered, the world a mere slit of light. Then, slowly, painstakingly, I managed to pry open my eyes.

One slow blink.

Then another.

The world grew sharper—still blurred, but recognizable.

I turned my head a fraction of an inch, but it was enough to catch sight of a figure huddled next to my bed. His head lay next to mine on the mattress, his hand gripping mine as though he was afraid to let me go.

I closed my eyes briefly and focused on breathing. When I blinked them open again, I stared at the mop of tousled dark hair. I moved my other hand, the one he wasn't gripping, and touched his head, my fingers sliding through his locks.

Gabriel lurched up, knocking my hand onto the bed. His eyes were wild, almost frantic, and they roamed my face, as though searching for something.

"Maddie?" His voice was a rough whisper, heavy with relief and a hint of disbelief.

I tried to smile reassuringly, but everything was still too hard, too heavy, and my body didn't want to cooperate. Instead, I squeezed his hand, hoping it conveyed what I couldn't express with words.

"Maddie," he repeated, this time the relief more pronounced. He returned my squeeze, the warmth of his touch seeping into my skin. "You're awake." He pressed his forehead to our entwined hands, and I saw his shoulders shaking.

I reached out with my free hand and touched the top of his head in an attempt to soothe him.

He lifted his head, then leaned in and kissed my forehead. "You're going to be okay," he murmured, cradling my face. "You're strong. You've got this."

I wanted to tell him, *hell yes I did*, but sleep was pulling at me, tugging me back into the abyss. I gave a heavy blink and felt my grip on his hand start to weaken.

Panic flared in his eyes. "No, Maddie. Stay awake. You need to stay awake."

His desperation stirred a determination in me that I didn't know I still had. If he wanted me to stay awake, I'd try. For him. I forced my eyes open, battling back the blackness that wanted nothing more than to pull me back under.

"I'm okay," I managed to croak.

"Here," he said. He pulled his hands away and reached for something on the table next to me.

My mouth ached at the sight of the glistening water.

He held the straw to my lips. "Slowly now," he said. "Little sips."

I pulled deeply from the straw, then coughed. Pain lit through my entire body.

Gabriel placed the glass back on the table and cupped my cheeks. "Shh. You're okay. That's why I said small sips."

Once I stopped coughing, he offered me another drink. This time, I was careful to take the smallest of sips. Relief soothed my sore throat, and I dropped my head back against the pillows with a sigh.

"What. Happened?" I wheezed.

"What do you remember?" Gabriel asked.

Broken memories surfaced, and I catalogued

them as best I could. It wasn't until I remembered the demon's hand plunging into my chest that I cried out and tried to sit up.

"Shh, Maddie." Gabriel clasped my shoulders and helped me back down. "You're okay. You're okay."

Hysteria tore through me, and I started sobbing.

Gabriel cursed. He pressed a palm against my cheek and spoke softly. "Listen to me, Maddie. The demon's gone. You're okay. You're safe. I've got you."

It took a few moments for his words to register. The image of that *thing* tore through my mind. The feel of its claws embedded in my skin, its hands breaking through my bones, its haunting voice echoing my failing heartbeat.

"Shh," Gabriel crooned. "Stop, luv, you'll hurt yourself."

But I couldn't stop. The tears just kept coming.

The hospital equipment mirrored my heartbeat, quickening until it set off all the alarms. The next thing I knew, my room was full of people, all trying to calm me down. But how on earth could I calm myself? I'd gone up against a demon and nearly died. That thing would haunt my nightmares for the rest of my life.

Eventually, my tears slowed, and the panic subsided. My watery gaze leapt from face to face, taking everyone in. Vlad, Anna, Lucy, Sam, Jaden, Josh...they were all here. And they were all okay. Chris's was the only missing face, but I hadn't expected to find him here, not after everything. The only person I didn't know was a woman standing in the back, but based on her lab coat, I assumed she was a doctor.

That made me look around. I knew I couldn't be in a hospital. It was against the rules for us to seek human medical attention.

"Where are we?" I rasped.

"My place," Lucy said. "And this here is Meredith, the pack doctor."

Right. I remembered her now. She'd delivered both of Lucy's babies.

Meredith stepped forward and checked the machines. "Vitals are stabilizing. Everything's looking good." She turned to face me. "How do you feel?"

I almost said I was fine, but I had a feeling no one would appreciate that answer, since it wasn't truthful.

"Sore," I admitted. "And exhausted."

"Understandable," Meredith said.

"Is Auntie Maddie going to be okay?" a small voice asked.

My gaze darted to the doorway to find my niece, Annalise, hovering there. Fear and concern twisted her face. A little boy clung to her legs. My nephew, Fynn.

Lucy hurried to her children and shooed them away from the room, but I heard her promising them I'd be fine.

"Let's let her get some more rest," Meredith said.

"I'm not going anywhere," Gabriel announced.

Meredith gave a faint smile. "Yeah, I expected as much."

The room emptied, and I found it a bit easier to breathe without everyone staring at me.

Gabriel lowered onto his chair and took my hand, rubbing his thumb over my knuckles. I had a feeling he was soothing himself more than me right now.

"Damn it, Maddie, you scared the hell out of me," he murmured, his voice barely above a whisper. He held my hand so tightly, as though afraid to let go, afraid I'd vanish.

"I know," I managed to croak. "I'd apologize but..."

"But it wouldn't be real," he said, his lips

quirking into a sad smile. "You jumped in front of me, Maddie. Sacrificed yourself for me."

"I couldn't let that thing hurt you," I replied.

He exhaled a shaky laugh. "Promise me you won't ever do that again. I lost one mate that way, I can't—I *refuse*—to lose you. I wouldn't survive that."

I stared at him, then turned my hand over and clutched his tightly. "You know I won't promise that."

He dropped his head down onto our intertwined hands and swore. "Maddie, please. Did you even stop to think about what you were doing? The demon didn't have a stake."

I frowned.

"Those were claws. Not a stake. It would have injured me, yes, but I would have survived and been fine. You, above all others, know what it takes to kill a vampire."

"Beheading, sunlight, fire, or treated stake," I recited, understanding dawning.

Gabriel brought our hands to his mouth and kissed my fingers. "Nowhere on that list is claws."

"Have you ever faced a demon?" I asked.

His expression shuttered. "No. I've never heard of anyone summoning one topside before. I suspect the witches called it."

"And have you ever had your heart carved out of your chest?"

If possible, he paled. "No."

"Then you don't know if it could have killed you. It was a *demon*, Gabriel. Is it dead? Did you kill it?"

Another expression, this one frightened. "No."

Fear engulfed me.

"Right before you fell, Sam and Lucy converged on the demon. Anna and Vlad weren't too far behind. Together, the five of us injured it enough that it vanished. But it's still alive."

Oh god. That thing was still alive, and out there. What if it came back? What if it hurt someone else?

"Vlad and Anna are looking into it," he assured me. "We think the coven summoned it. And if that's the case, they should be able to control it."

"But you don't know," I said.

"No."

"Then it could come back for us." My breath quickened as panic set in.

"Relax, luv. I won't let it touch you again. It's been three days since the attack, and a lot has happened since then."

"Tell me," I said, hoping for anything to distract me.

"I've kept my location a secret as best as

possible," he assured me. "In the meantime, I've appointed Vlad as the go-between for me and two council members, who I trust explicitly. I couldn't abandon my people. I'm sure you can understand that," he said pointedly when I scowled. "I seem to remember us having a similar conversation about your slayer friends.

"Anna is scouring the state for the coven's location and keeping an ear out for anything that might sound remotely like the demon. Lucy and Sam are helping as well. They're trying to pin down the identity of whoever wants me dead. Jaden and Josh also stayed, and they're working on a plan to expose the Academy's corruption."

My eyebrows rose.

"Hey, we're capable people," he teased. "I've also put together a small guard, all of whom I compelled to tell me if they're involved in any of this."

I stared at Gabriel. "You can *do* that? Why didn't you tell me that in the first place?"

"Because it isn't foolproof. Some people have very strong wills, making it impossible to compel them. For example, I doubt I could compel you to do anything."

"Let's not and say you didn't," I intoned.

Gabriel smirked. "But I feel safe with those I

chose. They'll guard me during the day, so you don't need to do anything except focus on healing."

"What about Jaden and Josh? Are they okay with everything?"

"They were a bit spooked," Gabriel confessed. "Vampires don't frighten them, but apparently, people turning into wolves is a bit beyond their comfort zone. They're coming around though."

"Did they see me shift?"

"Josh did," he said. "Jaden didn't wake up until a few hours after the skirmish. But Josh told her."

I closed my eyes and pressed my head into the pillows. "I'm sure the alphas will love this."

"Lucy explained the need for them to keep this a secret. Which is why I didn't compel them to forget again."

"That's something, I guess."

Gabriel rose to his feet, then leaned over and kissed my forehead. "You should get some rest. Don't worry about anything, okay? We're all here, and we'll take care of you."

Tears welled in my eyes. He didn't understand how much that meant to me, that I had people here who cared about me. I'd never had that growing up. Never knew the power of having loved ones.

"Thank you," I rasped.

"Oh." He straightened and tugged his shirt down. "One more thing."

I raised a brow. He sounded so serious, so a part of me feared hearing what he had to say next.

Gabriel looked me in the eye and said, "You're mine to keep. You know that, right? So if you ever pull a stunt like this again, I'll lock you up for the next ten years."

I smiled weakly.

"I think you're my forever," he continued. "I know we're mates, but I also know firsthand that doesn't always guarantee a happily ever after. You, Maddie, are my happily ever after. I have no doubts about that. So I need you to stick around so we can share our lives together, okay? No more jumping between me and demons, and no more fighting witches all by yourself."

I fought back a grin.

"Good. Glad to see you're not arguing about this. I'll let you get some sleep. But we're all in the living room if you need us."

He took a step toward the door, but I called his name, stopping him.

"I-I think you're my happily ever after too," I admitted sheepishly.

He grinned at me, then winked. "Of course I am. I'm awesome like that. Get some rest."

I couldn't help but laugh before settling back against the pillows. Even though I'd nearly died— *again*—I felt lighter than I had in days. There were people here to help us now. People who cared about us. I wasn't alone anymore.

Eventually, the chaos would resume. Our lives were still in danger, after all. Until then, I would rest and heal. But once I had my full strength back, I would find the person responsible for all this, and I would kill them. I refused to let anyone steal my happily ever after from me. It was mine. I deserved it.

EPILOGUE

Well, there you have it, folks. If my life were a soap opera, the ratings would be through the freaking roof right about now. Heroine meets her soulmate? Check. But hey, since she's a slayer, let's make it the Vampire King. Need more drama? Throw in some witches. Double-check. Oh, and a demon. Because the audience loves it when we spice things up. Check, check, and check.

Personally, I could have done without the witches and the demon. Total killjoys—literally.

I'm on bedrest, thanks to them and the autograph

the demon left permanently etched into my skin. Everyone keeps hovering and asking me a million questions. Am I comfortable? In pain? Need a drink? Something to eat? Pillow fluffed? I love that they're worried, but it's exhausting. I had to bribe my niece to break the doorknob just to give me a few moments of peace and quiet. She loved it, and quickly stuffed my five dollar bill into her piggy bank. Good to know she's financially motivated. That might come in handy in the future.

Meanwhile, the world keeps spinning.

Our mystery guy is still at large. Yes, the one with a taste for royal blood. My top suspect is still Gabriel's dear ol' dad. Nothing says "I'm upset" quite like trying to bump off your kid, right?

Last I heard, Gabriel and Vlad are working together to rally us up some allies across the pond. They're searching for people who can keep tabs on Adrian and report back his shenanigans. Nothing like some old-fashioned sleuthing to help us nail this asshat down.

Lucy and Sam are in demon-chasing mode, hoping to catch the creature who currently stars in all my nightmares before it harms any humans. No luck so far. The thing is slipperier than an eel.

As for the dynamic duo, Josh and Jaden?

They've started Operation Academy Exposure. While I was vacationing in coma-land, Chris, in an unexpected move, dropped Gabriel's bounty. And since I was out of commission, Vera assigned it to another slayer. No leads on their identity yet, but Jaden told me not to worry about it. Gabriel is well-protected by our motley crew of werewolves, vampires, slayers, and his own human guards. Apparently, I can cross "guarding my mate" off my to-do list.

Yeah, right.

The only item I want to tick off is 'get better.'

I need to get back on my feet. And pronto. Everyone knows the shit is gonna hit the fan. And when that moment comes, I need to be ready to kick some supernatural ass. I just found Gabriel. Ain't no one stealing him away from me. Not on my watch.

TO BE CONTINUED

HOOKED ON THE VAMPIRE KING SNEAK PEEK

I stood in front the bathroom mirror and stared at my sunken-eyed expression. The three bowls of gumbo I'd gulped down had brightened my complexion and filled out my hollow cheeks a little. But the shadows beneath my eyes remained, betraying my exhaustion and weakness.

Sighing, I slowly removed my shirt, exposing my torso to Gabriel and the harsh bathroom lighting. The bandages were white and crisp against my bruised flesh. I'd seen the wounds for the first time yesterday when Meredith changed my bandages. The sight had stolen my breath and brought tears to my eyes. And from the looks of it, things hadn't improved much since then. She'd warned me that they'd take longer to heal than normal, given the extreme amount of damage done, but I'd still hoped for a miracle.

With a deep breath, I reached for the edge of the tape. My fingers trembled, and Gabriel wordlessly took over. His touch was gentle and the adhesive tugged lightly at my skin as he peeled the strips of tape back, revealing the still raw wounds underneath.

My pulse quickened as I took it all in. The stitches were gone—dissolved—and the gashes sealed. But my skin still looked...*angry*. Red, welted, and bruising that spanned my entire chest.

I glanced up and caught Gabriel's gaze in the mirror. When a tear escaped and slipped down my cheek, he caught my chin and turned my head toward him.

"Hey," his soft voice cut through the silence. He brushed away my tears, then cupped my cheeks. "Scars are just a part of our journey. They don't take anything away from you. They add to your story. To your strength. Do you know what I see when I look at you?"

I shook my head.

"I see *all* of you. Your courage, your tenacity, your heart." His hands slipped from my cheeks to my neck.

Then he guided me forward until our foreheads touched. "These marks are just something that was *done* to you. They don't change who you are. Nor do they change how I feel about you. So they shouldn't change how you feel about yourself. You jumped in front of a *demon* to save me, Maddie. One day, you'll look at these and you'll see them as badges of honor."

A small, fragile smile tugged at my lips as his words washed over me. I absorbed his soothing reassurance and let it seep into the raw bits within me that the demon's claws had shredded.

"Thank you," I whispered. I only hoped he was right, and that one day I wouldn't feel such abhorrence when I looked at my chest. I would take it one day at a time.

Gabriel pressed a kiss to my temple. "How about that bath now?"

I nodded. A bath sounded perfect right now. I just wanted to sink into the water and forget about all this.

As Gabriel strode to the tub and turned on the taps, I kicked off the rest of my clothes. When the water started to steam, he stepped aside, then rifled through the cupboards.

"What are you looking for?" I asked.

"Aha," he replied, pulling out a few candles. "I knew I smelled something girly."

I smiled and watched as he laid out five candles. For a moment, I wondered if he'd done it purposely, to match the five marks on my chest, but I quickly realized he'd simply used all the candles Lucy had. He quickly lit them with a small lighter she left in a drawer for this occasion, then gestured me toward the tub.

"Climb in," Gabriel told me.

I lowered myself into the massive whirlpool Jacuzzi tub Lucy had insisted upon when they'd moved in. According to her, it'd taken Sam two months of renovations to design their ideal bathroom, including this oasis of a tub. Its soft curves allowed a girl to lay back, close her eyes, and just float. Even better, the size could accommodate two, even Gabriel's towering stature —not that we'd had a chance to experiment together yet. Thanks to my injuries, I'd been sentenced to sponge baths.

Once the water reached my waist, Gabriel turned off the taps, then activated the jets.

A happy moan slipped past my lips and I laid my head back against the back of the rub. Pure heavenly bliss. My muscles uncoiled as heat seeped into my tired body, while the scent of cherry and vanilla candles filled the air.

"Comfortable?" Gabriel asked.

He'd parked himself on the edge, his gaze attentive, yet casual. Candlelight flickered across his face, highlighting his striking features.

"Why don't you come find out?" I suggested, my tone entirely too innocent.

Gabriel lifted a brow as indecision warred on his face. He wanted to—I could see it in his eyes—but he also feared hurting me.

I sat up and scooted to the middle of the tub, my legs still stretched out. "Come on. Join me."

Apparently, I didn't need to tell him a third time.

Gabriel quickly stripped, discarding his clothes next to mine. At the sight of him, a chiseled work of art, my breath caught. He was the epitome of masculine perfection—at least in my eyes. His torso was a canvas of sculpted muscle and taut skin, marred only by the shadows the flickering candles cast, adding to the mystery of his allure. His arms, thick and defined, bore the evidence of years spent mastering the predator within. The sight of him, so powerful and beautiful, made my heart race.

I still couldn't believe he was mine. He was a force of nature, an entity of strength, speed, and beauty, all wrapped up in one perfect package that I wanted to unwrap with my teeth.

In a display of fluid grace, Gabriel stepped into the bath behind me. The water rippled and sloshed as he lowered behind me, his thighs caging me between his legs.

He settled in behind me, then pulled me back against his chest. The water had risen with his added weight, and it lapped near my chest, but I didn't feel any pain. Instead, a soft sigh escaped my lips as his arms slid around me, enveloping me in a cocoon of warmth and comfort.

I closed my eyes and allowed myself to drift, to exist in this moment of peace and quiet. Gabriel's and my relationship was so new, yet it was moments like this that made me feel as though we'd been together forever. Fate forged the bond between mates, and it was a connection I felt to the very depths of my soul. It'd frightened me at first, seeing as how I had zero experience with intimacy, but the less I fought it, the happier I seemed to be. I'd just needed to get out of my own way and stop sabotaging myself. That was easier said than done, but I was willing to to fight that battle. For Gabriel.

ABOUT THE AUTHOR

 Kinsley Adams is a thirty-something-year-old author who stopped counting when she turned twenty-five. When she isn't writing uproariously hilarious romantic comedies, she's raising her womb-gremlin with the hopes that he might one day become the world's first Supreme Leader (and yes, *Debbie*, that's a Star Wars joke). You can find her and her books online at kinsleyadams.com.

If you enjoyed this book, please leave a review! Your support and feedback are greatly appreciated. And be sure to sign up for Kinsley's newsletter at kinsleyadams.com/newsletter for updates on new releases, sales, and more!

ALSO BY KINSLEY ADAMS

DATING MONSTER MAIN SERIES

DATING DRACULA

LOVING DRACULA

MARRYING DRACULA

WOOING THE WOLFMAN

MATING THE WOLFMAN

WEDDING THE WOLFMAN

SMITTEN WITH THE VAMPIRE KING

HOOKED ON THE VAMPIRE KING

HITCHED ON THE VAMPIRE KING

DATING MONSTERS SIDE STORIES

WHEN VLAD MET ANNA

MR. & MRS. DRACULA

MONSTERS & CHOCOLATE

THE VAMPIRE KING'S NIGHTMARE

THE VAMPIRE KING'S ETERNAL KISS

QUEEN OF HELL SERIES

MATCH MADE IN HELL

www.ingramcontent.com/pod-product-compliance
Lightning Source LLC
Chambersburg PA
CBHW020251030726

47499CB00001B/160